A Rock And A Hard Place

A Tiger Lily's Café® Mystery

By Kathleen Thompson

A Rock And A Hard Place

Volume 5

A Tiger Lily's Café® Mystery

By Kathleen Thompson

ISBN-13: 978-0-9984023-4-5

ISBN-10: 0-9984023-4-6

Library of Congress Control Number: 2017904563

A List of Tiger Lily's Café® Mystery Series Books:

This cozy mystery series has everything you seek: an eclectic cast of characters, a mystery or two, and diligent detectives on duty. The detectives just happen to be feline.

Tiger Lily's Café is set in a Midwestern town nestled into the coast of a Great Lake. The setting itself acts as a character, bringing the reader into the sights, sounds and smells of the small resort community of Chelsea.

Read the series in order, or read any book alone. While characters grown and change, each volume stands alone with a clear beginning and a clear end.

- Turtle Soup (2014)
- Boo! (2015)
- Phishing (2015)
- Holiday (2016)
- A Rock And A Hard Place (2016)
- Splash (2016)
- Chasing A Butterfly (2017)
- Pumpkin Squash (2017)
- Snowblind (2017)
- Hearts On Fire (2018)
- Morel Of The Story (2018)
- Dragon Fire (2019)
- Beach Bunnies (2020)
- Shipwreck (2020)

Cast of Characters 9
1 19
2 43
3 56
4 63
5 79
6 85
7 100
8 125
9 130
10 147
11 163
12 176
13 195
14 222
15 228
16 236
17 249
18 266
19 273
20 287
21 290
22 294
23 305
24 310
25 319
26 327
27 340
28 346
29 349
Thank You For Reading! .... **Error! Bookmark not defined.**

Cast of Characters

Annie Mack, with the help of her "kids" and a talented staff, owns and manages a bed and breakfast, a cafe and other businesses on the south side of The Avenue. She has lived in Chelsea for only a few years, but her ancestral roots to the town date to the Civil War era.

Annie's SASHET Rainbow: (sa SHAY) a model that assigns color to each core feeling. **S**adness is blue; **A**nger red; **S**care green; **H**appiness yellow; **E**xcitement orange; and **T**enderness purple.

For more information, visit Liberation Psychotherapy: www.libpsych.com/articles/sashet/sashet.html.

Ben and JoJo are college students. They work part-time all over town, including most of Annie's businesses.

Boone is the person to call if you need anything: mowing, snow removal, landscaping, maintenance, preventative maintenance, and just about anything else. He is married to **Harriet (Hilly)**, who provides business cleaning services. His sons **Daryl** and **Donny** work for him. Their roots are in rural Appalachia, and they are so much more than people think.

Candice is the head waitress at Mo's Tap. She and George can't decide if they are dating or not.

Carlos is the manager and baker at Mr. Bean's Confectionary. He is a citizen of the US but was originally from Mexico. He supports his mother and younger sisters, who still live there. He is preparing to marry Isabel.

Cheryl inherited The Marina from her parents. It's a small deep water marina with basic amenities. Cheryl is married to Ray. She has known Annie since they were children.

Chris is Annie's special friend, although neither of them are ready to commit to a permanent relationship. He is the Officer in Charge of the Coast Guard Station. His stress relieving hobby is art. His sketches – in charcoal, pencil and pastel – are sold for charity.

Clara owns the flower and gift shop, Bloomin' Crazy. She is a citizen of the US, originally from Haiti, and has an ebullient personality. She keeps The Avenue decorated with fresh and silk flowers year-round.

Cookie probably has another name, but this is what he goes by. He cooks at Mo's Tap and learns what he can from Felicity at every opportunity. He's reticent at best, and he yearns to have his own restaurant. To keep him, Annie opened a fine dining restaurant, Bon Vivant Grille, on Fridays and Saturdays inside the Café.

Diana is the chief instructor at L'Socks' Virasana (Veer AHS ana). She is Mem's daughter. Diana left home right after high school and did not speak to her mother until her return ten years later. Their relationship, while tenuous, continues to grow stronger.

Felicity is the chef at Tiger Lily's Café. She is young, perky and extremely talented in the kitchen. She manages the Café, the upstairs catering facility and outside catering operations.

Frank recently moved to Chelsea to open an antique shop, Antiques On Main. He and Mem are in a relationship.

George is the bartender and manager of Mo's Tap. He is a top-notch bartender and can be counted on to keep confidences. He is a volunteer with the local Coast Guard.

Geraldine was the leader of the "it" crowd in high school, and somehow, life didn't turn out quite as she expected. Everything Annie isn't – perfectly dressed, perfectly coiffed, and perfectly awful – Geraldine is more than a thorn in Annie's side. **Everett** is her on-again-off-again husband.

Ginger is the daughter of Pete, the Chief of Police, and Janet. She works part-time at L'Socks' Virasana. Because she moved to town as a teen (when her father retired from the Marine Corps), and because she is one of the few African American teens in town, she sometimes feels like an outsider.

Greg is a progressive realtor in Chelsea. His goal is to get the right property to the right owner, always moving Chelsea forward.

Gwen is Annie's accountant. A motherly figure, her financial acumen is hidden from all but those lucky enough to have her in their corner.

Hank is a former member of the Town Council. He opposes Annie in every way.

Harry is the regular driver for the rental company used almost exclusively by folks on The Avenue.

Henrie manages the KaliKo Inn in an elegant manner. He does not invite confidences and speaks little about himself. Always formal in tone, people have difficulty pegging his accent. Is it French? Cameroon? Rwandan?

Holly and Jolly, twins, own DoubleGood, an electronics and hardware store. Holly lives in a wheelchair. Natives of Chelsea, they used to hate the names given them by their parents. Now, they enjoy the novelty of it.

Howard owns a bed and breakfast in town, the Sunset Breeze. The B&B is not in a location to see the sunset or to feel a breeze. Howard is president of the local B&B association.

Isabel is going to marry Carlos; she'll move from Mexico soon.

Janet is Pete's wife. She spent twenty years as a Marine officer's wife. She traveled the world and is now living in Chelsea. She is an outsider, not having grown up here like Pete. She is the ultimate community volunteer.

Jennifer and Marie, sisters and nurse practitioners, own The Drug Store and The Clinic. Folks call the sisters before calling nine-one-one. Chelsea natives, they know everyone. And their secrets.

Jenny is an attorney who focuses on family law. She enjoys taking on cases that will right an injustice. She is always ready to engage in battle with those who don't believe a woman, much less a woman of color, can dance with the big boys.

Jerry learned how to make candy in a minimum security federal prison. He was not an employee. Jerry works hard to overcome his shyness, particularly around women.

Jesus manages Sassy P's Wine & Cheese and also selects the wines. His family, famous vintners in the Napa

Valley, owned, farmed and made wine for generations before California became a part of the United States.

Joan is a member of the Town Council. She opposes Hank in every way. Clara's pet name for her is "Joan of Chelsea."

Laila owns Babar Foods. A traditional Pakistani, she is raising her children without the assistance of a husband. Her children are **James**, **Ava** and **Carl**, who lives with Autism.

Marco is a police officer in Chelsea. He is "second in command" because he was the only officer that didn't go off-kilter during a hostage situation. Marco prides himself on being one-hundred-percent-eye-talian-American.

Martha owns a bed and breakfast in town, the Snuggle Inn. Martha is older and considering retirement; the B&B is a cute cottage in a residential area of town.

Mem owns the health food store and cyber café, CyberHealth. Her wisdom is reassuring to everyone, including her daughter, Diana. She teaches the safe use of social media to all ages and has equipment and technology that is helpful to the small-town police department.

Minnie chooses perfect cheeses to accompany the rotating wine selections at Sassy P's Wine & Cheese. She comes from several generations of cheese makers in Wisconsin.

Nancy and Sam are Annie's mother and step-father. They have been married since Annie was a child. They come for extended visits in Chelsea and have learned to call this town their second home.

Pete is a native of Chelsea. He retired from the Marine Corps and is now the Chief of Police. Like Annie, his ancestors arrived in the Civil War era. His, however, came up via the Underground Railroad. He and his wife Janet have three children, the eldest of whom is Ginger.

Ramon (ra MONE) is Clara's boyfriend. A Jamaican by ancestry, he plays saxophone with a jazz fusion band called Bergamasco (after the breed of his dog). He and Clara work hard to maintain their mostly long-distance relationship.

Ray owns and operates The Escape, a yacht fashioned into a cruiser for fishing, diving and pleasure. He is married to Cheryl; Chris is his best friend.

Teresa is a newcomer to the area. She came to this community to serve. She pastors a small church, Soul's Harbor, and pastors the community through her outreach.

Trudie is the barista at Tiger Lily's Café. She is from Jamaica and ended up in Chelsea when a former boyfriend dumped her at the campground. Felicity saved her, and they have been the best of friends ever since.

Annie's Cats

Annie has seven cats. Most people would call them "rescue kitties." From Annie's perspective, each of them rescued her.

Tiger Lily is a beautiful tabby cat with soft green eyes. She is the titular manager of Tiger Lily's Café, the main gathering place for Chelsea. She is generally calm and logical.

Little Socks is a bright-eyed black cat with white socks. She has a commanding personality and is small and sneaky enough to serve as a cat burglar. She spends time at the yoga studio, L'Socks' Virasana (Veer AHS ana).

Kali, Ko and Mo are litter mates. They shared a secret language as kittens; Kali and Ko now speak "cat," but Mo still speaks "secret." Kali and Ko can be found at the KaliKo Inn, a lakeside bed and breakfast. Mo spends time at Mo's Tap, an upscale blues bar.

Sassy Pants is aptly named; it's difficult to keep this little girl's attention. She is overly sensitive and will react out of emotion instead of reason. She entertains at Sassy P's Wine & Cheese.

Mr. Bean is the baby of the family and is mostly gray with traces of tiger. He has two speeds: fast and love me.

Other Companions

Claire is a blue point Himalayan cat whose human is Frank. She's beautiful and loves people. She is stand-offish with other cats.

Cyril is an English setter whose human is Pete, the Chief of Police. Cyril is friendly and calm. He is an excellent hunter.

Fiamma is a Bergamasco. Dreadlocks cover her face. In fact, her entire body is covered with a combination of long dreadlocks and mats of hair. She is an outrageous flirt.

Honey Bear is a large, golden, long-haired mutt of a cat who believes it is his perfect right to be anywhere. Other cats hate him.

Jock is a Portuguese water dog whose human is Ray, the captain of The Escape. Jock is spirited and affectionate; he loves children.

Oscar McMurphy was a stray, named Scaredy Cat by the kids. Despite the name, she is a girl who now lives with Holly and Jolly. She claims Holly as her very own. She is often in and out of the Inn and other places on The Avenue with her brother, Simon Finnegan.

Simon Finnegan was a stray, named Fat Cat by the kids, who now lives with Holly and Jolly. He claims Jolly to be his mom. He is often in and out of the Inn and other places on The Avenue with his sister, Oscar McMurphy.

Tillie came to live on The Avenue with her dreadful family from England. She is a Jack Russell Terrier and now lives with Carlos above the Confectionary. She has free run of The Avenue, including the Inn.

Guests at the Inn

Fred Calendar has come to town to look for his daughter.

Georgia Jones and her daughter, **Frederica**, move from the KaliKo Inn to the Snuggle Inn, a more affordable B&B.

Rock And Gem Show Exhibitors

Dwight is the show's coordinator and he has a booth as well.

Garry sells elegant designer jewelry primarily from gems.

Gema creates uniquely designed jewelry from both gems and stones.

Nelson sells raw and polished Larimer as well as jewelry and other accessories made with the stone.

Guests At The Campground Or Other B&Bs

Adam sells stones and fossils. He is the most knowledgeable of the exhibitors but is quite messy.

Martin handles premium stones and stone products.

Kristina is a highly respected turquoise exhibitor.

Pattie deals with glass and synthetic beads and is looked down upon by the people who deal in stones and gems.

1

Mem's naturally calm demeanor was gone. Perhaps never to return. In a weak moment, she agreed to be the local organizer for the first annual Chelsea Rock & Gem Show. Mem could only hope this would be the first and the last that involved her.

Never again, she thought to herself. Never, ever again.

She stood, surrounded by carts of folding tables and folding chairs and nearly fifty crates of who-knows-what delivered by FedEx and UPS, all labeled "fragile," deciding whom to strangle first: Dwight, the main event organizer or the Gods of Fate that found her in this position.

The space was to be arranged by noon, as exhibitors were expected to start arriving by that time.

Nothing on the outside of the crates noted what was inside, or to whom they belonged. Even had she known to whom they belonged, she still would not have known where to place them.

She had secured the location and arranged for delivery of tables, chairs and a sound system. She arranged with friends to be on hand, strictly on a volunteer basis, to take money from event guests for the next several days. She arranged for the campground to hold a large section for the exhibitors that came in their RVs. She sent Dwight information about local B&Bs and other accommodations, as well as contact names and email addresses for advertisers. She personally passed out flyers of the event to every local business and to many businesses in a multi-county area.

In short, before this morning, she spent a significant amount of time in an attempt to make this a successful event.

She arrived early this morning expecting to meet Dwight and acclimate him to the facility and the town. She had not counted on this. This mess.

As she met the first delivery man, Harry, with the tables, chairs and sound system, she received a blithe telephone call from Dwight. He would be delayed until about noon. Just start setting things up. You don't need a floorplan, just set it up in a way that feels right.

Feels right? What felt right was a neck between her strong hands.

And then FedEx arrived. Followed shortly by UPS.

She didn't have a list of vendors. She didn't have notes that said how many tables individual vendors would need. She didn't know how they liked to arrange the tables. She didn't have a moving crew.

Now, two delivery men from some fly-by-night company stood in front of her. They had ten crates. Cash on delivery. That will be five hundred dollars, ma'am.

Mem stood firm. She would not pay for the crates. The fly-by-night gentlemen stood firm. One of them, a tall, full-bearded brute of a man, said, "They does this all the time. We gets paid before we goes. And we has a schedule. Pay up."

Mem called Dwight, supposedly still on the road. His response was, "Pay the men and I'll reimburse you."

"You've got me between a rock and a hard place. He's demanding cash. Five hundred dollars. I don't carry that kind of cash."

"Well, can you go get some? There have to be ATMs in that town. It's a tourist place!"

"What would be the problem if I told them to hit the road?"

"You can't do that! Those crates probably belong to Garry. He would have a fit if the delivery wasn't made on time"

"Well, maybe Garry needs to get here on time to pay for his own deliveries!"

"Please, Mem, just pay the man."

After a quick trip to her storefront across The Avenue, Mem paid. The brute then said, "Who's takin' this lot from the truck? We deliver. We don't unload. And someone has to get the lot upstairs."

Mem, on the phone again, nearly threw it across the room when Dwight said, "Well, don't you have people around that can do that?"

She caught herself, hung up, closed her eyes, breathed deeply for ten long counts, and called Frank. When she finished the conversation, she turned to the brute and said, "Go back to your truck. Someone will be here shortly."

Mem returned to her checklist, marked off items delivered by Harry and glanced out the second story windows from time to time. She looked at the podium with a self-contained sound system. Not what she had ordered, but in this facility, it would work. She checked "sound system" off her list.

Frank, a special friend to Mem and the owner of an antique store, was there within ten minutes with equipment for moving large crates. Mem saw him arrive from her vantage point and saw Ben coming from another direction. Ben was a college student who worked for Frank part-time. Thankfully, this was Monday, and this semester, he did not have classes scheduled on Monday mornings.

Mem watched as Frank directed the fly-by-night truck to the back entry so the cartons could be unloaded closer to the elevator. She turned as Harry came up the stairway with a to-go carton.

Harry, an employee of a rental firm used almost exclusively by Mem and her friends, loved his Chelsea deliveries. After dropping off his items, he went downstairs and now had a spinach and mushroom omelet with a rye bagel. A large to-go cup of coffee, blonde, flavored with chocolate and cashews, topped it off.

Mem smiled at Harry as he sat down to eat. Harry was a gem. He would help Mem place the tables and chairs, and with Frank and Ben, maybe she could at least take a stab at arranging the facility.

They were on the second floor of Tiger Lily's Café. This was the Café's catering and party venue. It featured a large, open space with a deck on the back overlooking a small park.

The Café was the main gathering place for the town of Chelsea, for locals and tourists alike. It was located at the corner of Sunset Avenue and Main Street. Sunset Avenue was one long city block, extra wide, with ample parking on both sides and a welcoming park area for a median. It started at the town building and ended at the lakefront where, given the right time of day, a brilliant sunset could be viewed year round.

To the locals, it was known simply as The Avenue. Sitting at the tip of it, Tiger Lily's Café acted as a gateway to paradise. Manager and chef Felicity was known for her eclectic and ever-changing menu. Trudie, the barista, was known for her coffee creations. The blonde bomb enjoyed by Harry was her newest spring flavor.

Harry said, "I shoulda brought a cup for you."

"Thank you, Harry. I have a carafe of tea. Thank you again for taking the time to help me arrange this mess. We'll start as soon as Frank and Ben are ready."

The two sat together, drinking their hot beverages and watching as Frank placed the crates at the edge of the pile. Frank looked around at the mess, shook his head, and walked slowly to Mem and Harry.

"Harry, did you load these tables and chairs yourself?"

"Nope. For once, the truck was already loaded when I got to the warehouse. Unusual, but it gave me time to eat breakfast."

"I'm not sure you really have any extra time. Did you look at this stuff as you unloaded?"

"Nope. Just brought up the carts. What's the problem?"

"Come over here and look. They seem to be marked as broken."

Harry and Mem jumped up and walked quickly to the carts holding the folding tables. They went through them, one at a time. Each and every table had a broken leg, a broken clasp, a broken hinge, or one or more brutally sharp feet. Many had what could politely be called substandard tops.

The chairs were similar. As Mem picked several up to place them, chairs leaned left or right or collapsed straight to the floor.

Mem walked to the self-contained podium. She opened the storage compartment and a bundle of wires, broken microphones and speaker connectors fell out.

"Harry, this has to be fixed right away!"

Harry was already on the phone to the warehouse. He walked to the far side of the room to talk to the warehouse manager, but that wasn't far enough for Mem and Frank to hear the suddenly raised voice speaking, as Mem kindly put it, in French.

Mem, eyes tightly shut against the next disaster, waited until Harry stood in front of her. She opened her eyes, looked up, and saw a face painted with a mixture of anger and sympathy.

"They gave me the wrong truck. And then, to make matters worse, they loaded my order on another truck that went to the landfill. Your order is already in the middle of that pile of trash."

Mem sank into a chair, not paying heed that a chair was not behind her. By the time she got there, however, Frank had grabbed a left-leaning folding chair to break her slow descent.

"Sam said we could have a new load here by tomorrow morning, but we can't do it before then. Your order cleaned out our stock; other things are coming back today, but we have nothing left at the warehouse."

Mem, numb and staring blankly at the floor, pulled her cell phone out one more time. She called across The Avenue to the hardware store. Jolly answered. Mem, in a rather wooden voice, told Jolly the problem, hung up, and a single tear traced down her cheek.

In a strange, choked voice, she said, mostly to herself, "The moon is waxing gibbous."

Henrie, serving only one guest at the KaliKo Inn this morning, laid out a variety of breakfast foods. His guest, a young single mother with an infant child, seemed to have an aversion to breads but denied an allergy to gluten. Wanting to provide a variety of foods she could eat, Henrie had talked to Carlos, manager and baker of Mr. Bean's Confectionary.

This morning, Carlos sent a fresh pan of cinnamon rolls made with spelt.

Henrie tried not to turn up his nose at the sight. The rolls were flat and looked tasteless. Remarkably, his guest seemed to think otherwise. Georgia looked at the rolls, nestled in between scrumptious meat and egg dishes, and placed one on her plate.

When Henrie looked in again, she had taken another roll from the platter. She smiled up at him. "Spelt. I love this stuff!"

Henrie, back in the kitchen, took a call from Carlos. "Did she like the rolls?"

"She did. Tell me about spelt. It looks atrocious."

Carlos laughed. "I should have warned you, but I was in a rush this morning. It's from the grass family. It contains gluten, but the gluten doesn't hold up well. It doesn't rise like breads made with wheat flours, but it's easier to digest."

"And it must have a pleasant flavor."

"You didn't try it?"

Henrie answered in his always-formal fashion. "I shall try it if my guest does not devour the platter."

Back in the dining room, Henrie almost tripped over Kali and Ko, resident cats and namesakes of the Inn. Big girls, they took to heart their newest guest, the baby, Fred. Well, Frederica. Fred for short.

The cats hovered around the baby whenever she was in a common area, and, Henrie thought, probably in the guest room as well. They worried as she cried, purred as she slept, and climbed onto Georgia's lap as Fred suckled from her breast.

Georgia's lap was always full during feeding time.

Henrie gave Kali and Ko a semi-hard look, then turned to Georgia. "Do you have plans for the day?"

"I'm still looking for work, but I really need to find another place to stay. I love it here, but I can't afford it. It's so hard, looking for work and taking Fred with me wherever I go. No one wants to talk to me if I can't get childcare."

"I know this is hard for you. You do understand all of the rooms are booked this week."

"I do understand, Henrie, and I appreciate everything you've done. Do you have any suggestions?"

Henrie thought for a moment. "I will make a call."

Henrie called a friend and colleague, Martha, an older woman who owned a small bed and breakfast a few blocks over. She picked up right away.

"Snuggle Inn. May I help you?"

"Martha, this is Henrie at the KaliKo Inn. Do you have a moment to speak with me?"

"Certainly. No one here but me today. That's more and more the case, you know. Everyone wants to stay at a larger place with, you know, more amenities."

"You have a lovely home, Martha."

"Thank you. And how can I help you, Henrie?"

"We have in residence a young woman with an infant. She moved to town to start over, to use her words. She is pleasant, seems an industrious sort, but she cannot afford to stay here while she looks for work and a place to live. Your rates are more affordable; do you have reservations that would preclude a guest for the next week?"

"Henrie, I don't have a single thing on my calendar until July, and that one is iffy. So, she has a baby?"

"Yes. Frederica, known simply as Fred. A pleasant child. You would hardly know she existed."

"You don't have to sugar-coat it, Henrie. Actually, I'm thinking of just getting out of the business. I can't afford the licensing fees, and it's tough to keep groceries on hand 'just in case.'"

"Would you consider taking her on as, perhaps, a last guest?"

"Tell you what. I'm not doing a thing right now. If she's there, I'll come over and talk to her, see what I think about her and the baby."

"Thank you, Martha. I will expect you shortly."

Back in the dining room, Henrie shared his plan with Georgia.

"Martha has a small bed and breakfast, just two guest rooms, and her rates are more affordable. Perhaps you can stay there while you look for an apartment, and I think we can find a college student to help with child care while you look for work. I have one in mind."

"Oh, Henrie, thank you so much." Georgia's face and voice didn't match the sentiment.

"What is it? Can I be of more help?"

"It's just that I don't think I can afford to pay anyone for child care. I had just enough to maybe pay for a place to live for a month, but..."

At that moment, the kitchen door opened and a woman's voice said, "Henrie? I have a delivery."

Henrie went again to the kitchen. "Laila. What on earth do you have there?"

Laila owned the grocery store across The Avenue. She carried two reusable grocery bags, one on each shoulder. As she placed them on the table, she answered the question. "I have some formula, diapers and wipes. Your guests get younger and younger, Henrie."

"Oh, goodness." He called over his shoulder, "Georgia, could you please come to the kitchen?"

Georgia appeared at the doorway. "Oh, thank you so much. I was just about out of everything."

"You didn't ask for a lot of formula. Will this do it for you?"

"I normally breast feed, but I was thinking I would have to have formula on hand if I'm ever to find a job. I thought I would try to get her used to it."

Laila looked at Georgia, then at Henrie. "Henrie, could you excuse us, please?"

More than happy to oblige, Henrie exited the kitchen to the dining room to begin the clean-up process. He picked up a plate, fork and cinnamon roll first. At his first taste, he thought, my, my. I have been neglecting my guests. This is delicious.

It was just another Monday in Chelsea, a small resort town on the eastern coast of one of the Great Lakes. Snuggled into the lake on one side and the wooded acreage of a state park on two other sides, it had the feel of a village separated from the rest of the world.

Tiger Lily's Café and the KaliKo Inn were just two of a number of businesses owned by Annie Mack.

The Inn had a prime location with a lake view and, from the back, access to a private, pristine white sand beach. The Inn was a former mansion with a wrap-around porch reminiscent of southern mansions. Through the years, it had morphed into a fine hotel and restaurant and now rode the typical tide of old homes in resort communities. It was the biggest and most well-respected bed and breakfast in Chelsea.

Annie and her family of cats lived on the third floor. Henrie, without whom she couldn't exist, had an apartment on the ground level.

The Inn and the building that sat to the east, a long, two-story brick building built in the same era as the home, had been in the Mack family for generations.

The long building held five businesses, all well-suited for a resort community. A wine and cheese shop, a confectionary with both baked goods and chocolates, an upscale blues bar, a yoga studio, and the Café were each named for one of Annie's cats. The cats served as titular managers, going to "work" every day to supervise the humans. Silly humans who thought they held the title of manager.

Annie was the only remaining Mack. When her father died, everything came to her. Victor Mack did not raise her. She spent summers with him, but she did not know him well, always considering her step-father to be the real parent.

In her young adult years, she came to know Victor better, and in the end, they were quite close. While his death came as a shock, he had, in his own way, prepared Annie to take over the family legacy.

Annie missed everything that Monday morning. She did not have breakfast at the Inn and she did not hear Henrie's conversation with Georgia, then Martha. She was not at the Café to witness Mem's distress. She was not at any of the places in between.

No. She was in a much less pleasant space. After walking up The Avenue with her brood of cats, each one peeling off to enter his or her own place of business, she had been stopped at the entrance of the Café.

Tiger Lily, sensing nothing amiss, walked through the cat door to take her place at the hostess stand while Annie stood on the corner, talking to Howard.

Tiger Lily watched out the window with curiosity as Annie walked with Howard to a bench on the median of The Avenue. There, Annie carried on an animated conversation that ended with her rising from the bench and storming off, walking up Main Street in the direction of Antiques On Main. Or maybe she was going to see Gwen, her accountant, at Beancounters. Or maybe she was just going for a walk.

Tiger Lily turned to her duties, greeting customers as they entered the Café, thanking them as they left, on occasion jumping to a table ledge to recommend a menu item to a new guest.

She was in her glory as the Rotary Club adjourned their breakfast meeting in the back room. As they filed out, there was no lack of pets, coos of adoration, and the sweet sound of loose change and dollar bills hitting the crystal tip bowl set up for the charity of the month. All thoughts of Annie's strange conversation vanished.

Martha arrived at the Inn, parked her 1971 VW bus, and made her way up the steps, pulling on the railing as that darned left leg decided to cramp up one more time.

If Henrie wasn't such a good friend, she wouldn't have made the trip. She didn't need a baby in the house. She did need the money, but how much could this girl afford to pay? And would she be stuck with the expenses without reimbursement? No, Henrie wouldn't let that happen. He would pay out of his own pocket if the girl, for some reason, didn't pay her bill.

Martha, thoughts rolling through her mind, finally reached the front door just as Henrie opened it. Beside him were those two big, beautiful cats, Kali and Ko, like bookends on either side of him. They must have thought they had a new guest.

"Hello girls," said Martha, leaning down to pet each soft head.

She received two loud purrs in reply.

"Thank you for coming, Martha. Come in. The coffee is fresh."

"Sounds great. The stronger, the better."

"And a cinnamon roll?"

"Oh, yeah. Now I remember why I like coming here in the morning. Leftover breakfast! Always excellent!"

As they walked from the foyer to the dining room, a loud wail could be heard from the back guest room. Henrie winced. Kali and Ko headed in that direction at a run.

"Truly, this is an unusual occurrence. Generally, the child is very quiet."

"Right. So tell me, Henrie, what's up with this girl? Why are you so involved?"

By now, they were in the kitchen. Martha winced as she sat on a tall barstool at the kitchen table. Henrie didn't notice; his back was to the table as he poured coffee and placed spelt cinnamon buns on small plates.

Martha looked at the buns with wide eyes. She looked up at Henrie with a question mark in them.

He answered the unasked question. "They are made with spelt. They have an unusual appearance, but I assure you they are quite good."

Martha took a bite. "They are! Well, Henrie, you got me here. Now spill."

"Yes. I will spill. Georgia has been here since the middle of last week. She found us through the website. Using her words, she thought a place that was so kind to cats could not help but be kind to a lost girl and her child."

"Lost?"

"That is how she described herself. She married at the age of twenty-one, and the young man soon deserted her. When she discovered her pregnancy, she left town. Her father, according to her, would not have approved. She moved to a city until the baby came, apparently taking advantage of the anonymity that comes with city life. However, living in a city is more expensive. She thought a resort town might have positions to match her skills, and here she is."

"Without a family, without the father."

"The father has never come up in conversation beyond her first explanation, and I do not believe it polite to ask."

"And you're nothing if not polite, Henrie. By the way, I haven't heard anything past that first wail. Why don't I go back and meet her?"

"Excellent idea. Do you know the way?"

"Sure. I've had the tour a few times." Martha got off the stool, carefully hiding any expression of pain from Henrie. On her way to the room, she stopped one time to lean against the wall and catch her breath.

Mem returned from the Café, a tray in hand filled with carafes of coffee, cups, condiments and a treat from Felicity. Breakfast Surprise wraps. They were whole wheat wraps with freshly cooked chicken and bacon, steamed broccoli and onion, cheddar cheese and raspberry preserves. The surprise was the preserves, an unusual addition to any breakfast or sandwich wrap.

Felicity's favorite was FROG preserves, a combination of fig, raspberry, orange and ginger. However, she was having an issue with her vendor, and the FROG was not delivered. Mem caught the tail end of that telephone conversation. Very un-Felicity-like.

Harry was still here, having dared the warehouse manager to force him to return. Frank and Ben were still here, as was Holly, Jolly's sister and co-owner of the hardware store across The Avenue.

And, bless him, Boone was here, responding to an SOS call from Holly. Certainly he knew what he was doing. Boone and his sons took care of most of the building maintenance on The Avenue.

The elevator pinged, and two young men stepped out. Boone's sons, Daryl and Donnie, carried tool boxes and a backpack that looked like it might contain a kitchen sink.

Prowling the room, examining the broken tables and chairs, were two cats recently claimed by Holly and Jolly. A boy and girl, Simon Finnegan and Oscar McMurphy, they were rescued from an uncertain fate by Annie's cats. Probably dumped at the state park's campground, they found their way to The Avenue, relative safety, and, eventually, a fur-ever home. Now, they examined the broken articles looking for all the world like they knew what they were doing.

Besides Boone and his boys, Holly was the most talented fix-it person in town, unusual for two reasons. One reason was the purely sexist one: she was a woman. Another reason was discriminatory for another reason: she lived in a wheelchair following a childhood accident. She and Jolly made do, and with a nip here and a tuck there, Holly was able to get around very well on her own in most situations. Daryl and Donnie were known to ask Holly for advice when they didn't want to let their father know they needed help.

Two of the newer pieces of furniture in the room were little red wagons. One was redone as a mobile tool box. It was light enough to be easily pulled by Holly from her motorized chair. Ben had recently returned from the hardware store pulling another wagon with spare parts requested by Holly.

Holly worked on tables, reattaching legs to bases, while directing Harry and Ben as they completed other repairs. Frank had a grasp of the situation and had taken over repair of the chairs, helped by Daryl. Some chairs were beyond repair. They went to a stack near the elevator. The most important repairs were to the tables, at any rate. Boone and Donnie tackled the tables in most need of repair. For today, they would do without a sound system. Harry would bring another tomorrow.

After delivering wraps and drinks, Mem went back to the floor plan she had made. She was going to set up tables with no information, and if exhibitors were angry, well, they could take it up with Dwight.

Holly finally declared, "I think we have enough of these repaired we can at least start getting the decent ones out of the way."

Mem put the almost-completed floor plan on one of the FedEx boxes, pointing out the general gist to the men, and they began to move tables into place.

"Once the tables start to make sense, let's move these crates somewhere out of the way. Maybe we can put them on the deck. It's a nice day. The exhibitors can figure out what belongs to whom when they arrive."

They worked steadily until almost noon. The room was nearly in shape when the elevator dinged arrival. A woman and three bad-tempered men got off. A disheveled man finished a conversation. "It ain't my fault I make more money than y'all do!"

The woman, well-dressed in an artsy style, turned away from him and looked around the room. She saw Mem and smiled.

A sporty-looking man put his hands on his hips and declared, "Dwight hires local people to take care of the set-up. They never get it right. And where are my display cases?"

The fourth man, in well-pressed blue jeans, walked around, looking at every piece of furniture, walked around again, then came to Mem. "Who's in charge here?"

"That would be Dwight, and he isn't here."

"Well, where is he?"

"I assure you, I don't know. But if you wonder who is responsible for the fiasco you believe you see, trust me, it is him."

"Who are you?"

"My name is Mem. I'm so pleased to meet you, Mr.?"

"Where is the sound system? It was supposed to be front and center."

"It will be. Tomorrow."

"Tomorrow?"

The sporty-looking man broke in. "Where are all of my display cases?"

"I don't know. Who was to bring them?"

"They were supposed to be delivered. They are very expensive, fragile, and most of my product is packed inside."

"Well, if anyone had display cases delivered, then they are out there on the deck."

Two men, distressed looks on their faces, nearly ran to the deck to look for their cases. Mem called after them, "Someone owes me five hundred dollars!" She turned to the disheveled man, who had yet to move. "Well, is it you? Do you owe me for the cash on delivery crates?"

"No. I carry all my own stuff."

The woman had strolled to the deck to look over the crates. She came back and said to Mem, "The boys are quite incapable of doing anything on their own. I apologize for their behavior."

Mem didn't have time to reply before sporty looking man returned to say, "Move this inside at once!"

Frank, who had stayed in the background, heard quite enough. "Excuse me. Could we at least back up and say hello? Meet and greet? This woman is Mem. She is the local organizer, not the event organizer. I'm Frank. I came over to…"

The man in blue jeans blustered into the group. "This needs to be fixed at once. At once! Get these crates inside, before it rains, and get these tables set up the way they were supposed to be set!"

"It won't rain today...." Mem's voice trailed off as a crack of lightening sounded, and the loud patter of a hard spring rain sounded on the roof.

"Oh no!" wailed sporty man. "Get this stuff inside!"

The men, well, the men from Chelsea, moved to the deck to push and carry crates into the facility. Sporty man, blue jean man and artsy woman stood by. Disheveled man, after a couple of beats, moved to help.

Mem stood her ground, glaring at the other three, now determined to be as rude to them as they were to her. Well, she would at least be rude to the men. The elevator dinged again, and a man in a suit disembarked.

Sporty man, blue jean man and artsy woman, backs to the elevator, turned to look. Three voices cried, "Dwight!"

"Hello there, boys and girls! It's going to be a great show!"

Loud male voices hit him. Disheveled man left the group on the now very wet balcony to join in the chorus.

Mem could hear various versions of how awful the set-up was, why was nothing done, who was responsible for this disaster, do you know our cases are out there in the rain, you promised me the best placement, and look at this place!

Every now and then, the woman would look toward Mem with a sympathetic face.

Eventually, the group quieted and Mem heard a male voice say, "I can't apologize enough. You know how it is. You come to these small towns, and you take whoever steps up to volunteer. I can't help it that she couldn't read the floor plan. I sent it three weeks ago. This should never have happened. I'll make sure she gets you twenty percent off on your accommodations, wherever they are."

Mem turned, picked up her carafe of tea, walked into the middle of the group, looked at the man in the suit and said, "Dwight, you owe me five hundred dollars."

"Oh, you must be Mem. So pleased to meet you."

"Five hundred dollars. Oh, and you owe the hardware store seventy-five dollars and thirty-three cents."

"Let's get these tables taken care of, and then we'll talk about that."

"Five hundred seventy-five dollars and thirty-three cents."

"You know I always expected you would take it from the money we take in at the door. Certainly we'll take in more than enough tomorrow."

"I see. You didn't expect to pay me today. You were late on purpose so you would not have to face that delivery charge or any other charges that might occur."

"Now, Mem. Let's not get carried away."

"I promised to have volunteers here to take tickets every day. I will not renege on that promise. But for now, Dwight, this mess is all yours. I don't care how you spin it to your friends."

She turned to the others. "Oh, and that percentage off your accommodations he just promised? Bite me."

Mem walked to the stairway. As she got there, she felt, more than saw, Frank and Harry behind her. She noticed Holly, Ben and the cats get onto the elevator, two red wagons in tow. Mem pointed down. Holly nodded, understanding they would meet for lunch at the Café below.

Mem laughed to herself as she heard Boone address Dwight. "My boys and I will help you. Let's see. That's three of us, so it'll be sixty dollars an hour, and we'll stay here as long as you need. You had a problem paying the lady, so let's just say you can give us a one hundred twenty dollar retainer before we get started."

Mem wished she could see the look on Dwight's face.

As Mem left, the woman looked around the space. The north windows covered the entire wall. The east wall was similar, as the building itself was on the corner of Main Street and Sunset Avenue. The walls were clean and devoid of decoration, probably to allow persons renting the facility to decorate it as they wished.

The space was completely open, with the exception of load-bearing beams painted in rainbow colors. There were six of them: blue, red, green, yellow, orange and purple.

The woman smiled to herself. The owner of the building, having everything else decorated in rainbow colors, probably couldn't resist, even though the space was supposed to be flexible.

She had come off an elevator, and there were stairs as well. Both came from the back dining room of the Café below. She went to the deck, now that the rain had stopped. It was large and it overlooked a small park area, either private or public, the woman couldn't tell, and further on, the woods of the state park.

This exhibit space would do nicely, she thought, as long as Dwight puts me in the right spot. I think on the aisle facing the north windows will be perfect. Well, no use waiting for him to do the right thing. She walked to the tables that had been set up and staked out three for herself, placing two on the aisle facing north and one to the side that faced the east. With those quick and painless moves, she placed herself in both a front booth and on a corner.

She took paper and markers from her purse, wrote in large block letters "Gema's Creations," and placed one piece of paper on each table.

The men had stopped to look at her. She looked back and smiled. "Oh. Was this not the right place, Dwight?"

The men turned back to Dwight and started a clamor about Gema always getting the prime locations. Gema shook her head. All they had to do was take some tables and arrange them. That was all. Men!

2

Henrie promised to get Georgia and Fred to the Snuggle Inn the next day. In the meantime, he called one of his part-time helpers, JoJo, to come over.

JoJo and her brother Ben had been full-time college students. Now reduced to part-time, both needing to fund their education, they worked for several of Annie's businesses. JoJo was familiar with the KaliKo Inn. She did not expect to see what Henrie had in mind for her today.

Coming through the kitchen door, she was surprised to see Henrie puttering around the kitchen. Well, that wasn't surprising. Henrie often puttered around the kitchen. The surprise was the car seat holding a sleeping infant in the middle of the butcher block table.

Sleeping beside her, but suddenly alert to a new presence, were Kali and Ko. Each touched the baby in some way. Kali's head rested on the baby's foot and Ko's tail was clutched by a tiny hand.

Henrie turned as she walked in. "JoJo, thank you so much for coming. I was not sure what I needed you to do, but things have crystalized a bit since we spoke."

"Henrie, you have a baby."

"Yes, well, that is the point. I thought, when I called, that perhaps I could ask you to help Hilly clean and I would care for the child. However, in the meantime, I find I am not proficient at some of the finer points of childcare."

"Like what, changing a diaper?"

"Exactly."

At that moment, a loud, somewhat embarrassing sound emanated from the baby. Kali and Ko, ever alert to baby needs, stood at once, looked at Henrie and meowed plaintively.

They said, quite clearly, *"She pooped!" "Change the diaper!"*

Henrie and JoJo heard, "Ew, what's that smell?"

Henrie looked at JoJo, actually begging her with his eyes to step in. She laughed. "Okay. Whatever. Where's her stuff?"

Henrie took leave of JoJo and Fred in the back guest room when the front door opened. He was two seconds from the foyer when he heard a loud voice, quite possibly rude but perhaps only raised, say, "Where is everybody? Anybody home?"

Henrie entered the foyer as Hilly, in the midst of her cleaning duties, looked over the second floor railing. She saw Henrie, nodded to him, and went back to work.

Henrie saw a pretty, artily dressed woman, a sporty man, and a man in pressed blue jeans. "Welcome to the KaliKo Inn. I am so sorry I was not at the door to greet you."

The man in sporty attire dropped two large bags on the floor and ignored Henrie. Turning to his companions, he said, "Let's hope this place is better put together than what we've had to deal with so far."

Henrie smiled and moved forward a bit, realizing the voice had been, in fact, rude. "I am Henrie. I will be your host throughout your stay. We expect several guests today. May I ask who I have the pleasure of greeting?"

The artsy woman moved forward. "How do you do? My name is Gema. I have a reservation for the week."

"Certainly you do. You will be on the second floor in a room that overlooks the Lake. I hope that will be satisfactory."

"Oh! I can't wait to see it!"

Sporty guy huffed. "You always get the best stuff."

"Oh, Garry. Stop it. We're going to be together almost nonstop for a week. Can you please put a cork in it?"

Henrie, heading off an argument, interrupted. "Garry, is it? You have a room with every amenity. It overlooks a garden in between the Inn and the wine shop next door."

Turning to pressed blue jean man, Henrie asked, "And you, sir, may I ask your name?"

"Nelson. I'm sure my room has every amenity as well." The voice had just the touch of a sneer.

"Yes, it does. You, sir, will be in a room overlooking the state park. A lovely room with a south facing deck."

"Deck! He gets a deck?"

Henrie, realizing this group had a get-it-done-now attitude, decided to speed up his tour. "Every room has a deck, deck furniture, HDTV, computer access, both wireless and wired, a queen-sized bed, a seating area, a dresser and locking armoire. Allow me to point out the features available to you on the lower level and the second floor landing, and then we will go directly to your rooms."

Gema listened with half an ear while she looked around. She hated these gem shows with a passion, but she had to continue to do them until she made her mark in the jewelry world. How dreary. But, she thought, this town was a pleasant surprise.

The downtown had been lovely. That cute Café, she would have to get back there, had definite possibilities. And there was a yoga studio. She would have to ask about early morning hours. Both sides of Sunset Avenue were adorable, attractively decorated, and spring flowers adorned the median and the sidewalks.

Cute tables, all painted the same color as the awnings above them, dotted the sidewalk on this side of the Avenue, looking much like the furniture on the porch of this lovely old mansion. Well, the website did say the same woman owned all of the places on this side of the street. And they all had cute cat names.

Henrie stood in the foyer and pointed out rooms and amenities. She assumed their rude entrance forced him to speed up what was probably a leisurely and gracious tour. Oh, well. That always happened with this group. This group. Oh, gadzooks! She would be so happy when she could move on!

From the foyer, she could see into both the library and the dining room. Furniture was both elegant and comfortable, upholstered in shades of slate blue and gray. Tables, bookshelves and other wooden furniture were of light-hued walnut. The walls of each room were a different color, but all were a light pastel. The entryway was blue; the library lavender and the dining room rose. The house was bathed in light from the windows, which had minimal coverings. The entryway had a large welcoming bouquet of fresh blue blooms, and a smaller but similar bouquet in the dining room could be seen from the foyer.

From his position, Henrie turned slightly and pointed out the coffee and snacks corner and the reading areas in the library, the foyer, and the second floor landing, quickly mentioning the televisions and computers in each area.

"I can tell you are in a hurry, but for a delightful view of the sunset from inside the house, please make use of the all-season porch, which can be found through this hallway."

"Now, let me help you with your bags."

Gema picked up the larger of her two bags. She would need two hands to carry it up the stairs. Henrie, without help from the men, loaded the rest of the bags into the elevator. He invited them to take the stairway up, thereby getting a better look at the Inn from another perspective.

When the elevator arrived on the second floor, and being Henrie, having remembered which bags belonged to whom, he picked up Gema's remaining bag to escort her to the lakeside guest room. The men walked in as well.

"Well, Gema," snorted Garry, "you certainly have the best view."

Henrie opened the patio door to show Gema the deck and pointed out the cat door. "Our resident cats, Kali and Ko, are busy now, but they will, from time to time, step into your room to make sure all is well. If you do not desire their company, you may latch the door from the inside. Every room has the same feature."

"Now, Garry, let us get you to your room." Henrie motioned Garry into the room across the hall, and again, all three went in. Henrie, going to the elevator to retrieve luggage, rolled his eyes. He could hear the argument continue as Gema said, "See? You have a great view, too. Grow up."

Finally, Henrie was able to invite Nelson to his room facing the trees of the state park. Again, everyone trailed along. In this room, while all were still in earshot, Henrie said, "Breakfast will be served at 8:00 tomorrow morning, unless you desire an earlier time."

Nelson answered for them all. "I think tomorrow we'll need breakfast at 6:00, but for the rest of the week, 7:00 will work out."

"Fine. 6:00 tomorrow it is. I will leave you to get settled."

At that moment, they all turned to look toward the hallway as the dulcet tones of a baby's loud wail reached their ears. JoJo, carrying Fred into the kitchen from the back room, had dropped the toy she was using to keep her attention. Fred was not happy.

Three guests turned back to Henrie. He smiled, shrugged his shoulders, and said, "One of our guests. She must be angry about something." He left the room.

Georgia, finally baby-less, walked purposefully through town. She stopped in almost every business, even places she had stopped before. She had a formula. Be polite. Be assertive, not aggressive. Smile. Say one thing, one thing only. Hello. My name is Georgia. Are you taking applications? I would be a great asset to, and name the place.

And, when the inevitable answer came, something along the lines of I'm so sorry, or no, not at this time, or didn't we have this conversation before, smile again, say thank you, and walk away. Don't look back. Don't let the smile leave your face. Don't let them see you cry.

Today, she didn't bother anyone on The Avenue. She made those stops two days running, every time with a baby in tow. But she was getting to know these people, and she knew they didn't really have anything to offer. At least, not now.

She stopped at Antiques On Main, Beancounters, a couple of realty offices, three law offices, a clothing store, a gift shop, a t-shirt shack. She was walking up the highway toward the big box store – for the third time in three days – when she had to stop to get a stone out of her shoe. She didn't realize how close she was to a mud puddle, left after an unexpected shower. A car whizzed by, paying no heed, and suddenly, her clean clothes, even her hair and face, were bathed in wet goo.

Could anything else go wrong?

Wiping her face, unable now to keep the tears from flowing, she turned around to go back to the Inn, feeling the hunger gnaw at her insides.

In the Café, Tiger Lily took time from her hostess duties to visit with special friends. At the big table in the corner were some of her favorite people. Mem and Frank, Ben, Holly, Harry from the rental company, and they saved a place for Mommy. Here was Mommy now.

Tiger Lily motioned to Simon Finnegan and Oscar McMurphy. She still called them Fat Cat and Scaredy Cat, the names the cats had given them when they first came to The Avenue. Nearly running over Annie, they scampered to the back of the hostess stand where a server had placed a bowl of something absolutely marvelous. Oscar

McMurphy purred, *"This is the best place for lunch in town. I love it here!"*

Annie, or Mommy, if you happened to be one of her cats, walked into the Café, waved to friends and acquaintances, balanced herself as three big cats raced from the corner table to the hostess stand, and made her way back to the table.

"How is your day going?" Annie stopped in mid-sit as she saw five faces staring back at her. Baleful. Yes, that was the look. No. Wretched.

"What's up?"

Mem spoke for everyone. "That group of rock and gem show exhibitors. That's what's up."

"Please tell me it's not going to be a fiasco."

"It's not going to be a fiasco. Except that it is."

Annie and Mem had talked at length about holding the show on the second floor. They worried about parking, accessibility, the ability of community businesses to handle the extra traffic this early in the tourist season. Both agreed it would work. It would be a stretch, but it would work.

Annie knew that many of the B&Bs, at least the ones with decent reviews, were grateful to be full for the week, and the campground at the state park was happy with the week-long bookings. Local restaurants had been warned and most had staffed and ordered stock to meet the extra need.

Life went on, however, and several other things were going on. Here at the Café, for example, this week was a huge one for Felicity and Cookie. Felicity and Annie worked out a plan to offer Cookie, the cook at Mo's Tap, an opportunity to open a fine dining restaurant.

Because the Café closed in the late afternoon, it was available in the evening for other things. Sometimes they rented the space, including kitchen facilities and often staff, to groups.

However, starting this weekend and going through at least the summer, on Friday and Saturday evenings Cookie would open his own restaurant, the Bon Vivant Grille.

Annie worried about doing it during the final days of the rock and gem show, but, really, life went on, and sometimes you just had to roll with it. The grand opening would be held Thursday night, no matter what.

Now she felt a little niggle of fear.

Mem continued. "Well, I don't know that the entire show will be a disaster. Certainly it won't. They do this all the time. They are disorganized in person, very unlike my impression over the telephone and through emails. Really! The audacity! And poor Harry, here, has a sad tale of his own!"

As everyone gave their orders for lunch, Harry talked around other heads and the ongoing I'll have the crab cakes or give me your sandwich special to tell Annie of the landfill blunder. By the time he finished, Annie had to wipe away tears of laughter. In fact, Harry had so embellished the story that everyone was laughing now. The day was too pretty to waste on bad energy.

Mem stopped laughing for just a minute. "Annie, frankly, you look a mess. What happened?"

"Who knew it was going to rain? There wasn't a cloud in the sky!"

Everyone laughed again, tears rolling down Holly and Mem's cheeks, as Frank explained the disaster of the packing crates.

As the laughter died down, Mem asked, "What were you doing, that you got caught in the rain?"

"I went for a walk. Well, I went to talk to Gwen about an issue that came up, and she recommended I talk to Greg, so I walked to his office, but he wasn't back from Rotary Club. I walked back to Gwen's office and she said, 'get yourself a lawyer,' and, well, while I was getting myself a lawyer, I got caught in the rain."

"You got a lawyer?"

"Yep. Jenny Howe."

"Jenny Howe? She's the saint of lost causes. What's going on, Annie?"

"Howard, you know, he has the Sunset Breeze, the B&B stuck in the middle of a residential area where you can't see the sunset or feel a breeze? He thinks he can force me out of the Inn. Among other things, he says the KaliKo Inn is bad for Chelsea, and he's going to fix it. And he thinks he can, because he's president of the B&B association."

Frank, incensed, said, "What does he think he can do? That association doesn't control anything regarding regulations or licensing."

"That's what I said. He doesn't seem to agree."

"What does he mean by the Inn's reputation?"

Annie looked around the table, a gleam in her eye, signifying that not only was she a fighter, but she was a fighter with a sense of humor. "What do a few murders and kidnappings have to do with anything, anyway? Who pays any attention to that stuff?"

The table laughed again, pleased that Annie was going to meet this new challenge head-on.

When the laughter died down, Mem got serious. "You know we have your back on this, no matter what, but what is your next step?"

"Howard 'invited' me to their meeting tomorrow morning. I told him that I was not available, and he intimated that if I were not at the meeting, whatever happened would happen without my input. So…Jenny is going to go in my place."

Mem, looking over Annie's shoulder, said, "Well, this doesn't look good."

Everyone turned. Diana, the head yoga instructor and manager of Lil' Socks' Virasana, made her way to the table, a look of consternation on her face. Only Mem could tell how bad the look was. Mem was Diana's mother and had been reading that face since its birth.

Diana made eye contact with everyone at the table in a silent hello, looked straight into Annie's eyes, and said, "Joseph's Crook just cancelled."

Everyone got silent, except Harry. Harry, confused, said, "Who's Joseph's crook? What did he steal? What got cancelled?"

Frank filled him in. "The block party is going to be held all over The Avenue this month. It's an open air jazz fest,

Jazz On The Avenue. Joseph's Crook was one of the two jazz bands lined up to play."

"Oh, you know, I noticed that on my delivery schedule. Lots of outdoor furniture for food and vendors, tents, a stage, that kind of thing. So you lost your band?"

"Well, one of them. Two were scheduled, one to play early and one to play later. Which one was this, Diana?"

"The early band. I guess we can get by with a band that starts as the sun goes down, but we'll miss a lot of folks that like to get out early."

"Maybe we can find another band."

"It's too late for that. It's less than two weeks away. Most bands will be booked already. I can call around, see what I can come up with."

"We can always go to plan B."

"There's a plan B?"

"There's always a plan B. This plan B would include CDs and a good sound system."

"That's not what we wanted. Give me a little time, I'll try to find another band."

"Thanks, Diana. Want to join us?"

"No, I'm picking up a to-go order. For some reason, a lot of my regulars that dock at the Marina are coming early this season. They're starting to come in today. I've spent all morning scheduling classes and calling in part-time instructors to cover."

"Why?"

"One of the messages said something about the rock and gem show. This is something that really brings in that crowd."

Annie and Mem shared a look. For the second time today, Mem said, "The moon is waxing gibbous."

Annie pulled out her cell phone and sent a text to all of her managers. "High alert. Marina boaters already here. Restock. Call part-timers. Moon waxing gibbous."

She thought about it, then copied the text to Laila.

Lunch arrived, everyone ate with relish and talked about things that didn't really matter, in the long run, to anyone.

3

As the group broke to carry on with the rest of the day, Annie went to the kitchen. The lunch rush was over, and she hoped to find Felicity with a free moment.

Felicity, normally perky, even in the face of servers and cooks coming and going and rogue turtles falling into soup, was anything but perky today. And Cookie, normally reticent, saying as few words as possible in Annie's presence, was also out of character.

Cookie aspired to more than he could ever hope as the cook at Mo's Tap. He showed such talent that Felicity convinced Annie to give him a shot at a fine dining restaurant so they wouldn't lose him.

Until today, Felicity had been nothing but supportive.

Today, Felicity had Cookie backed into a corner. She waved a butcher knife and punctuated her sentences with thrusts in Cookie's direction.

"I called three of my vendors today and cussed them out! Cussed them out! I have a Café to run, and I'm trying to get meals done for Ray's cruise. And we'll have hundreds of people coming through this week. Hundreds!

"We agreed, we agreed, that we would work together. We sat here together, and we made your orders for this weekend. Your menu was set. And now I find out you're the reason I'm missing stock? I cussed them out! I can't get meals ready for Ray! I don't have enough stock for the week! We agreed!"

"I didn't take that much! I had to practice. I've got so much on my mind, I come over here evenings, and I only took a few things, honest! I meant to leave you a note."

"Leave me a note! Leave me a note, sorry, Felicity, whatever you were using this pork roast for, just change it? Sorry, Felicity, that drawer of fresh vegetables shouldn't be a problem? Sorry, Felicity, for some reason, I just had to have four dozen eggs? Sorry, Felicity, you didn't need that bacon, did you?"

Annie tried to back out quietly to let her staff handle it on their own. After all, they had not asked for her intervention. Thankfully.

She didn't quite make it. Trudie came through the kitchen door with a quick step and a raised voice. "Annie! They need you upstairs!"

Felicity and Cookie turned. At the same time, she was able to hear, "Annie, he is ruining me! Ruining me!" and "She wants me to fail! I never should have listened to her!"

"Sorry, guys. It looks like the two of you are talking. That's half the battle, right? Um, Cookie, now that I'm thinking about it, who's making lunch at the Tap?"

Cookie looked down and mumbled, "George." It was a very soft mumble.

"Excuse me?"

He looked up and said a little louder, "George."

"George? My George? George, the bartender George?"

Nod.

"I didn't know he could cook. Can he cook? Who's covering the bar?"

Cookie looked down again.

Annie rolled her eyes, giving her head a roll for good measure. She turned and headed for the back stairwell and the next disaster.

Upstairs, a cluster of people she didn't know stood in a group and argued. The use of the word "stood" is something of a misnomer. It was an animated group, arms waving, heads rolling, voices raising, one ever louder than the next, and, actually, the group appeared to act like a wave. They waved and shouted in front of one table, then moved on, waving and shouting at another, then another....

Annie looked toward the corner of the room. Boone, Daryl and Donnie stood, faint smiles on their faces, silent and watchful. She moved to them.

"What's happening?"

Boone pointed. "See the guy in the suit?"

"Is that the Dwight I heard so much about at lunch?"

"The one and only. Seems he tried to hang Mem out to dry, but Mem was having none of it. Seems this group of people is onto his shenanigans and they are out for, um, maybe blood? But I think they would take a body part or two instead."

"And who are all of these people?"

"Exhibitors. Four of them were here earlier, then they left and checked into the places they're staying. I'm sorry to tell you that two or three of them went to the Inn."

"Know which two or three?"

"Definitely the woman with the flowy thing on, and that guy with a polo shirt. Maybe that guy over on the side with blue jeans and a big belt buckle. Looks like fake turquoise to me."

Donny added, "That guy that needs a bath and a haircut? I saw him pull his camper into the state park. These others, they got here later."

"I think Dwight is registered at the Inn. I remembered the name when Mem talked about him a couple of weeks ago. This ought to be a fun week."

"Maybe you can put him over in that carriage house."

"Can't. It's booked. Mom and Sam are coming for a month, and that crew is coming in for Ray's cruise."

"Yep. It's going to be a fun week for you."

"Any idea who asked for me? Trudie said I was 'needed.'"

"I think it was Dwight. Want me to introduce you?"

"No. I'll give it a minute and go over. What are you guys still doing here? Mem told me you were able to turn this fiasco into a minor payday."

"We're still on the clock. We're waiting to see where to move everything again. Nobody's happy, and no one told us they were finished with us."

Annie laughed. Daryl and Donnie were polite enough to look a little embarrassed.

Finally, Annie steeled herself, squared her shoulders, and waded into the group. With a raised voice, she said, "Dwight? I'm Annie. Did you need me?"

"Oh, thank goodness! Someone is finally here to help!"

"Help?"

"I haven't had time to check into the Inn, and I was told you might be downstairs. Thank goodness you were! I need you to take my bags over there and get me checked in."

"Excuse me?"

"My bags. They're over in that corner over there."

Annie looked. The luggage looked to be enough for a society maven for a month of outings and parties, no outfit worn more than once. Probably even a different pair of shoes and underwear for every day of the month. More like two pairs of shoes. Two sets of underwear.

"I'm sorry. We don't supply concierge service, and there are forms for you to sign."

Dwight waived a hand dismissively. "Don't worry about those forms. I'll get to them later, and surely you have people that can carry those bags."

"For a fee, I can supply 'people.'"

"Great. Get to it."

Annie pulled a cell phone out of her pocket. She called Henrie, told him the story, and they made a plan. She hung up. "Um, Dwight, you'll be up here for a while, right? I have to go downstairs. I'll be back."

Annie went to the kitchen and logged onto Felicity's laptop. The email was there, as promised. She made alterations to the lodging agreement as she and Henrie discussed, printed it out, and went back upstairs, heading straight for Boone and his boys, still waiting.

"Boone, I suppose you have no scruples about your boys double dipping? Being paid by the Inn to do work while they are on the clock, so to speak, for another person?"

"Normally, I would have scruples about that kind of thing, but today, I'll just have to set those aside."

"Great. Henrie has a full plate right now, but if one of you could nip down to the Inn to get a luggage carrier, I'll take care of getting the paperwork signed."

Daryl moved forward. "I could use the walk."

"Wait until I give you the word."

Annie met Dwight again, handed over the paperwork, which he barely touched before signing, and took the offered credit card. She used the card reader given to her by Felicity, plugged it into her phone, selected the Inn as the vendor, and ran the card for the number of days of residence plus extra expenses in the amount of five hundred dollars. Just in case.

It was denied. Four hundred dollars extra. Denied. Three hundred dollars extra. Denied. Two hundred dollars extra. Denied. Days of residence only. Denied.

"I'm sorry, Dwight, I'll need another card."

"What? What do you mean? That's the card I use for everything."

"Perhaps you need to check with the company?"

"Use this one." He flipped through his wallet, coming up with another card.

Annie tried again. Days plus five hundred dollars. Denied. Four hundred dollars. Denied. Three hundred dollars. Success.

"Sign this, please."

Dwight signed the credit card receipt and clicked "Okay." Then he realized what he had done.

"Wait just a minute! I shouldn't have to pay until I leave!"

Annie looked at him with a smile. "If you don't use all of the extra services placed on the card, you'll get a refund when you leave. Right now, you are being charged twenty dollars an hour for the amount of time it takes for luggage delivery, unless, of course, you would like to take your own?"

Dwight waved his hand again and went back to the group of angry exhibitors.

Annie motioned to Daryl to retrieve the luggage cart, checked her watch, and noted Boone checking as well. Their eyes met, heads nodding.

Annie took a breath and did the other thing Henrie had suggested. Guests had a habit of charging meals, wine, pastries and any number of items purchased at her string of businesses to their guest room at the Inn. Since all of the businesses on this side of The Avenue were connected, as a rule, the charges were accepted and sent immediately to Henrie for review.

In a final act of self-preservation, she sent an email to all of her managers. No charges would be accepted on Dwight's guest room account. Payment at time of service only.

Annie smiled at Boone and Donnie again, waving as she left.

4

Georgia went around the back of the Inn, coming into the all-season porch from the beach. This was close to her room. She would sneak in without being seen. She heard a young woman's voice and the cooing of her Fred coming from the direction of the foyer.

Georgia stripped off her muddy clothes, took a quick shower, redressed and went out the back way so she could enter through the front.

A woman, a little younger than she, had placed a blanket in front of the sofas in the foyer. Fred was on her back, alternately catching her own feet and reaching up for a dangling colorful toy, one of her favorites.

Kali and Ko lay on their stomachs, ever watchful that JoJo didn't drop the toy, or the baby didn't roll away. They were extra watchful for kidnappers.

Georgia sighed, wondering if she would ever figure it out. If she would ever get it right. Those cats seemed to do a better job of mothering than she ever could. The girl turned toward her and Georgia put the smile back on her face.

"Hi. Henrie must have gotten scared of the diapers. I'm Georgia, Fred's momma."

"JoJo. She's been so great. I came in right as she needed a clean diaper, so Henrie was spared."

At that moment, the cat door sprang open. Two cats and a little dog ran in, coming around the sofa to investigate. Kali and Ko stood up to hiss, but backed off as their friends came close, nosing up to Fred to investigate.

Georgia and JoJo laughed together. JoJo, glad to see the young mother didn't spook easily, asked, "So, you've already met some of the neighbors?"

"Oh, yes. They've been coming over since the first day. There must be some sort of jungle drum out there, letting the cats and dogs know if something exciting is happening. Do you know their names?"

"Sure. The large tabby is Simon Finnegan. The one that hangs back a bit is Oscar McMurphy. She's a girl, regardless of the name. They live across The Avenue above, and, well, I guess in, the hardware and electronics store. And this little dog is Tillie. She's a Jack Russell. She was left by some really awful people that stayed here at the Inn a couple of months ago. She lives up the street above Mr. Bean's now, with Carlos."

While the companions were being discussed, they completely displaced JoJo, who now stood next to Georgia, watching Fred giggle, coo and reach for noses, paws and tails.

Georgia nodded. "Oh, yes, I've seen her in there. She and Mr. Bean seem to compete for attention."

"It's the local 'big story.' Mr. Bean wants to be the only one to bring in foot traffic, but Tillie can be very engaging. They're working it out. The first time I went in, after Tillie moved in, I thought Mr. Bean was going to bite off Tillie's ear. But it's better now. At least a little bit."

Georgia let the silence stand for a while. "How long will you be here?"

"Henrie had to leave, and he just wanted me to stay with Fred. He said to stay as long as you needed me. I can stay a while longer if you need me, or if you're ready, I can go."

Georgia sighed. She really needed to go back to the box store to ask, again, for a job, but Henrie was paying this young woman. What should she do?

JoJo misread her silence. "It's okay, really. I'll go on home. Henrie asked me to come tomorrow. Is that alright with you?"

"Sure. Thanks."

"What time should I be here?"

Georgia thought about the day. She had to move to the new B&B, and there were so many places to go. "Can you meet me at the, I think it's the Snuggle Inn, at 10:00?"

"Sure."

"Do you know where it is?"

JoJo nodded.

"What kind of place is it?"

"It's a cute little cottage, and Martha is so nice. It's real small compared to the KaliKo, but you'll like it there."

Georgia gave a brief smile. She and JoJo remained standing, a little distance from the four cats and dog tending to Fred. Georgia, knowing how gentle the animals were, was still watchful. Just in case.

JoJo said her good-byes to Georgia, the baby and the companions and left.

Georgia sank into the sofa, elbows on her knees and her face in her hands. She was so tired. Bone tired. The muscles of her face hurt from the smiles, all the smiles that she kept plastered there.

With no adults near, she broke down again and cried, sobbing silently into her hands. Soon, she felt a wet nose on the one spot of her face not covered with a hand. She looked up. Tillie had come to her.

The sweet thing now settled next to Georgia with an anxious look. Georgia cupped a hand over the little head. She could make it. Certainly, if only she could find small kindnesses along the way. Like this one.

Kali and Ko jumped to their feet. Intruder alert! Footsteps on the porch! Georgia, roused by their alert, got on her knees to wrap the blanket around Fred. As she stood, Fred in her arms, the door burst open. Three loud, angry men and a woman entered.

They stopped short at the sight of a young woman with a baby and the sound of loud hissing.

The woman looked at Georgia. "Hello, there. We're all going to be staying here for the next several days. I'm Gema. I'm sorry we burst in like we did."

"It's okay," said Georgia. "I'm Georgia. This is Fred. Frederica. I'm here for one more night, so, um, maybe I'll see you for breakfast tomorrow?"

"Maybe. We're eating fairly early."

"Well, okay, then. Maybe." The men had already started to argue amongst themselves. Gema nodded as Georgia left. She chuckled to herself to watch the parade go down the hallway. Girl and baby, four big cats, a little dog, maybe a terrier. The dog turned to look every now and then, as if daring Gema to follow.

She left the men to their arguing to make a cup of tea at the Keurig corner. Henrie left a note about the snack in the refrigerator. Chocolate covered strawberries, ham and cheese roll-up sandwiches, a tray of fresh fruit and what looked to be a pitcher of fruit smoothie. She poured a small glass and sniffed. Mixed berry? Tasted. Mixed berry.

Gema thought about the girl. She looked lost. Poor thing, so young, with a baby. Just like me, thought Gema.

She put the thought away. No need to dwell on the past. She had found herself, and she was going nowhere but up. But in the meantime, karma placed this girl in her path.

Gema put a plate of snacks together: roll-ups, fresh fruit and chocolate covered strawberries. She could carry the plate without spilling anything, but just barely. Henrie had over-prepared. There was plenty left for everyone else.

She looked in the cupboard until she found a tall tea glass. She filled it with berry smoothie and went down the hallway recently taken by Georgia. She looked in the all-season porch. No one there. She knocked on the door at the end of the hallway. Georgia called out, "Come in."

Gema entered. Georgia had her back to the door and appeared to be wiping her eyes. Four cats and one dog stood guard around the baby in the middle of the bed.

"The boys were so rude, they probably chased you away. I don't know if you saw the snack Henrie left."

Georgia turned around. "No, I didn't even look. He always puts something out."

"Well, I brought you this plate and a smoothie. I hope it's okay."

Georgia, hunger gnawing, was able to hold it together. She said a gracious, "Thank you," took the plate and glass and placed them on the dresser.

Gema didn't leave. "So, you're leaving tomorrow. Are you going home? Vacation over?"

"No, no vacation. I'm going to another B&B, a smaller, cheaper one."

"So you're going to be in town for a while?"

Georgia didn't know why she felt compelled to answer. "I hope to find a job."

"What are you looking for?"

"Anything. I'm a good cook, a good waitress, I'm good with people. I could work in any store or shop. I'm not very good with secretarial stuff."

"Well, you're in the right town to find something to suit."

"But no one has an opening."

"All you have to do is wait them out. You know how often openings come up in restaurants. Cook asks server for a date and neither of them show up for work the next day."

"That's why I keep going back to the same places. So far, though, no luck."

"Well, here's wishing you luck. I'll be here all week, staying here and working the rock and gem show at Tiger Lily's Café. If you have a hard day while I'm here, look me up. I'm good for a hamburger and an opinion on the state of the world."

Back in the foyer, Dwight, Garry and Nelson were joined by Adam. Gema decided to play hostess. She invited the men to join her on the all-season porch. They didn't hear her until she waved her arms and whistled. Carried high, in a good waitress stance, were two trays with Henrie's snack. "Someone needs to bring the smoothie from the fridge."

She started walking, and like puppies, they followed.

Mem checked in at her own place, CyberHealth, then walked around The Avenue and Main Street to talk to her volunteers. She was going to keep her promise, darn it. She and Diana were to take tickets at the rock and gem show in the morning, and she needed to make sure everyone else was still committed.

At Lil' Socks' Virasana, she waited while Diana finished a class. Diana walked over, knowing what the conversation would be about. "Mom, I don't think I can be there. I've called all of my part-timers in for the week, but no one can cover tomorrow morning."

"But I thought you already covered it."

"I did, but with all these people coming back to The Marina early, I had to do some shuffling. There's a gap in the morning."

Little Socks lifted one lazy eye as she listened to the conversation. Very little got past her; lots of town gossip came through the studio.

Mem sighed. "Well, it just can't be helped. This just seems to be the week that everything will go wrong."

"Do you know the moon is waxing gibbous?"

Mem laughed. "Do I ever!"

"Well, it's my shift. I promised you. Let me call JoJo. I saw her walking down to the Inn earlier today. Maybe she's got some free time in between classes."

Diana picked up a cell phone and dialed. JoJo answered on the second ring. After a brief conversation, Diana rang off and turned back to Mem.

"She's babysitting in the morning, but Ben might be free." Diana was already dialing. After another conversation, she looked at Mem. "He's busy. I don't know who else to call. I've been calling people in all day, and of all those people I talked to, no one could come in tomorrow morning."

"I'll keep at it, dear. Don't worry. In a way, I caused your problem this week, so, anyway, don't worry."

Mem struck out everywhere she went.

Annie finally made it back to the Inn, cats in tow from every other place. The day had been long, filled with highs and lows. Now she needed Henrie.

No one greeted her in the foyer. No one in the dining room or kitchen. No snacks in the coffee and snack corner.

Annie walked to the all-season porch, hoping to find Henrie – or at least the snacks – out there. She found more than she bargained for. Dwight and several other people, more than could possibly be guests. She smiled, gamely, and welcomed everyone to the KaliKo Inn.

Dwight probably just couldn't help himself. He started on her again in a deeply condescending tone. "Are you going to take our breakfast orders, or do we just tell you what we want in the morning?"

Annie's breath caught in her throat. "Well, um, we don't really take orders. We do ask as you make a reservation if there are allergies or special needs. Do you have an allergy, or do you follow a vegetarian or vegan diet?"

"No, none of that. I just thought, you know, that you were more of a full-service kind of place."

"Oh. I see. Well, we are a full-service bed and breakfast, but that doesn't include menu services. Have you told Henrie what time you want to eat?"

Another man interjected himself into the conversation. "I don't think we met, I assume you're Annie, and the owner of this very nice place." He slid a sideways glance toward Dwight on this note. "I'm Garry, this is Gema, and over there is Nelson. We're staying here, and yes, we asked Henrie for breakfast at 6:00."

"I'm sure you'll find everything just the way you want it at 6:00, then." Annie looked around the room expectantly, silently counting five additional individuals. They said nothing. She assumed they were friends of her guests, so she said nothing more. Guests of guests were allowed, so long as it was not outrageous. She noticed that the snacks seemed to have emptied at tables next to the folks to whom she was not introduced.

Annie turned and went to Henrie's apartment. He didn't answer her knock. Next stop, the basement. Not there. She was puzzled, as he typically let her know, either by text, email or written note, if he left for an extended period.

On the second floor, she paused at the computer to check her email. Nothing there.

Someone was coming in through the kitchen door. Henrie and, was it Laila? Annie trotted downstairs and into the kitchen.

"Hi, Laila. Henrie. What's with all the boxes?"

Laila laughed. "You haven't seen what's already in the van."

"What's up?"

Henrie replied. "I am moving Georgia over to Martha's B&B tomorrow morning. She has not had guests in a while. I wanted to stock her pantry."

"And of course, we needed some empty boxes to pack Georgia and her baby."

"She doesn't have luggage?"

Henrie and Laila looked at one another. Laila finally looked at Annie. "She has a few more things than she did when she came."

"A few?" Annie looked at the pile of boxes. "What stuff?"

"Well, I've given her some of the kids' toys, and she needs diapers and things for the baby, so I've given her some things. Well, she thinks she bought most of it. I just maybe kind of doubled up."

"Think she'll forget what the value of a dollar is?"

"Well, to be frank, you did agree to…"

"…I know, Henrie. She's had her room here at half price. I'm glad she's going to the Snuggle Inn. Martha could use the business, and frankly, I think Georgia will be better off away from our new guests."

"Yes, our new guests do not endear themselves."

"To anyone, apparently. Well, it's a great idea, and I'm sure it was all yours, Henrie. What time will you move her?"

"I will take the food, already in the van, and some boxed items shortly. Laila will help Georgia pack some things now, and those boxes will be out of the way. We will have a leisurely breakfast tomorrow morning and leave afterward."

"Leisurely? With the rock and gem folks around?"

"They are dining at 6:00. They will be gone by 7:00." Henrie smiled.

"Well, while Laila is helping Georgia, might I have a word?"

"Certainly. Laila, when you finish, bring Georgia out for some coffee. I will get snacks from the refrigerator."

"The one in the Keurig corner?"

"Yes."

"Think again. Some guests of our guests polished those off."

"Well. Hmmm. Certainly I have additional here in the kitchen."

Henrie busied himself, Laila took a couple of boxes, and Annie wondered why the house was so quiet. Did she leave the cats at work?

She didn't know they were all in the back guest room, cooing in their cat voices at the baby.

Annie and Henrie heard, "Shoo! You leave this poor woman alone for just a minute, now!"

Nine cats and a dog skippered out of the room, down the hallway, and up the stairs to the second floor.

The telephone rang. Henrie was busy and Annie was the closest. "KaliKo Inn. May I help you?"

Annie held the phone away from her ear as Cheryl nearly screamed, "I need help! I haven't had time to call until now! Annie! Help!"

"Cheryl?"

"It's a disaster!"

"What's wrong?"

"You would think I didn't have a telephone, email, text, website, Facebook or any other method of communication. I even have a couple of cans connected with a string in the corner. And radios! We have radios! We have people coming in from all over, and only a couple let me know!"

"What do you need?"

"Everything! We need to clean and stock our restrooms and laundry, and our snack bar, and the little grocery store, and clean up the playground. And The Escape is still being repaired! Ray has a cruise this week, and that boat is still in dry dock!"

"Take a deep breath."

"Stop it with that breathing stuff!"

"It works! Take a deep breath!" Annie took a deep breath herself, helping to get Cheryl going in that direction. It worked.

"Okay. I'm breathing. I can think now. But I still don't know what to do next."

"First, give me a grocery and supplies list. I'll shop for you and bring things over right away. Now, who else do we need to call?"

Annie worked through the problems with Cheryl, and armed with a grocery list, left Henrie and Laila to deal with Georgia.

At the grocery store, Laila's eldest, James, was at the cash register. "Hey, Annie. I think Mom's over at the Inn."

"She is. I'm on a different mission. Do you have any more boxes?"

With James' help, Annie filled Cheryl's order, barely. "Your shelves are getting a little bare."

"All the B&Bs waited until the last minute to stock up, and a bunch of folks have come over from The Marina. Aren't they early this year?"

"Yes, that's part of the problem. How long will it take to get these shelves stocked again?"

"Mom gave me a list early this afternoon. Somehow she knew about the boaters. She said something strange about the moon. Anyway, tomorrow morning, I'm taking the van to Marsh Haven to pick up a lot of supplies. We're going to pay premium prices, but, like Mom says, when you're between a rock and a hard place, you have to punt."

"Punt? That's part of the saying?"

"I think she made it up."

"Speaking of your van, since my van is filled with stuff your mother put into it, may I borrow yours to take this to Cheryl?"

"Sure. Keys are in it. Pull it around front and I'll help you load."

At The Marina, Annie pulled into the common area. It was filled. People caught up with old friends, walked through the little grocery store with empty shelves, complained about the lack of stock.

Annie and Cheryl quickly stocked the shelves, then Annie took laundry and restroom supplies to finish the job. Cheryl stayed on the cash register.

Once the first rush had been satisfied, Annie asked, "You don't have your help yet?"

"It's not time! I have two starting next week, just to get things 'ready,' but we're past that. Neither are available until next week."

"And The Escape? How far from finished is it?"

The Escape was a yacht fashioned into a fishing and cruising ship by Cheryl's husband Ray. A couple of months before, it was docked when a severe winter storm came through. Damage was taken to the hull as well as deck areas.

Annie decided not to tell Cheryl that the provisions for Ray's scheduled tour had also taken some damage. In the form of Cookie practicing for his big debut. Hopefully, Felicity would fix that mess and Ray would be none the wiser.

"Well, the good news would be that The Escape is fixed and leaves on time. The bad news would be that we don't get it done and you'll have six guests at the Inn with nothing to do. Except to be angry about not going on a cruise."

Annie rolled her eyes. "I don't know which to hope for more." She paused, then continued. "Let's think this through. Let's assume The Escape takes off and you don't have to worry about that. Who can you call to work at The Marina?"

"I already tried the folks that work with Diana. She got to them first. I can get some of them some of the time. Ben said he could be here toward the end of the week. JoJo is busy doing something for Henrie."

"For Henrie?"

"That's what she said."

"I'll check that out. Henrie could probably get along without her if he knew what was going on."

"You have a full house."

"You're right. Maybe I'd better not beg Henrie to let her go. Have you called Ginger?"

"Yes, well, I texted her. She hasn't answered yet."

"What about Janet?"

"Janet?"

"Yes. She doesn't have a job. Maybe she wouldn't mind helping you out."

"I'll call her this evening."

Janet was Ginger's mother and the wife of Pete, the Chief of Police. She was the ultimate volunteer.

"You'd better call her now. I think Mem is looking for volunteers for the rock and gem show."

Cheryl got her cell phone from a pocket and dialed. After a brief conversation, she hung up, only slightly less dejected.

"Mem just asked her to work every day at the show, but she'll have Ginger call. She might be able to help. I know Ginger will have some of the yoga classes as well."

"This is an all-hands-on-deck week. We'll get through it."

By the time Annie got back to the Inn, Chris, her very special friend, waited to take her and Henrie to supper.

5

The argument on the all-season porch had moved to Mo's Tap. Sitting at a large table was a group of people that appeared to be at one another's throats one minute and best of friends the next.

Candice, the floor manager, took the table herself. She could smell trouble and thought that some of these people were staying at the Inn. She recognized the rock and gem traffic, having watched them walk from the Café to the Inn and back a few times.

Through the evening, serving sandwiches and drinks, she picked up the names of most of them and figured out who was staying at the Inn.

She pegged Dwight right away and cringed inwardly when he said, "Put the first round of drinks on my tab, sweetie."

Part of the cringe was for the "sweetie" comment; the rest was for the knowledge that the tab might be tough to collect at night's end.

So he was the organizer of the rock and gem show. If she and George were "on," she might cruise the show to see if she could find a suitable ring for a possible engagement, or even a potential promise of maybe we'll talk about it in a few years. But no. She and George were "off" again.

Last month, a…let's not call her that "s" word…came in every day for a couple of weeks and worked on him. And worked on him. And worked on him. One night, drunk beyond getting herself home any other way, George drove her. All the way to Marsh Haven. He was supposed to be home within the hour. He drug in at 9:00. In the morning. By 9:00, Candice was in her own home, in her own bed, cell phone set to disregard all calls and texts from his. She came to work every day and worked with him as she always did, but really. This was the limit.

George had tried to talk to her several times. She cut him off as soon as she saw where the conversation was headed with a curt, "You could have called, you could have texted, you could have messaged, you could have pulled into a twenty-four-hour gas station and asked an attendant to call. I don't want to hear it."

Doing her job, she let George know as soon as she realized Dwight was in the house and pointed him out.

"Bummer," he said, and handed her a tab from the round Dwight picked up at the bar.

George was back and forth, sometimes in the kitchen, picking up the slack from Cookie's distraction. When Candice noticed, she slipped behind the bar, asking other servers to cover her tables for the time she had to pull bar duty. The servers didn't care. This happened on occasion and Candice always made sure to share tips. Giving good service to Candice's customers meant better tips all the way around.

Moving from bar to floor and back again, Candice identified Nelson, who wore pressed blue jeans. They even had a crease. She gathered he was one of the major exhibitors and showed primarily stones and jewelry made with Larimar. From the conversation, she picked up some tension between Nelson and the major turquoise exhibitor, a woman named Kristina. Kristina called Larimar the "fake" turquoise. And that argument went around a few times. It appeared Nelson was staying at the Inn while Kristina had a trailer at the campground.

She picked out Adam, a disheveled man also staying at the campground. He seemed to command a great deal of respect and animosity at the same time. It appeared, from the snippets she heard, that he was an expert on stones, fossils and minerals of all types. He was willing to help anyone, even those at the table that didn't like him. It also appeared his prices were lower than anyone at the table. This was apparently one cause of the animosity.

Candice heard Adam's retort on this as well. "If you didn't put so much money into your fancy display cases and your fancy tools, you wouldn't have to charge so much."

On one occasion, she heard a woman whose name she didn't catch say, "I hate it when they put me next to you. Your tables are such a mess that people don't want to come near us."

A large part of the discussion had been about placement. Who deserved to be in front. Who deserved a prized corner position. Who deserved to be as far away from Adam as possible. And where should he go? Of course, according to Adam, in one of the prime spots.

Candice picked up that Mem was to be called to put together volunteers to rearrange the facility before 7:00. The show was to start at 9:00. Candice chuckled to herself, having heard all about Mem's morning. She sent a text to Mem as forewarning.

Pattie, another woman in the group, stayed at another B&B in town, Sunset Breeze. Candice knew the owner and manager, Howard. He sat at the bar, alone tonight, apparently people-watching.

Pattie seemed to have a difficult time working her way into any conversation. From what Candice could pick up, her stock was mainly glass and synthetic beads and jewelry. She gathered the exhibitors who carried stones had little respect for her product and even less respect for the individuals who flocked to her as an affordable alternative.

This night seemed to go on forever. The large table was still drinking when the kitchen closed to all but the bare minimum needed to keep a liquor license: sandwiches and soups that could be pulled from the freezer and microwaved on demand.

Most of the servers began to clock out. Their regular customers tended to go home about this time, leaving the bar to tourists and a few late-night prowlers.

George got Candice's attention. "I have to go back and check inventory in the kitchen. I don't think Cookie has been taking care of it."

Candice took the bar, motioning to the one remaining server to keep an eye on her last table, Dwight's table. Howard and a couple of others sat at the bar. Howard motioned Candice over.

"Would you like another?"

"No, I'm done for the night. I just wondered if you could tell me what it's like to work for Annie."

"Annie?"

"Yeah. What's she like? As a boss, I mean."

"She's a great boss. She pays us well, makes sure we have benefits, at least if we're full-time. That's unusual in this business."

"How can she afford to do that?"

A little birdie told Candice she had probably said too much already. "Don't know, Howard. Maybe you need to talk to her. Sure I can't get you another?"

As Howard shook his head, Candice walked to the far end of the bar, pulled out her cell phone and sent a text message to both George and Annie.

And then the bottom fell out of the evening.

Her table got up and walked out, en masse. The server, from the far side of the room, looked at them wide-eyed, then looked at Candice.

Candice left the bar and followed them out, calling Dwight by name. "Dwight, you all have a pretty big bill here."

Dwight, headed down the sidewalk toward the KaliKo Inn, turned around, continuing to walk backward, "Well, sweetie, you just put all of that on my tab at the Inn."

"I can't do that, it doesn't work that way."

"Make it work, sweetie. I'll probably see you again tomorrow."

When Candice got back to the bar, George was out of the kitchen. He knew what was happening. "How bad is it?"

Candice stood at the adding machine, totaling meals and drinks for seven people. They had been in most of the evening, and the drinks bill alone was high.

"A little over three hundred dollars, plus tax."

"I suppose no one left a tip?"

"Not a penny."

George took the bill, added the tax, added a twenty percent tip, logged it into the account for the Inn and sent a text to both Annie and Henrie. He sent a second text. "I know, I know! Couldn't be helped!"

6

Annie, Chris and Henrie took a tall table at the back of the main tasting room. By the time they arrived, the back garden area was already full with boaters from The Marina, locals and a few rock and gem show exhibitors. Annie waved to Felicity and Trudie, sitting at another tall table, through the doorway and around the corner from their own.

Mem and Diana joined Annie's group. They had to drag the last available chair from the tasting bar to fit five at the table.

"I guess we're all going to be a little bit busier than we planned," said Diana. "Do Jesus and Minnie have things under control?"

"It appears they're having to scramble tonight. I'll get up and help if they need it. Minnie said she was able to get extra staff in for the rest of the week, and she thinks they over-stocked, at least with food. She rolled her eyes when I asked about wine, but at any rate, they should be in better shape than the Café. And the Grille." Annie put her head in her hands at that last thought.

Chris asked, "Trouble in paradise?"

"Yes. I need a glass of wine before talking about it, though."

"Fair enough."

Jesus took time to stop by the table. One of Annie's trusted managers, he and Minnie, together, made Sassy P's a premier evening spot. Their partnership extended to their personal relationship as well.

"Let me know if you need me to step up tonight, Jesus. I can serve tables, serve wine, whatever you need."

"I think we will be fine. The only problem I have is that the wine we planned to feature for the next two weeks was not delivered."

"Will it be here tomorrow?"

"Nope. Mix-up at the winery sending it. They sent it somewhere else, and that place accepted delivery and is not inclined to return it."

"So what will you do?"

"I've called around. We won't have a special going on for the next couple of weeks, but I'll take a quick trip through the region tomorrow morning and get enough to cover us."

Annie looked around the room. "Let me know if you need anything tomorrow, but for now, let me at least serve this table. I'll leave a list for Minnie of the bottles and food we use. Will that work?"

"It will. Thanks!"

Diana got up. "I'll set the table."

In no time, Annie and Diana served a chilled viognier and a zinfandel, a variety of white and yellow cheeses, salami, prosciutto and two types of crackers. Annie left a list of items served at the cash register for Minnie to take care of later.

While they took care of serving, Mem told Henrie and Chris about her morning. She was just finishing as the meal was set. "Tomorrow morning, the first dollars out of the till will be five hundred dollars to me. And the next seventy-five dollars and thirty-three cents go to DoubleGood.

Mem looked up as two familiar individuals walked into the winery. "What are they up to now, I wonder?"

Geraldine and Hank. Hank, through some shenanigans two months earlier, had finally been removed from his seat on the town council. Geraldine, a wilting socialite, had committed a variety of offenses, some criminal, against Annie and her businesses. They were both currently free of judicial encumbrances and apparently as free as ever to spend money they didn't have. They walked through the tasting room and into the garden dining area, not looking right or left.

"They aren't going to find a table."

"Maybe they're meeting someone."

Diana leaned over to watch their progress. "They're sitting down with a couple. I don't know them. Oh, wait. The woman came in to get a schedule of classes. I think she's staying at the Inn. She's an exhibitor."

Henrie said, "That would be Gema. I wonder who she is with. I did not get the impression she knew anyone in town."

"Probably another exhibitor."

"Possibly. She did not appear to get along well with the others at the Inn. Excuse me."

Henrie got up from the table and appeared to head for the restroom. He glanced casually into the dining area, stopped, turned around and sat back down.

"I do not believe it. She is with the man she argued with most forcefully. Garry."

"Garry," said Mem. "He's the reason I'm taking five hundred dollars out of the till. That cash on delivery was for him."

"This seems to be a presumptive lot," added Henrie.

"A presumptive lot who somehow have managed – already – to acquaint themselves with the finest citizens Chelsea has to offer. Henrie, what do you think about locking up the china and silver for the week?"

Henrie gave Annie a stare. "I shall do an inventory count daily."

"Good enough."

The group lapsed into silence while cheese, crackers, meats and wine were enjoyed.

Mem picked up her vibrating cell phone and read a text. "Oh, no. Oh, no, no, no, no, no."

"No?" asked Chris.

"Candice picked up a little tidbit at Mo's. It appears Dwight is going to call me tonight and tell me to rearrange all of the tables before 7:00 tomorrow morning. He will, of course, expect me to get a crew, for no charge."

"What are you going to do?"

"First, I'll not answer my phone unless I know who it is. Second, I'm going to sleep in. CyberHealth is taken care of tomorrow; I'm supposed to be at the gem show a little before 9:00 to start selling tickets. I'll show up a little before 9:00 to start selling tickets."

The group laughed, talked some more about nothing important and laughed some more. Eventually, the conversation was halted by raised voices from around the corner. Felicity and Cookie.

Annie said, "Uh oh."

Diana asked, "Where did Cookie come from? I thought he was working tonight."

"He was." Annie looked at her watch. "Wow. We've been here a long time! The kitchen at Mo's is closed now. He must have come in through the garden."

The garden, when fully opened for the season, shared space with Mo's Tap, allowing guests to go from one place to the other. And allowing Cookie, obviously, to move around as well.

Chris smiled. "So there is trouble in paradise. How bad is it?"

"They'll get through it. I'm trying to not get involved. This was, after all, Felicity's idea. And now, Cookie has apparently been going into the Café at night to get supplies, and he has 'practiced' with those supplies. This means that Felicity, with several things on her plate this week, is short."

"Isn't one of those things catering a cruise for Ray?"

"Yes. The Marina has their backs to the wall this week as well."

"I know. Ray came over to the Coast Guard Station this afternoon. He had to blow off some steam about his contractor. He doesn't even know if The Escape will be ready in time for the cruise."

"I wonder if Felicity needs to worry about preparing the meals?"

"I think she should go ahead. If I know Ray, he'll be out there working on that boat through the wee hours of the morning to get it ready on time."

Henrie looked at Annie. "Is it possible the crew coming in this week will not be able to go on a cruise?"

"Oh, certainly Ray will do something. If he can't get The Escape fixed, perhaps he could borrow another yacht."

Everyone looked at Chris, as if he would have knowledge of yachts for rent. He decided to act as if he were informed. "At worst, you're looking at a day's delay while Ray gets something else. Maybe. Probably."

Everyone looked up as Cookie stormed past the table on his way out of the winery.

Diana's phone vibrated. "What now?" She read the text message, and then stared at it for a while.

"Diana?" said Mem.

"Well, Sahara just cancelled."

"Sahara, too? I haven't even asked, were you able to find a band to replace Joseph's Crook?"

"Nope."

"So now we're down to zero bands?"

"Zero. None. Nada. Zip. We're going to have a great time during Jazz On The Avenue, seeing as how there won't be any jazz on The Avenue."

It was Annie's turn to receive a text. This was from Candice. "Howard asked Candice about me, what kind of an owner/manager I am."

The group commiserated for a while as they finished their wine. They decided to go home for the evening before more bad news could arrive. They didn't make it. Annie and Henrie both reached for their phones.

Annie spoke first. "Well, Henrie, we need another plan. Doing the math, with the bill from Mo's and what we owe Boone and the boys, Dwight has definitely exceeded his three hundred dollar budget."

"I have been thinking about that. I will be ready in the morning."

Mem had one parting statement. "The moon is waxing gibbous."

Geraldine and Hank joined Gema and Garry at a table in a corner of Sassy P's. Geraldine greeted Gema warmly. "Darling! It's so good to see you here in Chelsea!"

"I'm glad to be here. You know how important this is to me."

"I do, dear. And Garry, it's good to see you, too."

"Hello, Hank, Geraldine. Will your husband be joining us tonight?"

"No, not tonight, dear. He hopes to see you several times throughout the week, though."

"Well, I hope he comes by early. I've got quite the ring to show him. I want to encourage him to buy this for you. It's perfect."

"Well, perhaps I should see it first and let you know if I agree."

"I'll show you first thing in the morning!"

Hank inserted himself into the conversation. "Let's talk about this little deal you have for us."

"Oh, yes," said Garry. "Gema, why don't you explain it to them?"

"Well, as you know, I want to get out of the gem show game and open a storefront design studio. Garry loves this life. I can't stand it. If I can get a storefront, I can carry Garry's fine lines along with my more artful line."

"So you both have something at stake here."

"Yes. And we will both make an investment, so it would be easier all the way around. But I have to make a splash. I have to have a big sale at this show. People have to get to know me and my work."

"Do you really think Chelsea is the place you'll make it?"

"Oh, yes. If I can keep Garry from diverting the big money to himself, like he just did with you."

"Well, dear, I'll spread my money around this week!"

Geraldine didn't bother to tell either Gema or Garry that her credit cards were at their limit, or that the mortgage on her house was at the maximum limit with two additional loans. The home had been a gift from her wealthy parents when she married, some twenty years ago. A mortgage wasn't taken on the home until Geraldine and her husband, Everett, had run through her inheritance several years later.

Geraldine hoped to be a backer in the planned jewelry store without actually giving any money to anyone. She had stars in her eyes once again, imagining financial security.

"Hank, why don't you tell them our plans for the storefront."

"Well, yes, you see, this street is the perfect place for a jewelry store. Lots of opportunity from well-to-do locals, and people from all over the region come here often. And tourists! People dock at The Marina for several months at a time, people in the campground. We have bed and breakfasts and a couple of hotels. They're generally at ninety to ninety five percent capacity during the tourist season."

Gema's smile was radiant. "Do you have a place in mind? Is there a vacant storefront, or is there an opportunity to build?"

Hank answered. "I think we could find you a place right here on The Avenue."

"Yes," said Geraldine. "As a matter of fact, one very close to this winery. I think the winery would be a draw for your store, and the bar up the street. Even the bakery would bring people by your front windows."

"Well, that leaves the yoga studio and the Café, at least on this side. I haven't looked closely at the other side of The Avenue."

"You're right. And you hit the nail on the head. I think the storefront that could most easily be made available would be the yoga studio."

"I'm going there tomorrow. She has an early morning class. I'll talk to her about the possibility of a change."

Geraldine and Hank spoke at once. "Oh, no! Don't do that!"

They looked at one another, then Geraldine looked back at Gema. "The woman that runs the studio doesn't own it."

"Oh, I know that. Garry and I both have a room at the KaliKo Inn; we know everything on this side is owned by the same woman. I just thought..."

"Well don't think about it. Please don't say anything to either woman. At least, not yet. Look around while you enjoy the class. Be sure the building will suit your purpose."

As they chose wines and cheeses, Gema took the time to look around. They were in what looked like an extended dining room. That back wall appeared to be moveable, so perhaps this space expanded into a garden dining area once the weather was warmer. She could see through to the main tasting room. It was bright and modern with a healthy amount of wooden touches. Display counters, shelving and the bar had a light walnut finish, and the bar had delicate hand-carved trim. The wall behind the tasting bar was painted cranberry red; the other walls were lavender. At the end of the bar were a few café tables; several men and women sat at the bar in highly polished wooden stools with seats resembling hollowed out wine barrels.

This garden area was casual but elegant at the same time, with regular dining tables in the center and taller café tables around the edges. A second tasting bar was available, unused for the moment, against the wall that must be attached to the Confectionary. Potted plants, miniature trees and flowering shrubs were available in abundance, sitting around and near load-bearing beams, lending an air of privacy to most of the tables.

Gema gave a start when someone walked past the table, coming from behind. She watched as the man approached a table close to the door to the tasting room and sat down.

Cookie, tense, approached the table with Felicity and Trudie. They had just finished a tray of meats and cheeses; both had a glass of wine.

Felicity looked at Cookie, took a deep breath, and said, "Okay. Let's start over. Have a seat."

Cookie gave her a tentative smile and sat.

"So, I'm really sorry, Felicity. Really. I didn't think. I saw you were filled to the gills and I thought surely you didn't need everything. I didn't think. Just didn't think."

"I'm sorry for yelling at you. We're all on edge this week. The moon is coming full, and that gem show may end up being a giant thorn in our sides. What a week for you to have a grand opening."

"I appreciate everything you've done. Really."

Minnie approached the table. "Cookie, what can I get for you?"

"Do you have a Zin open?"

"If not, I would open it for you. Coming right up."

Cookie turned back to Felicity. "You were doing something about the ambiance."

"Yes. Let's get that out of the way first. I know you wanted something that popped, and I think I've got just what you need. I hope so, anyway. No one had what I wanted as a rental, so I purchased linens for you."

"Linens?"

"Yeah. Table coverings, napkins. You know how the tables at the Café are painted in bright colors, and the chairs have those same bright colors?"

"Yeah."

"Well, Trudie and I found linen table coverings in all of Annie's rainbow colors, and napkins, too. We'll make sure that we mix the napkins up, so the only way a napkin will match another one at the table will be if two or more tables are pushed together. That way, you will have the elegance of linen but keep the artsy nature of the Café in place."

"Wow. I can see it! Rainbow colors all over the Café. Thanks! I would never have been able to pull that off."

"You're welcome. And Trudie thought…"

Trudie took over, "We have to keep Tiger Lily's table ledges available, just in case she comes in, so I've been spending evenings at the sewing machine. We've made hemmed cut-outs in each side, so the cloths will fit over her ledges exactly."

"And your dishes will work out for me?"

"I worried about that. We aim for casual at the Café, but really, everything is either white or colorful, all china or crockery or glass. On linen, they should appear elegant as well."

"So we're set."

"The ambiance is set. Let's talk about your staff."

"My staff? Your people won't help?"

"Cookie, I told you they can't work that many hours in a week! I need them. I have a business to run. I have one big catering order and a couple of small ones, and that gem show is bringing huge numbers in. I've had to call everyone in to work extra hours this week already."

"But who's going to help me cook? I need servers, and a host or hostess!"

"I told you, and told you, and told you, that you have to hire your own people."

"I don't know how to do that!"

"I would help, but you haven't done the first thing!"

"What was I supposed to do?"

"I told you! Call the paper, place an ad, put flyers at the community college…but it's too late for any of that now."

"What am I going to do?"

Felicity's voice raised, high enough for Annie's table to hear, "I frankly don't give a rat's hind end what you do!"

Cookie, angry, held his temper. He looked down at the table. He knew if he didn't hold it together, he would lose everything. He was counting on Felicity to get him started.

He took a few deep breaths, then looked up, first at Felicity, then Trudie. "I'm sorry. I've been concentrating on the cooking, just assuming everything else would come together."

Felicity responded. "You thought we would do everything else for you."

Cookie nodded as he again looked at the table, wondering where to take this, how to say it.

He looked up again. "If you could just help me through this first weekend, this grand opening, I promise I'll get an ad in the paper tomorrow and hire people for next weekend."

Felicity started to relent. Trudie interrupted. "Cookie, do you know how many times you have promised to do something and then let it go, expecting Felicity to fix it for you?"

"Yes, I do. I know. I know. I've been a rat. I promise. I promise I'll run that ad tomorrow."

Trudie and Felicity looked at one another. Trudie relented. "I was planning on spending the weekend helping you wherever you needed me. The coffee bar won't be open, so I can cook or serve or whatever."

Cookie stared at her. The smile that had started to widen froze, midway.

Felicity didn't notice. "I was going to help you, too. I'll do whatever you need, and I'll try to convince some other folks to commit to working this weekend."

Cookie still stared at Trudie. "What do you mean, the coffee bar won't be open?"

Trudie, eyes wide, said, "Oh, no! Oh, no! I'm not standing behind that bar all weekend, not for you and not for anyone else!"

Felicity cut in, "What do you mean? I thought you were going to just make straight coffee and decaf coffee. The bar was never in the deal."

"You said the Café would be open to me. The coffee bar is part of it!"

Felicity could do nothing but stare.

Cookie got up from the table and stormed out the door, being careful to leave by the Winery door. He didn't want to run into George by leaving through Mo's.

7

Henrie was up early Tuesday morning. He looked outside. The moon, still waxing gibbous, was visible in the western sky. Carlos brought an early delivery. Fresh bagels and a warmer containing hot cinnamon rolls – one pan of regular, one pan made with spelt – were on the kitchen table.

Henrie prepared an egg casserole. This morning, the casserole contained prosciutto and scallions. He also filled a warming dish with asparagus and soft cooked eggs on toast. While bacon, sausage and ham sizzled in separate skillets, he made regular and decaf coffee, put out cereals, fresh fruit and yogurt, and made sure the plates and silver were free of cat hair. He checked condiments: salt, pepper, hot sauce, cream cheese, honey, jams and jellies.

Slices of fresh wheat, white, rye and multi-grain breads were in a basket beside a toaster. A steaming pan of oatmeal with cranberries and walnuts graced the middle of the buffet.

Pitchers of orange, cranberry and grapefruit juice sat in chillers.

Kali and Ko appeared just as the meats went into their warming servers. Right on time. He took a piece of bacon and crumbled it into two dishes. If he put treats in one dish, Kali would never get a bite.

They ate, then trotted down the hallway to check on Fred.

Breakfast was served. The hands of the clock moved past 6:00. Henrie went to his computer to do a web search. He sent some emails and printed out a few pages. It was now 6:20. By the time the clock reached 6:30, Henrie struggled to stay awake. He had nothing to keep himself busy, so he sipped on a third cup of coffee, hoping for a caffeine rush.

He stepped into his apartment to get a book and heard someone in the dining room. Rushing out, he saw no one. Someone had gotten something to go, however. The to-go containers were in the kitchen, untouched, but some of the meats, some egg casserole, a helping of eggs over asparagus and toast, half a pan of cinnamon rolls and several bagels had been carried away.

At 6:45, he heard someone come down the stairs. It was Gema. Henrie greeted Gema in the dining room, pot of coffee in hand.

"Good morning. Did you sleep well?"

"Yes, thanks! Just a bagel for me! I'm taking an early morning yoga class!"

Gema was gone.

Henrie put the pot back on the warmer, wondering if he should pour it out and make a fresh pot. Not yet.

At 7:00, Nelson came downstairs. Henrie greeted him in the dining room, pot of coffee in hand. "Good morning. Did you sleep well?"

Nelson looked into the warmers and poked through the serving dishes with his fingers. "Huh? Oh, sure, sure. I'll take a cup of that coffee to go, cream and sugar."

"Nothing else?"

"No, I don't go in much for breakfast. I have to set up my exhibit."

Nelson took the to-go cup offered by Henrie and left without another word, licking his fingers.

Henrie decided not to make a fresh pot of coffee. He spooned out the areas with holes made by Nelson's fingers and threw the food into the trash.

Just before 7:30, Dwight and Garry came down together, not speaking to one another. Henrie greeted them in the dining room, a less-than-fresh pot of coffee at the ready. "Good morning. Did you sleep well?"

Garry said, "Yeah, sure. Smells good. Too bad I slept in. Maybe I'll get up in time tomorrow." He left.

Dwight sat down. With his typical swagger, he said "I'll take a cup of that coffee, my good man." His cell phone rang.

"What? Who? Mem! Good! You got my message. Is it all set up now? The right way?"

Dwight got up and started to pace. "What do you mean, you just got the message?"

He continued to pace. "The show opens in an hour!"

He continued to pace, phone held tight against his ear. Henrie did not react.

Dwight clicked off the phone, angry. "I have to get over to the show. I can't believe that woman didn't get over there! I left a message for her last night! I need to go fix this."

Henrie realized he was going to lose his chance.

"Excuse me, Dwight. I am so glad we have this moment alone, and I know you are in a rush. I will be brief."

"What is it?"

Henrie reached into the buffet and pulled out a printed web page. "Well, you see, my goodness, you do photograph well. I found this likeness on your website. I took the time this morning to conduct some research. Quite impressive. You must be very successful."

"Yeah, yeah. So?"

"So, you see, you left Mo's Tap last night without paying the bill, the bill that you requested be put on your tab. The staff thought, of course, that you were running a tab there. At Mo's Tap. It appears you intended the tab to come to your room. While, for many guests, that is a reasonable expectation, here at the KaliKo Inn, we will be unable to accommodate any future expense."

"What?"

"You see, your credit card was debited for the nights of stay plus the three hundred dollars the card would allow. Given the expense to porter your bags from the Café to your room and the bill from the Tap, the three hundred dollars has more than depreciated."

Dwight seemed to think about it, probably running the last sentence through his mind a couple of times. Finally, he said, "I'll get you the money."

"I am sure you intend to. As I said, your photograph is quite good. Very natural. I took the liberty of sharing the photo with all of Annie's managers. I am afraid that for the rest of your stay, you will be asked to pay for anything you purchase up front."

"Up front?"

"Yes. If you order a meal from the Café, they will present a bill before preparing the meal. As with all of the other establishments."

Dwight stared at Henrie.

Henrie continued. "Unless, of course, you can offer another credit card?"

Dwight gave Henrie one last stare, turned and left.

Henrie finally emptied the coffee pots, both regular and decaf, and made fresh ones.

At 8:15, Mem arrived at the gem show with Janet. Both were prepared to sit at the ticket table until 1:00, at least.

Mem was surprised to see that Dwight's booth, the very first booth as guests entered the hall, was completely set up. Displays were attractively arrayed and prices displayed. Larger pieces, hard to carry away without notice, were in front. Smaller pieces were inside locked glass cases. Dwight was not visible.

Mem was not surprised to see many of the other exhibitors in a flurry of activity. She noticed some of the tables had been moved, but not all. Exhibitors were "making do" with the final placement from the day before. She and Janet left the chain out, signifying the exhibit was not yet open, and took a quick walk around the room, making notes as they walked. They wanted to be able to direct inquisitive customers to the correct booth if asked.

Gema had some outstanding, artfully crafted pieces of jewelry. She calmly put finishing touches on her display. "How lovely," exclaimed both Mem and Janet. They spent a minute at the booth and promised to return before the week was out.

Gema was gracious and relaxed. She leaned in close. "Don't let Dwight get to you. He's a horse's hind end."

"So I gather. By the way, how early did he arrive to get his booth in such good shape?"

Gema laughed. "He hires it done. He doesn't think we know. Since he always has a key to the space, he sends in a crew of three men in the middle of the night, the night before a show. Those same men will hang out in town throughout the show, just in case he needs them, and in the snap of a finger, when the show is over, they'll tear his booth down and load it on the truck for the next show."

"No! Why didn't he have them move the tables?"

"He doesn't want anyone to know he has them at his disposal. I don't know what the big secret is. We all know. Those men will even come to the show every day. We all know who they are. I even know their names, but of course I'm not supposed to."

"One more reason to do absolutely nothing when he calls with another imperious demand."

"You've got that right!"

Mem and Janet moved on. Mem laughed to herself to see Adam behind piles of what looked like produce crates, large covered bins, plastic freezer containers, and who-knows-what covered in plastic tarps. The tops of his tables were filled with single layers of the same items, dusty, jumbled, and in no order that she could tell.

Adam waved hello with a cinnamon roll. A Tupperware container sat on the table with the detritus of what looked to have been a large and delicious breakfast.

Nelson was busy with an extensive Larimar display. Next to him was a woman Mem had seen but to whom she had not been introduced. Kristina could not hide her distain at her two neighbors, Adam and Nelson. Her turquoise exhibit appeared to be top notch.

Making a slight turn, they saw another exhibit. Fully put together, this set of tables held an attractive and distinctly singular display of stones: polished stone jewelry; animal carvings, fish, birds and mythical creatures, from miniature – the size of a fingertip – to large – up to four feet tall; lamps and other items made using natural stone; and stones and artifacts used to develop and enhance individual personal powers.

A handsome man, tall, slender, and dressed in casual business attire, sat in a comfortable canvas folding chair, a small table to its side with a lamp and some books. Several bottles of water sat in what looked to be a large champagne chiller.

Attracted as much to the relaxed man as the display, they stopped.

"Good morning. I'm Mem, this is Janet. We'll be working the ticket desk this morning, and, well, for most of the week."

"So you're Mem. I've heard so much about you, and let me say that your appearance does not match the, um, descriptors that were used. I'm Martin. I try to stay out of the way of most of the other exhibitors. They probably use similar descriptors for me."

"I didn't notice you yesterday afternoon. I thought I had seen almost everyone."

"I came into town last night, but didn't check out the show space until this morning. From experience, I know to get here early on the first day and stake my claim for a good spot."

"And it looks like you've been ready to go for quite a while."

"I like to be ready before the clowns arrive." His eyes roamed over the room at that comment, looking at the frenzy of set-up going on just minutes before the show opened.

Mem wasn't sure what to think about his attitude. "Well, you have lovely items. I'm sure we'll be back."

Mem and Janet had gone full circle around the room and approached the fine jewelry stand. Garry, owner and designer, struggled to finish his displays. They were wood and glass, lighted on the inside, and filled with what appeared to be very expensive designer jewelry.

Garry looked up with a smile. He saw it was Mem and turned it to a scowl. Mem smiled sweetly and turned to look at the booth of Garry's neighbor, Pattie. Long rows of glass and synthetic beads were on display with costume jewelry.

Mem thought to herself, point and counter point.

Once they reached the ticket table, Mem looked at Dwight's exhibit. Now that she had walked around the room, she realized that Dwight's exhibit appeared to be a pale example of several of the other booths. It looked as if he had purchased items from others and placed them in his booth with enhanced prices.

At 9:00, Mem and Janet settled behind the table and admitted the first guests, a party of five. No one was in line behind them. The expected rush at 9:00 did not occur. Several people dribbled in throughout the morning, however.

They did not have the ability to accept debit or credit cards. Cash and checks started to fill the drawer. Most of the income to this point was in checks, made out to the Chelsea Rock & Gem Show.

Mem counted out one hundred fifty dollars in cash, wrote a note, and asked Janet to sign as a witness. The money went into her purse.

Harry arrived with the sound system. "I'll just set that up here and go back to the truck for the chairs." Harry looked around. Very few people walked through the displays. "I might stop for coffee first."

Dwight finally showed up for his booth at 10:30.

"A few people have come in. Since your booth is the first one they see, everyone has stopped there, looked around and moved on."

"Well, they'll be back. The folks that come to these shows can recognize quality when they see it."

"Surely," said Mem, dryly.

Dwight took a look at the sound system, checking that it worked.

Mem asked, "What are you going to use that for?"

"You're going to use it," he said. "At 12:00 and 3:00, you're going to announce door prize winners."

"Door prize winners? We haven't sold or given out door prize tickets."

"Yes, you have. Each ticket that you sell has a number. See?" He pointed to the lower right hand corner. "You're selling them in order, and at twelve and three we're going to run a random number generator. We'll always start with zero-zero-zero-one, and we'll stop with the number just before the ticket on the top of the pile."

"Oh, how clever," said Mem.

"I'll come over here and help you with it at noon today."

"You don't need to do that, Dwight. I can pull up a random number generator on my phone and run it. I suppose the winners have to be present?"

"Yes. We don't deliver. So you may have to go through several numbers before getting a winner. Just one each time."

"Where are the door prizes?"

"Top shelf of my front display cabinet. The winners come and make a choice. Any one piece that they want."

Mem walked over to look. To her, the prizes seemed incredibly cheap. She held her tongue and went back to her seat.

Dwight moved to the cash drawer and opened it. "There's hardly any cash! All checks! What gives?"

"You will see the note there. I've taken one hundred fifty dollars, and I will continue to take from the drawer until the five hundred seventy-five dollars and thirty-three cents has been reimbursed."

"I need that cash! I have bills to pay for this show!"

"And one of those bills is five hundred dollars. To me. And another is to the hardware store, whose owner pitched in to cover for you. Once those bills have been paid, the rest of the money will be yours to distribute as you see fit."

"But the five hundred is really Garry's bill. Go collect from him."

"My deal was with you. I'll collect from you. You collect from him."

"Are you going to make me call the police?"

"Oh, no. As a matter of fact, the police just arrived."

Dwight whirled around. A tall, distinguished, dark-skinned man in a police uniform was coming from the elevator, a large, happy English setter at his side.

"Cyril!" cried Mem. "Come here and say hello."

Cyril obliged, coming behind the table to give both Mem and Janet licks of joy.

Mem turned to Dwight. "Allow me to introduce Pete, our Chief of Police. He's probably just checking in to see what's going on."

More people arrived. Mem, Dwight and Pete moved to the side to allow Janet to continue to take ticket money.

Pete picked up the conversation. "Well, actually, I've come to see the paperwork for your permit for this event."

"What?"

"Permit? I've been dealing with any number of traffic and parking issues this morning, and the first thing I did was ask Marco why we didn't have extra staff on duty. Guess what he said."

Mem, trying not to smile, said, "What did he say?"

"Marco said, 'I didn't know we needed extra people.' Guess what I said?"

Mem again, "What did you say?"

"I said, 'Whenever we have a permit for an event like this, it tells us we need to consider extra staff. Especially since all of the boaters seem to have come back early, just for this show.' Guess what he said?"

"What did he say?"

"He said, 'We didn't get a permit.' Then he went on to say he had gone to The Marina yesterday to help Cheryl, and she didn't know what everyone was doing back early. And then…"

"What did you say?"

"I said, 'Call the Town Clerk and find out what happened to that permit paperwork.'"

"I suppose Marco did that?"

"He did. He called, he asked, he hung up the phone, and he said, 'Well, boss, there is no permit.'"

At this, Pete and Mem turned to Dwight.

"No permit? Mem, can't you get anything right?"

Now, Dwight and Pete looked at Mem.

Mem took a deep breath. "Dwight, how computer literate are you?"

"What?"

"How skilled are you in the use of your computer, email, things like that?"

"I do okay, what's that got to do with this permit?"

"Well, I'm better than okay. I'm an expert. I will stand right here," she pulled out her cell phone, "and pull up that email I sent, oh, probably three months ago. The one that sent you the information, including the form from the Town Clerk's office, for the permit that you were to request. You know, I might even find your response, thanking me for the information."

Mem's hands had continued to move as she talked. Soon, she held her phone to Pete, who looked at the email, the message, the attachment, and the date. He moved to the next email, a response, thanking Mem for the information.

"I think you'll need to come to the town office to fix this before the day is out. There will be the cost for the permit and a late penalty."

"Well, officer, I'm going to have to tell you that this woman," he pointed to Mem, "has been taking money out of my till, so I'm not sure I'll have enough to pay you."

"Is that right?"

Mem nodded to Pete.

"There, see, she even admits it!"

By this time, Janet was clear of customers. She joined them and handed Mem another one hundred dollars. "I updated the note, showing that you now have two hundred fifty. You're almost halfway there."

"So you're both taking money?"

"No, just Mem."

"Officer, I want you to arrest them for theft!"

"Mem, can you talk to me about this?"

"Certainly. While I waited for Dwight to show up yesterday, a cash on delivery came in. The bill was five hundred dollars. Dwight told me to 'pay the man' and he would reimburse me when he arrived. He arrived with nothing. No money. I told him I would take it out of the till this morning."

Dwight spluttered, "What drivel!"

Pete looked at Mem. "Do you have witnesses?"

"Well, as a matter of fact, I do, and one has just arrived. In the nick of time."

Harry backed out of the elevator, chairs on a dolly in tow.

"Here are your chairs, Mem. And I think our delivery is now final. Who do I give this invoice to?"

Mem took the invoice and gave it to an astonished Dwight. "Harry, could you please tell Pete what happened when that last delivery arrived yesterday morning?"

"Sure." Harry went through the story, including the telephone call Mem made, ostensibly to Dwight, and her trip across The Avenue to get five hundred dollars to 'pay the man.'"

"And was there conversation later about the five hundred dollars?"

"Oh, yeah, when Dwight got here and Mem asked for her money, he started to make an excuse, like it was supposed to come from the till here today, and pretended like that was the plan all along."

"So, if Mem is taking money from the till today, she had permission to do so? At least from what you observed?"

"Oh, sure."

"Thanks, Harry."

"No problem, Pete. Well, I'll deliver these chairs around the room."

Pete and Mem looked at Dwight. Dwight looked at the invoice. Then he looked at the floor. Janet came up with another one hundred dollars. "Three hundred fifty. Slowly but surely."

This time, Mem returned to the table and Janet stayed with Dwight and Pete.

Dwight looked at Janet, an attractive woman, perhaps in her forties, well-dressed. Possibly well-to-do. Volunteering here during a week day. A society woman. She would do nicely.

"So, Janet? That's your name, right?" Not waiting for an answer, he pushed on. "It looks like I might need another local coordinator, someone to help me with local issues. I don't think Mem's heart is in it anymore."

"Oh, no. Mem signed on to be the local coordinator, and she'll see it through to the end. She'll be here every day. So will I, actually."

"Well, I might be in the market to replace her. If not this year, then next. I can tell you've got what it takes. I'd put you down as a…well, you tell me. What's your sign?"

"My husband carries my sign. It says, 'not available.'"

"I'm just talking about the show, but, you know, if something happens, it happens. But, hey, we could have lunch, surely your husband won't mind."

"I'm sure he won't, but I don't care to, thank you."

"I'll just call him and ask for you."

"I don't care to go, but if you insist on calling, all you have to do is turn your head."

Janet went back to the table. Dwight turned his head. Pete first looked at him with a stony expression, then sent him a smile that could have melted a glacier.

Pete noticed a flyer on the table. He picked it up and started to read. "This flyer says 'municipal buses will provide shuttle service from the public parking lot to the event.' Well, that's great, because you would have to have that in place in order to get your permit."

Dwight got a pained expression on his face.

Pete continued. "I haven't seen the shuttles yet. Our local buses are provided by the senior center. Of course you contracted with them, right? When will they start running?"

Dwight realized he was caught in between a rock and a hard place. This knowledgeable Chief of Police on one hand and Mem on the other.

"Mem sent me the contract. I must have forgotten to fill it out and send it back."

"You forgot? And the signage directing attendees to the public lot? Did you forget that as well?"

Dwight sighed and looked at his feet.

"Tell you what. Why don't you take care of those things by noon today, and we'll expect you at the town office by 1:00 to get that permit. By then, of course, the signs will be up and the buses will be running. Well, I take that back. They may have to call people in to work. Those buses might not start until tomorrow. But you let us know at 1:00 what you have arranged. We'll consider your efforts when we tack on the late fees."

One man walked around town on his own. He was a tall, thin man, clean-shaven and dark-skinned. At his side was a large dog with hair a mottled combination of brown, gray and black. Those who saw the dog face-on thought they could catch a smile, but it was hard to tell. Tangled, curly hair covered the face completely. Long mats of hair, some resembling dreadlocks, covered the dog's body. Most dogs with matted hair would have a problem. Not this fine dog. This was natural. On occasion, the dog would send a look of adoration at her human. They resembled one another, except the man's dreadlocks were held back from his face.

The man sat on one of the benches of the median. He had an ulterior motive for being in town, but he was in no mood to reveal himself. First, he wanted to take in the aura of the town. The aura would be important. The man had a feel for color, rhythm and style. He took in everything. First, he took in the totality of the street.

Sunset Avenue ran from the town building to the lake, one long city block. He knew the nickname for the street. The Avenue was wide, deep enough on either side for angle parking from one end of the street to the other. The Avenue ended at the expanse of parking lot, a city park, a campground connected to the state park, and beaches fronting the eastern shore of one of the Great Lakes. The man knew how Sunset Avenue's name was derived. The view of the sunset from anywhere on this street would be priceless.

Today, the town bustled. Every parking place was full. As one car made an exit, another car waited to fill the space. The public parking lot was full; parents and children too young for school dotted the park's playground. Campers pulled into the state campground, but none pulled out. To his left, boats entered and left the small marina. His skilled eye noted the marina must have a deep harbor, as some of the boats were better described as yachts.

He sat on a wide median. It, too, bustled. He noted clusters of people obviously seeing one another as after a long spell away. Many of those had walked to The Avenue from the little marina. The median itself had a number of benches, small game tables, cement flower pots filled with live spring blooms, midget trees, and a brick walkway up the center. He noted the attention to detail, the accessible curbs both on the median and on the sidewalks.

Even the town circle was attractively maintained, with trees and flowering shrubs. A tulip tree sat in front of the police department. A large dog had been napping there but now looked intently in their direction.

Flower carts dotted both sidewalks from the town center to the lake. They held greenery and fresh spring flowers. The man was fairly certain he knew who maintained them. As he breathed in, he could smell the mixture of fresh lake water and the floral essence.

Enough of the big picture, he thought to himself. He turned to concentrate on the south side of The Avenue. Most of the block was taken up by a long two story building, circa 1880, well maintained. The town had been a lumber and shipping hub, growing to prominence after the

Civil War. This building spoke of a prosperous post-war period.

The original brick façade was set off by colorful awnings that separated one storefront from the next.

The first storefront had windows and awnings on both the north and east sides. The awnings were bright purple with mint green stripes. Somewhat higher than the awnings, at the corner of the building was a sign with the name, Tiger Lily's Café, and the picture of a pretty tabby cat looking over The Avenue. The man had heard good things about the food at this place.

The second awning was bright orange with a white silhouette of The Hero pose on the right hand side. The accompanying sign, in contrast, showed a black cat with white markings in a pose only a cat could make. This was Lil' Socks Virasana, the yoga studio.

The next storefront had a bright yellow awning sporting a black beer tap on the left side. The sign showed a long-haired gray cat with, yes, it was actually a sexy stare, proclaiming the business to be Mo's Tap. The man knew this to be an upscale blues bar with artisan beers he would certainly try soon.

On the next sign, a muscular gray kitten danced on hind legs, reaching for the top of a letter proclaiming the name of the business, Mr. Bean's Confectionary. This awning was bright green with white stars. This would be the man's next stop.

The last storefront of the long building had a sign with the picture of a small, spunky cat curling around the name of the business, Sassy P's Wine & Cheese. The sign sat atop a bright red awning accented with purple wine glasses. The man knew about this place as well.

Underneath each awning were café sets, wrought iron tables with chairs, painted to match the color scheme of the awning. The bright, primary colors gave The Avenue a sense of whimsy.

Each table was in use, some by four or five people, others by one or two. He people-watched for a time, moving his eyes from the tables outside the café all the way down to the tables outside the winery. Then a gap, a small garden, and another building from the 1880s. A former mansion, the house was outstanding for its hint of southern glory in a northern town. The man knew this was a bed and breakfast. The most prominent in town.

Bright blue awnings with narrow stripes in a multitude of colors surrounded the lower level of the building, setting off a long, wide front porch. That porch also had café sets as well as settings of wicker furniture, including gliders, rocking chairs and Adirondack chairs, cushioned in every color imaginable. The sign, with a picture of two large dilute calico cats standing back-to-back, proclaimed the name of the KaliKo Inn.

The man knew everything on the south side of The Avenue was owned by one woman. He thought he had picked her out of the crowd, leaving the B&B and walking up to the Café. She was an unassuming woman, clothed in a colorful, flowing top, capris and sandals. Her hair was graying uniformly, but it was hard to tell her age. High cheekbones gave just a hint of Indian heritage.

The man turned in the other direction. The north side had a similar building, a long, brick two-story building with seven storefronts. The building had seen more wear and tear than the one on the south side, but they were possibly built at the same time. The original brick was painted over, however, probably to hide a history of poorly-made repairs.

Being a man taken in with details, he started again at the east end. The first storefront was painted pale lilac and had a modern art rendition of the cross in a dark purple. The sign said "Soul's Harbor." He knew this to be a nondenominational church established to minister to both locals and tourists. Much like a hospital chaplaincy, the church embraced many faiths.

He knew something about the pastor. She was a relative newcomer to the area, quiet, private. She had a heart for service and had recently renovated her apartment above the church, making a small living area for herself and an efficiency apartment for persons in need. This was proving to be a good option. Before the renovation, she had allowed persons in need to live in a spare bedroom. The efficiency apartment allowed for privacy for everyone concerned.

The next storefront was called CyberHealth. He knew this to be a combination cyber café and health food store with a tea room thrown in for good measure. The exterior was painted pale peach and had a bright Mayan sunburst under the name. He recalled what he knew about the owner. She was a mature woman, the mother figure of The Avenue, wise, dating the owner of an antique store on Main Street.

Next was a grocery store, Babar Foods. The man knew the woman to be Pakistani. He watched as she came outside to tend to the flowers. She was dressed in traditional Pakistani garb, loose trousers and tunic topped off with a dupatta. The outfit was colorful, bright orange with accents of bright pink. The exterior of the store was painted butter yellow. A graphic of an Indian elephant laden with baskets of fresh produce appeared to lumber toward the lake. The man had a longing thought for some of the traditional Indian and Pakistani dishes that he knew could be found in the deli section.

The next store, DoubleGood, was a combination hardware and electronics store. The man knew about the owners of this place also, young women, twins. One lived in a wheelchair. The store was painted mint green and had two 3D graphics. On one side, a woman sat in front of a plumbing disaster. On the other, a man multi-tasked with a computer, cell phone and laptop.

The man looked at the flower and gift shop, Bloomin' Crazy, a rose pink storefront with a graphic of red tropical blooms. He knew all about the owner of this place. She was a dark-haired, dark-skinned Haitian beauty, looking for love in some of the wrong places.

The last business had a double storefront. The man knew the story behind this as well. Two sisters again, older than the twins, were licensed practical nurses and owned both a drug store and a clinic, called simply The Drug Store and The Clinic. Painted light slate blue, the clinic side boasted a cartoon of an old fashioned ambulance. Two men ran toward it carrying a stretcher holding a woman who obviously wanted off. The other side was more sedate. It was set off with a bottle with pills bursting into the air like fireworks.

The man took one more look at the lake. He watched as people walked to and from the lighthouse, poised at the end of a half-mile long jetty.

The man got up to walk with his dog to Mr. Bean's Confectionary. He said a quiet word to the dog, who sat obediently at the door. The dog, Mr. Bean and Tillie stared at one another through the window. While the man made his order, Mr. Bean turned to look at Carlos, then ran to the cat door. He stuck his head out first, for an easy, backwards escape into the Confectionary if the big dog proved unfriendly. When that was not the case, Mr. Bean bounced out, Tillie following.

"I'm Mr. Bean. Who are you?"

"I'm Fiamma."

"I've never seen a dog like you before. Did your daddy forget to cut your hair?"

"No, it's supposed to look like this. It's sexy."

Tillie laughed. It looked like a sneeze to passers-by. *"Really?"* The little dog was just a little jealous. It was a glorious coat. *"I'm Tillie. I live here."*

"I'm visiting."

Tillie breathed an inward sigh of relief. *"How long are you staying?"*

"I don't know."

The man came back out, a bag of pastries in one hand and a bag of designer dog treats in another.

"Did you find friends already?"

Fiamma looked up at the man, adoration in her barely visible eyes.

"Come on. Say good-bye. We have to go."

Fiamma looked at her two new friends. *"Good-bye. Maybe I'll see you later."*

The two crossed to the median and, as Mr. Bean and Tillie watched, they walked to the end, into the park, onto the beach, and toward the lighthouse.

Before going in, Tillie said to Mr. Bean, *"Is it true that dogs look like their humans, or that humans take on the look of their dogs?"*

"I don't know. It's sure true for them. They have the same hair."

Both stared at Tillie's reflection in the window. The little terrier had a longish nose and smooth skin. Then, almost as one, they looked up at Carlos. His dark head of hair, dark mustache and short, dark beard didn't look very terrier-like.

"Well, we haven't lived together for long. Maybe he'll change." Tillie hoped fervently she wouldn't sprout a dark mustache.

Georgia, preceded by Kali and Ko, meowing loudly to announce her presence, appeared for breakfast at 8:00. "Oh my, Henrie, you have so much food!"

Henrie couldn't help himself. He took Fred in his arms and bounced her just a little bit. Very unlike Henrie, he answered Georgia in a baby talk voice. "We made way too much food for the people today. They said they wanted breakfast very early and no one ate anything. Except for a phantom person who took quite a bit."

"Really? Someone slipped in to eat?"

Henrie put Fred in the baby chair and answered in his formal tone. “Yes. At first, I wondered if you had come out, but several breads were taken, none of the spelt.”

“Thank goodness whoever it was left that for me! Henrie, I can’t thank you enough for everything you’ve done. I’m still not sure how I’m going to get a job, but I’ll figure it out.”

“Allow me to give you a referral. Our cook at Mo’s Tap will open a fine dining restaurant this weekend, here on The Avenue, evenings only. After this Thursday, Friday and Saturday evening only. I thought his staff was hired, but as it happens, he is in need of someone to help him get started as well as cooks, servers, and a hostess. In short, he is up the proverbial creek without an essential paddle. By the time you get settled with Martha, he will probably be at work. You should go to the bar to talk to him.”

Georgia’s smile was all he needed to see.

“Now, eat up. I will put your things in the car.”

8

Pete hired a couple of reserve officers to handle traffic issues on The Avenue. As he made the calls, he worried about telling the Town Council of the additional expenditure. He was sure there was money to handle it, but the Council did not like to hear of these things after the fact.

Pete couldn't blame them. He didn't like it either.

In the meantime, the police department had to make some decisions. The first was whether or not to enforce the two-hour parking limit on cars parked on The Avenue. The public lot was a long city block away, and most people could be expected to walk that distance. That did not, however, allow for accessible parking for people attending the show that could not walk that far.

If they didn't enforce the two-hour limit, storefronts on The Avenue could expect to see a slow-down in their regular business. Parking, and the appropriate management of the space to assist both patrons and businesses, was always a delicate situation.

Before making a decision, Pete tasked Marco with talking to business owners on both sides of The Avenue. Their concerns would guide them as they made a decision for today.

"Tell them we're just worried about today. By tomorrow the shuttles will be running. I talked to the senior center. They don't have a contract with the show yet, but they're calling in extra drivers. I can pull out the parking signs we use for other events. We'll just have to tape over the event name and write in the Rock & Gem Show."

"Is the town going to have to pay for those buses, boss?"

"Nope. If the senior center doesn't get a contract, they'll have to charge for each ride. That won't go over well, but what can we do?"

Annie made quick stops at each of her businesses. She then drove to Marsh Haven and went into a boutique she had – to this point – only walked or driven past. She hated to shop. Hated it with a passion. It was worse when the shopping was for herself. But she had let this dreaded trip wait until the last minute, and she had to push forward.

With the help of a kind attendant, and after trying on what must have been fifty dresses – at least it felt that way – she chose the perfect one. Plus accessories.

It was a strapless, shimmery, low cut, tight-fitting dress in tones of rose and lilac. She found strappy, glitzy sandals, purple, with a two inch heel. She also picked up two items meant to accessorize a man's tuxedo.

Getting into the dress and walking out of the house with it on would take some personal talking-to.

She then met Jenny Howe at Mr. Bean's. Over pastries and coffee, they talked about the meeting Jenny had attended. "How bad is it going to be?"

"He's going to make trouble, that's for sure. It could get bad in the short term. He claims the bad publicity generated by the Inn has caused local B&Bs to lose customers. We may have to prepare a defense in case the

Association or its members sue you for lost business. I'll start by getting tax records for the last five years, maybe ten, to show that you have nothing to do with their lack of clientele." Jenny looked at her and smiled. "I love a good fight."

Martha waved Henrie out the kitchen door and turned to look around the kitchen. The groceries from yesterday were put away and her menu for breakfast planned for the next several days. She had cleaned the guest room and the dining room, rarely used recently, and was ready for this.

Except that she couldn't quite remember what she was supposed to do next....

Georgia came to the kitchen, Fred crying in her arms. The child could not be consoled. She had cried so hard her little sobs came in fits and starts. Her whole body was red and her face wet with tears.

Georgia did her best to function while hugging and bouncing Fred on her shoulder. "Do you need me to sign in or anything?"

"Oh, goodness me, that's what we need to do." Martha chuckled a little. "I would just forget my head if it wasn't attached. Let's go to the office."

As Georgia followed Martha, she noticed the older woman dragged a leg as she walked. She said nothing. Perhaps this was a long-standing issue, and she didn't want to appear rude. Plus, it was hard to have a conversation given Fred's current condition.

Martha tried but failed to keep up a conversation as the paperwork was completed. Georgia apologized often, and hoped fervently this fit of crying would not lead them to the street again.

Just as they finished, they heard the door open. From the entry, JoJo called, "Hello?"

Georgia, stressed, got up to greet her. Fred's wails reached a higher pitch as she walked from the office to the entry. "JoJo, maybe I should stay with her today. She just won't stop crying. I think she's reacting to the change."

"Oh, no. Well, I can handle it, if you can handle being away from her."

"Really?'

"Sure. I've seen some real criers at the day care center. And if I get stumped, I can call my Mom."

"Or Henrie."

"Henrie. Now there's a thought. Besides trying to calm her down, is there anything special you need me to do today?"

"No, I guess, if you can, please ask Martha where you can take Fred. Obviously my room, but I don't know where else."

Martha was just behind her. "JoJo, it's good to see you, dear. You have the run of the house."

"Great. Come here, Fred. Let's you and me have some fun today."

Fred wailed louder, put her arms around Georgia's neck and refused to let go.

"Oh, JoJo, I almost forgot. There's a cooler in my room. Laila got a breast pump for me, so I've left enough milk for the day, I think."

"That will help, I'm sure."

JoJo tried to move closer to take Fred. Georgia held Fred tight and wished with all her might she didn't have to go. But she had to get a job. She just had to. With one hand, she loosened one of Fred's arms from her neck and leaned into JoJo to turn over the bundle of, well, not joy.

As JoJo took her, she wailed even louder and reached out her arms to Georgia. Georgia's heart gave a tug, then she said her good-byes and left for what she hoped would be a stellar job interview. Once again, tears streamed down her face.

At the Inn, Henrie could barely stand to hear the plaintive cries from Kali and Ko, who seemed to be bereft of all happiness. It would be easier to bear if they were in any other room but the room he was in. But, no, they had to stay at his feet, jumping out of his way as he walked or turned, sad faces peering up to his with their incessant cries. Perhaps he should take them for a visit to Martha's....

9

As Ray and his contractor worked on The Escape, Ray tried to distance himself from the anger he felt. He had hired this man two months ago, when the damage was first incurred. And after a rogue pretender almost made off with a lot of money.

The boat had been in the harbor when high winds, ice, hail and every other thing that winter can send battered the boat against the dock. Holes in the hull were the main sources of damage, but other repairs were also required before The Escape could go out.

The cabins and topside interior areas took minor damage from the sudden shift of furniture that had come loose. Ray had completed those repairs nearly a month ago and had been chomping at the bit to finish the rest of it.

The contractor, a heavy-set, full-bearded man with tobacco stains on his lips and chin, strolled over to Ray, on his knees and bent over a section of wood with a sander. Ray sensed his presence and looked up.

"Me and the boys is a-goin' to lunch. It might take us a while. There seems to be a lot of traffic up yonder." He motioned with his head toward The Avenue.

Ray stared at him. "You do know I have a cruise this week, right?"

"We's a-workin' as fast as we can. We has to take breaks. Can't overwork the men. You unnerstand."

"No, I don't understand. You got here two hours ago. And it's already time for lunch?"

"Well, we's accountin' for the wait time at that there café."

Ray sat back on his heels. He surveyed the dock, where a load of lumber and other supplies lay. "How is the work on the hull coming along?"

"Well, it's gonna take a little time."

"How long is that?"

"I suppose, well, maybe a couple days."

"A couple of days?" Ray did the math. A couple of days was Thursday. The crew arrived in Chelsea on Thursday. They were to leave early Friday morning.

"And taking it out for a test run?"

"Well, we could do that maybe, let's see, that puts us about to Friday."

Ray closed his eyes, breathed deeply and counted to ten, then twenty. This was the only construction crew he could get. If it was an insurance job, there would have been plenty lined up, but he was paying for this repair on his own. He was up against it, that's for sure. And that left all of the other repair work to him. He could get it done, but he wouldn't get anything painted or stained.

"Well, then, you'd better get on to lunch."

The crowd had been lighter than expected at the rock and gem show. Gema put a sign on her display noting the time she would return from lunch, but if someone wanted to see a particular piece before that time, please call her cell number.

Garry watched as she put up the sign. She caught his eye and they nodded to one another. Gema took the back stairway to the Café where she saw Geraldine at a corner table for two.

Gema took a second to go by the hostess stand and pet the beautiful cat. "Hey, big girl. My name's Gema. I'm staying at your place. We'll be seeing one another all week."

Tiger Lily purred. She decided she would have to stop by this woman's table to recommend a menu item.

A server approached. Gema said, "I'm joining Geraldine at her table." The server nodded, and Tiger Lily wondered if she should take back her initial positive assessment of Gema. All the more reason to stop by the table.

Once Gema was seated and looking at a menu, Tiger Lily hopped down and trotted over to the table. Geraldine, a regular, had started to talk as Gema perused the menu.

Tiger Lily heard Geraldine say, "What did you think about the yoga studio?" Tiger Lily had learned that she heard the best gossip if she jumped early and stayed at the table, luring guests into forgetting she was there. She jumped to her ledge and waited to be acknowledged.

Gema was startled by her sudden appearance, but she gathered herself and looked more closely at the table. Four ledges, one on each side of the table, were attached, about six inches from the table top.

Geraldine snorted. "You have just been graced with the vaunted Tiger Lily Tabletop Hop. She will now attempt, if you believe the gossip, to suggest an entrée for you.

Gema looked at Tiger Lily and received a slow blink. In this instance, this was kitty cat for "yes." Gema smiled and put the menu down. "Do you have a suggestion for me?"

Tiger Lily put her two front paws on the table and leaned in, looking closely at the menu. This looked like a woman who liked a good, adventurous salad. Tiger Lily put her paw on just the right one. A quinoa power salad. The baby spinach, quinoa, strawberries, blueberries and sliced avocado were topped with a dressing made of olive oil, lime juice and honey and garnished with chia seeds.

Gema read the selection, looked at Tiger Lily and said, "Perfect." As in a choreographed production, the server appeared at that moment. "I see Tiger Lily made a suggestion. Are you going with that, or would you like something else?"

"I'm going with her suggestion." Gema gave her order; Geraldine ordered the special, a grilled chicken curry pita pocket sandwich, with onion, yogurt, cucumber, lemon peel and shredded romaine lettuce. On the side, she ordered the roasted sweet potato salad with apples and cranberries.

"That sounds good," said Gema. Do you recommend anything to go with the salad?

"We have some warm pretzel bread with cinnamon and raw brown sugar butter."

"Great. That's what I'll have."

As the server went away, Gema looked at the table. Their table had a ceramic top, painted with a tropical scene of a large parrot in the jungle. She looked around the dining room. It appeared all of the tables were similarly painted, but in different designs.

She could see only hints from her seated position, as all of the tables were in use, but it looked like there were cats, dogs, other animals and outdoor scenes of every variety. The chairs were colorfully painted and cushioned, none of them matching at any one table, lending to an air of casual chic.

The Café, the main floor of the building hosting the rock and gem show, was on the corner of the street and had two walls that were mostly knee-to-ceiling windows with no coverings. Excess lighting was deflected by the awnings outside.

Her eyes were drawn upward to the ceiling. My, she thought. That looked to be the original tin. If not, it's a great reproduction. The walls were mint green with the exception of an accent wall behind the coffee counter and server station. That wall was bright purple.

At night, or on a gray day, an eclectic mixture of track, recessed and pendant lights could be used. The pendant lights were colorful and unique in shape and design, just like the tables. And she saw Tiger Lily's platforms on all of the tables.

Her hand went involuntarily to Tiger Lily and stroked her back. She realized Geraldine had been talking.

"So, did you go this morning? Did you see the space?"

"I'm sorry, what? I've been in a daze. Haven't heard a word you said."

"I was just talking about the yoga studio. It's perfect for you. Did you look at it this morning?"

"Oh, yes. It's an adorable space. Of course, I didn't go into any of the back areas, but the front is just perfect. I would even keep that mirrored wall. It would add to the illusion that the store was a large one."

"Right. That's what I just said." Geraldine pursed her lips. "Well, you have had a long couple of days, but there are things we must work on, and quickly, or we'll miss our window of opportunity."

"And explain to me again why we have a window now?"

"Well, I don't think I explained that in the first place. I believe I said the space could be made available. First, though, I wanted to make sure you approved."

"Could you at least tell me why Annie would let go of the yoga studio? I assume I would be renting from her? She owns the whole building, correct? I mean, from here, the Café, down to the winery?"

"At the moment, she does, yes."

"Has she put it up for sale?"

"Not yet, but I have reason to believe she will, very soon."

The food arrived and conversation ceased. When it started again, they talked about the differences between Gema's artistic jewelry pieces and Garry's elegant ones.

Tiger Lily couldn't bear to listen to this drivel. She jumped down and ran back to the hostess stand. She jumped into an enclosed shelf at the back of the stand, so she could not be seen by customers entering and leaving.

Mommy was selling the building?

At Mo's Tap, lunch rush was in full tilt by 10:30. Cookie didn't have time to worry about all the things he wasn't getting done. His new restaurant was going to be a fiasco! Just a fiasco!

Georgia got to the bar a little after 10:30, hoping she had missed the rush. She didn't make it. Shattered, she stood at the end of the bar, all the stools taken and every table in use.

George caught her eye and, with a twist of his head, asked for her order. She put him off with a gesture that could have meant, "I'm waiting for someone."

She stood, considering her options, as she watched servers hurry from table to table to table to bar to kitchen window to bar to table to table to table. They were good. She would be good at this, too. She knew how to wait tables and could out-earn most servers in tips.

Georgia watched tables empty and fill, bar stools empty and fill. Still, she stood where she was, out of the way and mostly out of sight of employees.

She watched the kitchen window. It filled up, emptied out, filled up, emptied out. Then it was empty for too long. Servers approached the window, asking for the order for table two or table six or booth ten. Then orders came up. Servers took them away, brought some back. One server, a pretty woman with long, lush dark hair, went back to the kitchen for a while, came out and had a conversation with the bartender. He was busy, too. His face showed frustration, but there was nothing he could do at the moment.

Finally, Georgia hit upon a plan. She walked out, looked to left and right, then turned right toward the Café. She rounded the corner, and when she reached the back of the building, she turned right to walk down the alley.

The doors weren't marked on the back, so she counted. One, the Café. Two, the yoga studio. Three, it felt right that this would be Mo's Tap. The alley stopped here, as the garden shared by the bar and the winery spread beyond the area.

Georgia took a deep breath, turned the knob, and sighed in relief as the door opened. Immediately, she heard the chaos. She entered the kitchen area to see three people furiously reading tickets and putting orders down. In the few seconds she watched, two different cooks read the same ticket.

Georgia pulled her hair back and into a ponytail, using a band from her pocket. She went to the sink and washed her hands. With an air of authority, and pretending she belonged there, she strode to the tickets at the server's window and pulled off the first one.

She turned to the kitchen and said in an authoritative voice, "Who's working on table four, burger medium, ahi tuna small plate and meatball sandwich?"

Two cooks said "Me!"

Everyone stopped. Georgia stayed in character. "You," she said to the man at the grill. What's your name?"

"John."

"What do you have from that ticket?"

"Burger medium, fries and meatballs, headed for the tuna now."

"John, keep going with that burger medium and add," she consulted the next two tickets, "a burger well and a grilled chicken. Don't do anything with the meatballs. You're going to do all the deep fries, so add three more orders of fries to that."

"What's your name?" She was looking at a man at the prep table, tuna steak in one hand and packet of meatballs in the other.

"Cookie."

"Keep going with the tuna, put those meatballs away, get the ones John started. Add another tuna and get a portabella mushroom out."

Then she turned to a man who seemed out of his depth, but who was gamely trying to slice vegetables for sides and garnishes. "And who are you?"

"I'm George Two."

"George Two?"

"George One is the boss."

"Okay. What do you normally do?"

"I wash dishes."

Georgia looked at the sink, piled high with dirty dishes, dishes they would need right away. As she looked, a server came back to drop another bin of dirty dishes on the sink's counter.

"Then do that, and hop to it. I'll take over here."

Georgia took the knife and moved the cutting board to just under the ticket counter. While she chopped what had been ready to go, she read tickets.

"John, tell me when you have room on that grill."

"Yes, ma'am."

"Cookie, let me know when you can do another tuna and another mushroom."

"You got it."

About that time, a handsome male face peered in at the window. It spoke. "I recognize you now. You've been in here a couple of times looking for work."

Georgia nodded, read another ticket, and said behind her, "George Two, we're going to need plates for these portabellas. Put them at the top of the pile."

"Yes, ma'am!"

George watched her for a bit. "You always had a baby with you. Not the best way to look for a job."

Georgia nodded, took the plated burger medium and added the fries and garnish, plated the ahi tuna and the meatball sandwich.

She put the plates on the service counter and called out, "Order up, table four!"

George said, "Well, I guess we'll talk after lunch."

George looked past her at Cookie. Cookie nodded, George shrugged and turned back to the bar.

Cookie, John and George Two continued to respond to directions from their newest triage expert. The lunch rush continued until 2:00. They didn't miss a beat, didn't make a mistake with an order, and didn't keep the servers from making their hard-earned tips.

Pete finally stopped at the Café for a late lunch, but the Café was still busy. He backed up to look down the sidewalk; Mo's and Mr. Bean's looked to be just as busy.

Cyril had already trotted in and was sitting behind the hostess stand, so Pete decided to wait until a table was ready. He didn't have to wait long.

Ray and Cheryl had a table and beckoned him over. Now he saw Rays' dog, Jock, behind the hostess stand as well. Both dogs had their noses poked into a shelf area. For a minute, he thought about taking a look, but he just shook his head and walked to the table.

"What a mess!" exclaimed Cheryl. "What's up with this police department that they can't keep the traffic cleaned up?"

Pete resisted the urge to take both hands to her neck. Instead, he got in a dig of his own. "It's the fault of that darned marina down there. They over-loaded their slips too early in the season. With no notice."

Ray said, "Well, I understand, from a good source, that the moon is waxing gibbous."

"Who's your source?"

"Chris. Speak of the devil."

Chris walked in, spied his friends, and after a quick trip to the coffee bar to give the barista a kiss, joined them.

"Who's the new dish at the coffee bar?"

"Oh, some hotty that decided to pick me up last night. I'm stringin' her along. You know. Love 'em and leave 'em."

"I hear the owner of this place doesn't go in for that stuff."

"What she doesn't know won't hurt her."

The server appeared at the table. "Annie said you wanted the blond bomb, extra spicy. She said to tell you the tabasco is on the house."

Chris and the others at the table turned to give Annie a hello salute. She didn't have time to acknowledge them, as she was buried in orders for iced teas, slushies, special coffees and blond bombs.

Chris and Pete gave the server their orders, and she left. Chris took a sip. They watched him. He put the cup down. "False alarm. No tabasco."

"How is the repair coming, Ray?"

Ray looked darkly at the table. Cheryl answered for him. "I dragged him here to get him away from the contractor. Do I need to say any more?"

"Not really."

The friends continued to chat but, spurred by the tables emptying and filling as fast as they could, ate quickly to make the table available for others.

The last table to fill before they left was a small one against the window. A man sat by himself. Well, by himself except for the big, hairy dog.

Pete looked over, looked back at his friends and laughed. "So who got the dreadlocks first? The dog or the man?"

Chris gave the dog an admiring stare. "Pretty dog. Lots of hair. Must be hot in the summer."

Cheryl, gathering her purse and phone, said, "Pretty man, too." She ignored the stares from her tablemates and continued, "You know, most strangers who come to The Avenue have to put their dogs on a leash. The new dogs get so excited to see other animals out and about. This dog must be well-trained to be here for the first time without restraint."

"You're right. Never thought about that. The dog didn't even bother Tiger Lily."

"Well, it would be hard to bother her. I haven't seen her."

They all looked around. She was right. Tiger Lily was nowhere to be found, at least within their sight.

Chris said, "She's probably hiding somewhere."

How true his words were. The friends said their good-byes and left.

As they got to the door, Ray saw two of the construction crew, who had returned from lunch before he left, playing cards on the median. He stormed out the door, leaving both Jock and Cheryl. Cheryl followed him, turning to say to Pete, "I have to stop a murder."

At that moment, Pete saw a fender bender. A driver backed into another parked car. The driver of that vehicle wasn't around. The first driver pulled away to drive off. Pete was out the door in a shot, headed to stop the hit-and-run driver before he got away.

Chris shook his head, waved to Annie and left.

Jock and Cyril couldn't believe their luck. Both of their humans left them right here at the Café!

They had commiserated with Tiger Lily, heard all about the possibility that Annie might sell this building, and then a vision of loveliness had entered the Café. She was gorgeous. She had hair, lots of glorious hair. Curly hair. Matted hair. She had an air of mystery. You had to look closely to see her eyes.

She had seen them through the window as she and her human walked to the door. She threw both of them a sexy, sultry stare as they entered and stopped at the hostess stand. As they were seated, she walked with a pronounced wiggle and sway. From their table in the corner, she sent flirty glances in their direction. Jock was sure he was the recipient of the beautiful girl's attention. Cyril was sure it was he.

When they were able to breathe again, they talked to one another, never taking their eyes off this vision. Cyril remembered it first. *"I know where we saw her kind. Hers was a new breed at the Westminster this year."*

"Yes," said Jock.

Cyril continued, *"I think she was in the herding group."*

"You're right. She's beautiful."

All of a sudden, the two realized they were rivals for the affections of this new, beautiful dog. They looked at one another and growled, low enough not to be heard by any humans.

Tiger Lily rolled her eyes. *"Not again, boys. Wasn't the last Westminster tiff enough to do it for you?"*

Pete recorded the Westminster Dog Show every year; watching it was a special treat for Cyril and Jock. Jock, a Portuguese water dog, was from the working group. Cyril, an English setter, was from the sporting group. In general, with the exception of the show a couple of years ago, they rooted for one another's breeds.

As the big boys continued to glare at one another, Tillie ran into the Café from Mr. Bean's. From the window she had seen Tiger Lily and their big friends behind the hostess stand. She started to trot around to sit with them, then she spied the beautiful dog.

She turned and went to the table. *"Fiamma!"* said Tillie. *"It's great to see you again. Did you have a nice walk?"*

"I did. I always enjoy walking along the water. What are you doing here?"

"I come into all the places here on The Avenue," said Tillie proudly. *"It's my home. The whole avenue."*

"How nice for you. Say, since you live here, do you know those two big boys over there?"

Tillie didn't have to look around, but for show, she did. *"Oh, those two behind the hostess stand? The ones that are pretending to not be interested in you?"*

"They're both doing a poor job of that."

"Well, they would. They're both nice enough. They're my friends. Want to meet them?"

"Sure."

Fiamma nudged her human in the leg, looked up at him, then turned and followed Tillie.

"What did you just do?"

"We have a kind of sign language. I just let him know that I wasn't forgetting he was here, so he wouldn't get up and follow me while I walked away."

"That's pretty good. How long did it take you to teach him?"

"Months and months."

Tillie sighed. *"None of them are as smart as they look."*

When they reached the hostess stand, Tiger Lily came out from behind and sat in front of Cyril.

Fiamma took a step back, then tentatively reached her nose in. She and Tiger Lily touched noses, acknowledging the mutual friendship with Tillie.

And for once, Tillie had the upper hand with the big boys. They stood, tongues lolling out of their mouths, and begged for an introduction.

Tillie took her time. *"This is Tiger Lily. This is her Café. Her human is Annie, back there behind the coffee bar. Remember Mr. Bean? Annie is his human, too."*

"Good to know," said Fiamma. *"And who do we have here?"*

"This is Cyril. He's with the police department. And Jock, here, has a yacht that goes out on the lake."

"Oh, my. Both of you are so distinguished."

Tiger Lily chided Tillie just a little. *"I'm sorry. We didn't catch your name."*

Tillie laughed. *"I'm sorry. I'm nervous. I don't often get to introduce folks. This is Fiamma."*

Fiamma, thought Cyril, dreamily. What did the name mean? What was its origin?

Fiamma, thought Jock, eyes slightly crossed. A vision. A blaze. A flame.

Both were brought out of their reveries when Chris came back inside. "Boys, your daddies want you outside."

They continued to stare at Fiamma, love-besotted.

Chris misunderstood. "Now, now, let's not get excited. It's just a dog." Chris got between the two and took a collar in each hand. "Come on, let's go."

He got two low growls. He thought the growls were for the interloper. He was mistaken.

Tillie, realizing the problem, said to Fiamma, *"Come on. Let's go back to your human. You'll see them again."*

Tillie nudged her, and she turned to go, sending back a long, sexy stare right between the two of them, making each of them think the stare was for him. As she reached the table of her human, Cyril and Jock finally allowed Chris to take them outside, turning to stare until they were finally forced to walk forward.

10

Upstairs, most of the vendors stopped by the registration table to pick up box lunches that Dwight had arranged. Of course, they had to pay for their own, and he only ordered enough for those that paid up front.

While Dwight took orders for lunches, Mem took telephone calls from the two people that were to take tickets that afternoon. Both had to beg off.

"Will this week ever end?" wailed Mem.

She made a quick call to her part-time helper and begged him to stay for the afternoon. When Mem got off the phone, she looked at Janet.

"Don't worry. I'll stay. I was just going to do laundry this afternoon. I think Pete has enough clean underwear to go another day or two. In fact, he can learn to use the washer himself. I'll stay all day for the rest of the week."

Mem and Janet added their order to Dwight's list. When the orders arrived from the Café, they ate grilled four cheese, tomato and bacon sandwiches on Texas toast with sides of pasta salad and cole slaw. They handed out lunch boxes for the next hour, each with a name written on the outside. Each vendor, needing a bit of peace and quiet, placed an "out to lunch" sign at their counter as they ate, and they sat at the registration table to do so. They came in ones and twos. Mem and Janet learned a lot.

Many of the vendors had to introduce themselves, as Mem had not yet met them. They were considered minor vendors by Dwight, not worthy of inclusion in decisions about placement. For the most part, they kept to themselves. From glances made toward the major vendors,

Mem could tell few had positive thoughts for Dwight, Martin or Garry. Most spent time talking to Adam, who appeared to work with them and help them with their products. They were also drawn to Pattie, who spent time during the day walking through their booths and talking to them.

When Pattie came to eat, she had plenty to say, and none of it positive, about several vendors. Dwight would not consider giving her a better placement in the shows, even though she was one of the more profitable vendors; Nelson carried fake product with his genuine Larimar; Adam was a complete mess and brought shame to the show, particularly to the vendors placed near him; Garry's 'originals' were purchased from wholesale vendors and were mostly fakes; and Martin didn't respect her art.

In a fit of pique, Pattie said one of the only unkind things said that day about Gema. "After she threw Martin away, I helped him pick up the pieces. But that lasted only as long as I could take his condescension about my glass."

Mem gave her a sympathetic glance. "It must be hard to be so close to him at the show."

"Oh, no. That was years ago. We've been doing this circuit so long, I barely think about it."

Right, thought Mem.

"Anyway, as it turns out, we're staying at the same B&B this time. That happens sometimes, too."

"Where are you staying?"

"The Sunset Breeze. What a name. On the web, it looked great. In person, you can see the sunset if you walk to the corner, and that's about where you catch the breeze, too."

Mem held her tongue and didn't ask about the owner, Howard. Before Pattie finished her lunch, Mem's reticence was rewarded. Pattie said, "You know, the guy that runs my B&B said something about buying this Café."

"Really? I didn't know it was for sale."

"I looked for the for sale signs this morning. Then I tried to remember what he said, exactly. He said, 'Real soon that place is going to be mine.'"

"Really!"

"Yeah. I know the woman that owns this owns all the places here. You must know her?"

"Oh, yes, I do, but we aren't close enough to talk business." Mem figured a little lie could be forgiven. If it was told for a good reason, that is.

"Well, I tried to book into her B&B. It looks like the best one in town. But I was too late; it was full. I was doing a web search, though, and it looked like she owned everything from the Inn all the way up to here. I wonder if he is buying all of it?"

"Well, I wonder! If I knew her better I'd ask."

"Just because I'm curious, if you hear anything, let me know."

A few minutes later, Martin dropped by for his lunch. "What was the she-devil filling your heads with? Probably telling you how wonderful her product lines are."

"Yes, something like that."

"Well, it's nice to put a few feet between us. This week we are just way too close. By the way, I figured you for a person who appreciated the psychic nature of stones. I have a piece of selenite that you may want to see."

"Really? I'm always looking for nice pieces of selenite. What do you have?"

"The one I had in mind for you is a tower, about six inches high. The shape is unusual; the edge is almost pencil sharp. You could place it near any item you wanted to restore and the aim will be perfect."

"I'll have to take a look! Thank you!"

In the few minutes he stayed to eat, Mem and Janet learned that Martin could never understand why so many people gathered around Pattie's table and why she made so much more profit than he. And Adam! How that man made so much money was beyond him. He was such a mess!

Martin didn't evidence any particular like or dislike for Kristina and Nelson, but he believed they would be better business people if they learned how to market the differences of turquoise and Larimar. Dwight was an incompetent idiot. Garry was a fake. Martin had similar comments about all of the other vendors as well, both major and minor. He said nothing about Gema.

Adam trotted over just as Martin left. "I had to wait for that dag-nabbed excuse for a human being to leave. And I'm starving!"

Mem handed him the lunch box and said, "It's not nearly so much as what your breakfast appeared. Hope it's enough."

"My breakfast?"

"It looked good. You had a large Tupperware container full. Maybe a couple. You must do a lot of cooking in that camper."

"Oh, yeah. Well, some things I brought ready-made, like, you know, the rolls and things."

"I notice a lot of the smaller vendors seem to spend time at your exhibit."

"Yeah. I grew up with this stuff, and my folks were really talented. They left me everything, so I started with a good deal of inventory. They taught me how to find the real stuff, how to find bargains. I pass on anything I can. Figure I owe it to the people who love it to get good product."

"That's great. It's good to know someone that really knows his craft."

"Unlike some of the others here."

"Really?"

Apparently, Mem asked the question just as Adam felt the need to unload. He unloaded.

"You want to stay away from Garry. His stuff is fake. And Dwight. He buys from other vendors, doesn't care if the stuff is real or fake, marks up the prices. If you look around, he doesn't have anything unique at his booth. Nelson has good stuff, but if you aren't careful, you'll end up with a really expensive piece of fake Larimar. You need to do a burn test with his stuff. Kristina has good product, and she's a talented artist. Can't go wrong with her stuff. Or Gema's. Gema has a great gift. She's going to go far, but not in shows like this. She needs to settle down, get a storefront, spend more time designing and less time packing and unpacking. Martin? He's talented, and his product is genuine, but it's over-priced. And he's such a horse's patoot. You have to watch him around the ladies. Loves 'em and leaves 'em. He'll leave a trail of heartbreak here in, where are we again? Oh, yeah. Chelsea."

Adam seemed to run out of energy about the time his container of cole slaw emptied. He got up to leave, saying, "Well, ladies, thanks for lunch!"

Garry didn't come empty-handed. He had a small case filled with smaller boxes. As he ate, he showed Mem and Janet the items he had chosen as things they just had to have. All vestiges of his seeming dislike of Mem were gone. Or covered up. He showed Mem a pearl necklace.

"How lovely!"

"This is a bridal necklace, eighteen karat gold, cultured pearls, Swarovski crystals. This floral design is meant to be offset." Garry demonstrated by taking the necklace out of the box and holding it the way it would lay on her neck. "See? The flower is centered on your breastbone, putting the floral vine in the center. I made earrings and a bracelet," Garry lifted those boxes to show them to Mem, "and I'm working on the design for a ring."

"What do pieces like this cost?"

"When you come over to my exhibit, we'll talk. I can make you a deal."

Garry turned to Janet. "I thought you might like this." He extracted a simple pendant, a ruby, square cut but offset with a swirl of silver over the top to hold it in place. "This is one and a half carats set in sterling silver."

Janet was drawn to the necklace, simple but elegant. The length of the chain would have the ruby dangling just below the hollow of her throat.

"This is lovely."

"And so are the matching earrings." Garry passed the box over.

"And I'm sure you'll give me a deal, once I come over to your exhibit?"

Garry laughed with her. Then he turned to Mem. "I understand you own the cyber café across the street."

"Yes."

"So you must know everyone around here."

"I know almost everyone in town. It's not hard in a town the size of Chelsea."

"So you must know the woman that owns this place."

"Annie? Sure."

"What can you tell me about her?"

The lies seemed to come more and more easily for Mem. "Well, I can tell you she's a nice woman, and that's about all. If you've seen her, you'd see she's almost young enough to be my daughter, so we aren't that close."

"I've seen you together a couple of times."

"Well, yes. We serve on community committees, and right now we're planning for a jazz festival. Committee members get together whenever we can, especially on weeks like this. So you've probably seen us at lunch or supper."

Garry nodded almost to himself and left.

Katrina and Nelson came together to pick up their lunches. Somewhat surprised at the pairing, Mem handed them their boxes and tried to keep the conversation light, "How is the show going so far?"

She got more than she bargained for.

Katrina and Nelson, both usually sniping at one another, took potshots at Dwight (a pompous so-and-so); Garry (a complete fraud); Adam (his messiness is an act); Pattie (she follows Martin around like a love-sick puppy but pretends to hate him).

As Kristina and Nelson left, Janet leaned down to her purse. "I have some paper in here. I'm going to start making a list of who hates whom or I'll forget everything!"

"And why do you have to remember?"

"I don't want to say the wrong thing to the wrong person, you know, like say how pretty a piece of Garry's jewelry is to Martin."

"Maybe we need to make a relationship chart."

"A what?"

"A chart that shows everyone in the show, and then draw lines that show who likes whom. Then we could use another color to show who dislikes whom. It would be a study in...well, it would be a study."

"I think I'll start it right now." She brought out a small laptop.

Mem said, "We'll need something larger. I'll get some printer paper from Felicity."

When Mem returned, the two women got started.

Mem suggested, "Let's write each name on the page in a circular pattern. Then we'll start drawing lines. I got three colored pens from Felicity. We can put the 'likes' in blue and the 'dislikes' in red. And if we need to, we can draw something in green. We'll call it the 'something' line. We may or may not know what it means."

"There are so many people!"

"Let's take the easy way out right now and put all of the minor vendors into one circle. We can change it later if we need to."

"It feels like we're, I don't know, doing something illegal or immoral."

"We're doing something fun."

As they drew lines based on the lunchtime conversations, patterns became apparent. Mem said, "Did you notice Garry didn't say anything about anyone?"

"Yes, I did. Can we make any inferences?"

"I don't know, but he had dinner with Gema yesterday. Maybe we should put a green line in there, something to watch for."

"Yes. Oh, and how about another green line from Gema to Martin, because of that comment Pattie made?"

"Good idea."

"Oh, and a green line from Pattie to Martin, as well as the red one."

"Right."

The women sat back to look at their chart.

"One more thing," said Mem. Those three men that Gema mentioned that help Dwight. We should put a little note there, and connect them only to Dwight."

"I think we've got it."

"Interesting."

"Very."

At that minute, Gema walked by. "Hello ladies. Doodling?"

Janet looked up, a little embarrassed, but certain Gema couldn't tell what they had drawn. "Just working on our lists of things to do." She folded the paper and put it into her purse.

Gema laughed. Her laugh had a tinkling quality to it. "Well, let me just clue you in on how the rest of the week will go. We had a pretty slow morning, which allowed me to take a longer than usual lunch break, but starting in about one hour," she stopped to look at her watch and amended, "in about one half hour, you will be busier than you can imagine. And it will stay that way until the end of the week. I've got to get ready!"

Dwight finally came up from the stairway. He looked at the empty table behind Mem and Janet. "So everyone got their lunch?"

"Yes. Did you order one for yourself, Dwight?"

"No, I had a sandwich downstairs when I put the order in. You know. Before I went to the town offices to take care of the permit."

"Oh, yes. The permit. You know, Dwight, if you had additional expectations of me, like filling out the paperwork for things like that, all you had to do was ask. I would not have fronted the money, but I would have done the paperwork."

"It's just this town. Everyone else overlooks it. You know. We bring in a lot of business for the towns. This town, man, this town expects a lot."

Mem and Janet held their tongues, knowing this was not a battle worth fighting.

Henrie could take it no more. He called Martha and asked if he could bring lunch over for she and JoJo, and could he please bring Kali and Ko.

Martha was happy for the company and JoJo, almost at wits end, was grateful to have another adult to help with Fred.

Henrie got out of the Inn's SUV and went to the back. Two screaming cats were not going to let him get away with this! He shuddered to think how hard it had been to corner, then get them into the carriers, and hoped he would never have to do it again.

All of a sudden, the cats grew silent. Above even their own howls were the cries from Fred. Anxious now, they started in again, urging Henrie to GET US IN THERE!

Henrie finally made it to the kitchen door, set the carriers down, unlatched them and stood back as they leapt out, running to save Fred from imminent disaster.

They surrounded JoJo, who had not once set the baby down, except to change her diaper. JoJo, sensing she was about to witness a miracle, got to her knees to allow the two big cats to nuzzle and paw the baby.

Fred struggled to quiet down, her sobs coming to a final blissful end while the two cats kneaded her little legs and nuzzled her arms and cheeks. JoJo finally placed a blanket on the floor and put Fred down. The cats snuggled up against her and they all got comfortable to take a nap. Kali was on Fred's right side, her face in between the crook of the baby's head and shoulder, her paw draped over her stomach. Ko's back was cradled into Fred's left side; Fred had a firm hold on the long, soft tail. Her other hand lay softly on Kali's paw.

JoJo, Martha and Henrie stood and stared. They left the room quietly, and Henrie made another trip to the vehicle to get lunch. They ate at the kitchen table, not saying a word, each of them staring into the front room at the vision of peace and contentment.

By late afternoon, most of the cats were back at the Inn. Tillie followed them in. Tiger Lily and Mo led the search for Fred. They looked everywhere. The guest room was empty, the porch was empty, the library, the dining room, the kitchen, the second floor computer and television area. The baby was not here!

Henrie came in and was met with wails and tails. He misinterpreted their angst. "Don't worry! Kali and Ko are visiting Martha's B&B. They're with Fred."

This started a new round of yowls. The reason? Why should Kali and Ko get to stay with Fred and not them?

Henrie finally shook his head and left for the kitchen.

Tiger Lily called for silence. *"Does anyone know how to find Martha's B&B?"*

No one knew.

"Then for now, we'll just have to deal with it. We'll deal with Kali and Ko later."

Mr. Bean piped up, *"And while we deal with them, can we deal with Tillie?"*

Tillie popped up from licking her leg. *"What?"*

Tiger Lily looked at Mr. Bean sharply. *"Are you still jealous?"*

"No, I'm not jealous, it's just that, um, well, um, she gets a lot of attention, and it's my store!"

Little Socks spat, *"Everyone knows it's your store. It has your name on it."*

"But the people that come in, they don't know if I'm Mr. Bean or if he's Mr. Bean!"

Sassy Pants had a moment of brilliance. *"If dey duzn't know dat, den dey isn't lookin' at da sign."*

Mr. Bean looked at the floor. Of course. The new signs, from last Christmas, had his picture. He was obviously the Mr. Bean of the name.

Tiger Lily said softly, *"Mr. Bean, it's not Tillie's fault. She belongs to Carlos. Where else is she going to spend her day?"*

Mo trilled. Mo, a litter mate to Kali and Ko, never progressed past speaking in their secret kitten language.

Tiger Lily sighed. She could still never understand the boy, and neither Kali nor Ko were here to translate. She turned to Sassy Pants. *"What's he saying?"*

"Oh. I forgets you duzn't understand him. He sez dat's da problem."

"What's the problem?"

"She belongs to Carlos."

"Oh." Tiger Lily finally understood.

"Mr. Bean, is Carlos less loving to you?"

The strong young cat shook his head, still looking at the floor, a little tear falling to the tile."

"Does he spend less time with you?"

The little head shook again.

"Does he in any way treat Tillie better than you?"

The little head shook again.

"So, is that what you're concerned about? Are you afraid Carlos is going to change?"

The little head nodded slowly, a few more tears trickling to the floor.

Tillie came up close to Mr. Bean. *"You know, I really belong to Isabel. It's just that I'm living with Carlos until Isabel comes to town."*

Isabel and Carlos were engaged to be married. Soon, Isabel would arrive from Mexico. She would stay somewhere else, possibly the Inn, until the wedding.

Little Socks piped up, *"You may live somewhere else for a while, then Isabel and Carlos will be living together, and you'll be right back."*

Tiger Lily bopped Little Socks on the nose.

"What?"

"You're not helping!"

"He needs to grow up!"

"He's still a baby."

"Well, he still needs to grow up."

Mo said, *"Trill!"*

"Oh, alright!" Little Socks stalked off to the library to find the softest chair.

Tiger Lily looked at Mr. Bean. *"Don't worry, little guy. Carlos loves you, and he always will. And you have us, and Mommy, and Henrie, and, well, everyone else on The Avenue. You don't have anything to worry about."*

Tillie piped up, *"Yeah. You don't have anything to worry about. I'm an only dog. I don't have siblings to love me, just you guys. And I love you, Mr. Bean, I really do. I'm not so sure about those big dogs, though."*

At this, Mr. Bean looked up. *"What's wrong with the dogs? You can't mean Cyril and Jock!"*

"I do. Those brutes don't pay me any attention, but some big pretty girl comes along and they're all ga-ga."

"You like Cyril and Jock that way?"

"Well, no, not really, but it would be nice if they would be nice to me."

Tiger Lily was concerned. *"They aren't nice to you?"*

"They don't look at me like I'm pretty."

"How do they look at you?"

"Like I'm a…dog."

Mo said, *"Trill."*

Sassy Pants was ready. *"He wants to know wot big pretty girl? Mo's de onliest dat likes pretty girls."*

Tiger Lily answered. *"It's a big pretty girl dog, Mo. She's got lots of hair, just like her human. They must be tourists."*

Tillie said, *"She's a flirt, but she's a really nice girl. It's hard for me to be jealous."*

"Well, it sounds like we all have a case of the jealousies, including me. I was jealous of Kali and Ko. Let's get it together.

There's enough weird stuff happening on The Avenue this week."

11

Annie got home and noticed the group of companions hanging out in the foyer. "Really? Are you the welcoming committee?"

Tiger Lily gave a quick "Meow," and they all ran to different parts of the house, in search of soft beds or toys or dropped crumbs.

Annie laughed. "Henrie, are you home?"

Henrie was already on his way to the foyer. "I am. How was your day?"

"I shopped, but I don't know if I will ever be able to get into that dress, met with Jenny about the meeting, and worked at the Café. Now I'm going to clean up a little and take my tired feet to the gem show."

"Are you looking for anything in particular?"

"Nope. Just looking. You know, my finger is still feeling pretty bare."

Annie had a beautiful ring from Chris. It wasn't exactly an engagement ring or even a pre-engagement ring. It was more of a promise to be faithful and loving. It was a deep purple oval-cut amethyst surrounded by white topaz and garnets of various colors. The smaller stones swirled around, encasing the amethyst in pinwheels of color.

Currently, the ring was in an evidence locker waiting the trial of a man who had mugged her and taken the ring from her hand.

"I think I need something to wear until I get my ring back."

"You can fit it to your right hand and continue to wear it even when your special ring is returned."

"Henrie, you look a little dazed. What's up?"

Henrie told Annie about the curious behavior of Fred, Kali and Ko. "I did not know what to do. I left the girls at Martha's, but surely, this can't become a permanent placement."

"Well, they didn't spend twenty-four hours a day with her while Georgia was here. Certainly there were hours of the day that Fred was cat-less. Maybe she settles down in the evening."

"Perhaps. I shall call Martha and arrange to pick the little dears up."

"Henrie, you're a gem. But what are you going to do tomorrow? Deliver the little baby sitters back?"

"That is a bridge we will cross tomorrow morning. By the way, how did that meeting go?"

"Just as we thought it would. He wants it all, from the Inn to the Café. I have to say, Henrie, we may be in for the ride of our lives."

The show was open until early evening. Mem and Janet were relieved mid-afternoon by high school students who planned to stay at the ticket booth until the show closed every day.

The two women were at Garry's exhibit when Annie and Laila arrived.

"I thought the two of you would be long gone."

"We didn't have time to look. Things got busy this afternoon. So we're looking at some things Garry put aside for us."

Annie and Laila looked at the pearl set and the ruby set. Laila gave her polite-to-people-who-didn't-know-her smile to Garry. "So pretty."

Mem and Janet caught the meaning. Both told Garry they would "have to think" about the purchases and that they would be taking tickets all week.

When they got a few booths down, Mem and Janet turned around, making the group a little circle. Laila asked, "How much?"

Mem took a deep breath. "Five thousand dollars for my set."

Janet said, "Four thousand, but mine didn't have a bracelet."

They looked at one another and said, together, "I'm making you a real deal."

Laila laughed. "I like to shop on the web. They are lovely pieces, but I saw the pearl necklace on Etsy. It's not really pearl. You can get the same thing for forty-nine dollars, maybe a little under one hundred if you add the extra pieces."

"You know, some of the others said his pieces may not be authentic."

"How can you tell? Are all of these booths going to try to take us for a ride?"

"No. Let's see. Janet, which are the reputable booths?"

"The turquoise, some of the larimar, but not all, so stay away unless you know how to tell, the artistic jewelry, we'll show you the booth, and, believe it or not, that messy guy."

"And the handsome man over there," Mem pointed to Martin, "has very nice things but his prices may be high."

"It pays to shop with someone who knows," laughed Annie. "So tell me, Mem, how is all of this going?"

"I think they have settled into a good group, with the exception, of course, of being liars, cheats and scam artists."

They all laughed again and wandered through the booths. Annie wanted to go past Gema's booth but decided to wait until she was alone.

Back at Garry's booth, Annie was taken by a lovely aquamarine ring with a price tag of fifty-nine hundred dollars. Garry told her the ring was set in eighteen karat brushed gold and white gold. The aquamarine itself was twenty one carats; the sides were inlaid with sapphires, rubies, diamonds and emeralds.

Annie tried it on. "It's lovely. Look, you can see my finger through the stone, and it's so big. It's very clear."

Garry said, "This is one of my masterpieces. I only make one item of each, and I have to tell you another person is interested. If she gets to it first, you will never have the opportunity again. And look. I made a matching necklace. She's interested in that, too."

Annie looked at the necklace, now draped on a velvet mat in front of her. She gazed at her hand with the ring on it. In her mind, she was thinking, why would I spend this much on a ring that meant nothing? I wonder if it's all fake? Forget fake; it's gauche!

What Chris saw, when he came up behind her, was a look of bliss. He gave her a kiss from behind and got a look at the price tag. To his credit, he managed to keep his reaction to himself.

"What do you think?" he said. "Do you want it?"

Annie laughed. "No, I'm happy with my ring. I'll just be happier when it's on my finger again."

Garry turned to Chris. "I was just telling her that someone else is interested in the ring and matching necklace. I'm working on the earrings now. It's possible all of it will be gone soon, and this is one of a kind."

Laila angled her body to put her back to Garry in such a way Chris could see her face. Her eyes said, "Don't do anything without talking to me."

Chris looked at Garry. "Maybe I'll come back on my own a little later."

Annie gave the ring back, and the group walked away.

"I've seen enough."

"Me, too."

"Beer at Mo's Tap?"

"Sounds good to me."

"Frank is already there. He got a table."

As they were almost into the stairwell, they heard Geraldine. Turning, Chris saw Geraldine put on the same ring, smiling, cooing and modeling it for her husband. The necklace was once again on the counter.

Annie tugged on Chris's sleeve and said, "Let's get out of here."

Chris's mind tumbled around as they walked downstairs and around to Mo's. When the conversation came around to the gem show, Laila told the group what she thought. "We're going to have to be careful if we buy. Take that ring Annie saw. The aquamarine is a fake, but a good one. The brushed gold and white gold are plated. The other stones are a toss-up, and my best guess is that they're fake as well. Even if some of them are real, the price is outrageous."

"And I didn't even like it. I want my ring back."

Chris smiled and kept up his end of the conversation, but in the back of his mind, he wondered if he shouldn't have gotten Annie something nicer, with precious rather than semi-precious stones.

Annie was still talking. "Can you imagine? Where is Geraldine going to get that kind of money for jewelry? She's in hock up to her forehead."

"Geraldine buys first, thinks later, then commits some kind of a crime to get what she needs."

As laughter at the crime was dying down, Pete and Cryil joined the table.

"What a day, what a day, what a day."

"Parking? Fender benders? Angry motorists?"

"That, and a couple of burglaries."

"What?"

"Yep. Over in the hotsy-totsy lakefront section of town. A couple of houses were broken into while everyone was away during the day."

"What was taken?"

"So far, the only items noted as missing were pieces of jewelry. Expensive jewelry. The kind you will never get to wear, my dear." That was said looking at Janet.

"Well, I found a pretty piece of expensive jewelry today, but unfortunately, the price tag probably doesn't match the value."

"Really?"

"Really. But they were beautiful almost-rubies."

While Candice brought Pete a glass and Cyril a bowl of water, Chris got Pete back on track. "How long has it been since Chelsea had a burglary?"

"Oh, it happens, but it's rare. Maybe two, three years ago. But I understand the moon is waxing gibbous, so that probably has something to do with it."

Cyril's attention was caught when the beautiful Fiamma entered the room. He stood up, tongue lolling out, tail wagging. Pete noticed the distraction.

When he saw the group entering Mo's Tap, he did a double take. His mind had wandered to the man with dreadlocks when investigating the burglaries. New man in town, new crime. The hair didn't help.

But now, what he saw stunned him. The man walked in with Clara on his arm. Clara!

Annie cried, "Clara! Come join us!"

Clara had grown restless in the last few months, and she had taken to going out of town on blind dates. Only a few people knew this, and those few people included everyone at this table. Pete, a police officer to the core, was immediately concerned. No one else seemed to be, however, so he decided to play it cool.

Clara made introductions, beginning with Fiamma, whose attention was already drawn elsewhere.

"Well, I'll be darned," said Chris.

"What?"

"Those two met at the Café today. I thought we were going to have a dog fight, but instead, it appears I was only seeing two dogs falling in love. Well, three. Jock was there, too. Maybe that was the problem. Maybe they were jealous of one another."

"It looks like those two are taken care of. Let's get chairs, more food, and a couple of glasses," said Clara.

When they were settled, Clara introduced the table, then her friend.

"This is Ramon. And before I tell you about Ramon, let me tell you how we met."

Ramon looked down at the table with a smile on his face. He then looked up and said, "I'm going to jump in whenever I believe she is going to tell an outrageous lie."

"Only then, darlin', not before." Clara turned to the full table. "Well, you know how I've been going out on these blind dates? Some fixed up by friends, but mostly internet dating? Really, it was kind of fun, but goodness me, how the computer matched me up with some of those guys is just, well, unbelievable."

"So you weren't an internet date, Ramon?"

"Nope."

"Shut up. I haven't started to lie yet. Well. Where was I?"

"Nowhere. Move a little faster."

"Okay, okay. Well, I was out on one of these blind dates, and he was a disaster! I mean, he was shorter than me, he does accounting in his own home, so he rarely sees anyone unless it's on his TV screen, he can't dance, he not only doesn't drink but he was put off that I ordered a glass of wine, and he hated the music!"

"What music?"

"The music at the club. He chose the place to meet. He chose this little jazz club, well, a medium, well, probably a large jazz club..."

"It's huge. It's a huge jazz club," said Ramon.

Clara closed her eyes and shook her head. "Okay. A jazz club in Marsh Haven. And he hated the music. He chose the place!"

"So you were at this jazz club?"

"Yes. Well, after dinner, when the waiter asked if we wanted anything else, he said, 'No, thank you.' But then he made no move to leave, so I asked if we were going to stay for a while. He said the band was changing, so maybe the music would be better, we should stay. So I got up and went to the bar to get a glass of wine."

Clara stopped, took a drink, took a few bites, and asked Annie, "When are you going to get your ring back?"

"What? You were telling us how you met. So far, you went to the bar to get a glass of wine."

"Oh. Well, the band was changing, and I noticed that the saxophone player from the first band was at the bar, so I kind of went to where he was, leaned over, showing off my particular good looks, asked that bartender for a glass of Zinfandel, and while I was waiting, I introduced myself."

"To the saxophone player."

"Yes. A very good looking saxophone player."

"And?"

"And he said, you're the fifth woman in five days to come in with this guy. What is it with him, and how can he get all of the hot ones?"

"I'm sure my line was a lot smoother than that."

"Not much."

"But it worked."

"Yes. It worked. I left my glass of wine at the bar, of course asking Mr. Handsome here if he would please wait for me, went back to the table, picked up my purse and said, 'I'll pay for my own meal. Thanks for the evening.' And I did – pay for my own meal – and he left. End of date, end of story, beginning of new story."

With that, Clara sat back with a smile, picked up her glass and had another sip.

"Annie, where's your ring."

"Still in evidence. So, excuse me, Ramon, tell me about your jazz band."

"What do you want to know?"

"So, you play places, right?"

Ramon replied with two long, drawn-out words. "Um, yeah?"

Mem took over. "Excuse my friend. Sometimes she doesn't think or speak clearly. We have a problem, and you may be able to help."

"Shoot."

"Okay. We're having a block party a week from Saturday. It's something we've never done before. It's called Jazz On The Avenue. The only problem is that we don't have any jazz to put on The Avenue."

Clara jumped in. "What? I invited Ramon to come down that day. He and the band have that weekend off. What happened?"

"We had two bands, and they both cancelled. So we have no jazz. None. For Jazz On The Avenue. What a way to make a splash!"

Ramon leaned forward. "So, it's an outdoor venue?"

"Yes. We have the stage, and if we need it, we have access to an outdoor sound system. We have everything we need. With the exception of the jazz."

"Clara told me about your block parties. They're for charity, right?"

"Yes. The other bands had agreed to play at no charge, which is why they probably felt free to ditch us for paying venues."

"That's not right. A commitment is a commitment."

"That's what we thought, but it wouldn't do us any good to argue the point. They won't come, and that's that. For them. We were beginning to look into jazz CDs, but…."

"I can't speak for the rest of the band, but I'd be up for it, playing without a fee. I can call them and find out if they're available. What's the charity?"

Mem answered. "The Ronald McDonald House. We change it up for each event, share the love, so to speak."

"It's a great charity. Excuse me. I'll make the calls. Saturday the thirtieth, correct?"

"Yes."

"And we would be the only band?"

"Unfortunately."

"Not necessarily. If you would allow us a few breaks. We can bring some great CDs to play while we're on break."

Annie and Mem could hardly contain their glee while Ramon left the table. Annie asked, "Clara, what's the name of the band? Are they any good?"

"They are great. Really, really great, and I'm not just saying it. They're called Bergamasco."

"What?"

"Bergamasco. You know. The dog."

"What dog?"

"That dog." Clara turned to point to Fiamma. "She's a bergamasco."

Ramon returned to the table in less than fifteen minutes. "We're in."

Pete leaned in to ask, "So tell me, Ramon, where does Bergamasco play?"

Annie felt Chris pulling away. She asked him quietly if everything was okay.

"Sure," he said.

"Nothing going on at work?"

"No, everything's fine at work. I'm just tired."

"Want to stay at the Inn tonight?"

"No, not tonight. I'll talk to you tomorrow." He gave her a brief kiss and said good night to everyone. Annie started to follow him out the door. They passed four people heading for the table they just vacated. Geraldine and Hank, and the man and woman from the gem show. Wonderful.

Annie veered to the bar, called George to the end and talked to him briefly before walking out.

12

Henrie arrived to pick up the girls, and he came with food. "I assumed you did not have time for dinner. I brought a selection of items. I'd love to hear about your day, Georgia, if you have time to tell me."

"Oh, Henrie, thank you. I haven't eaten anything since breakfast."

"And I haven't eaten anything since you fed me at lunch, Henrie, so sit yourself down."

They settled at the table, Fred in her chair on the floor. Her ever-present nannies stopped worrying about her long enough to beg for some food from Henrie. They ate what he offered and went back to their charge.

"Please tell me. Were you able to talk to Cookie?"

"Better than that." Georgia described for both Martha and Henrie her bold insertion into the kitchen at Mo's Tap. "And when the rush finally ended, I sat down with both George and Cookie. I have two jobs!"

"Two?" exclaimed Martha. My goodness, child. How are you going to manage?"

"Well, I talked to JoJo, and she said the school has a daycare service that maybe I could get into. It works on a sliding scale fee, so maybe it will be affordable. And she said she and a couple of her friends can help, too, really cheap."

Henrie was nothing, if not practical. "What are the jobs, Georgia? What are the hours?"

"Well, tomorrow and Thursday I'm going to help with the lunch rush in the kitchen at Mo's, since this is a particularly busy week. Then, in the afternoon tomorrow, really I started this afternoon after the lunch rush, I'm going to help Cookie get started with his new place. He doesn't have anyone to help with anything. He said the people at the Café will help with the front, but he has no one in the kitchen, so I guess I'm going to be the main help there. At least this weekend. We'll have to find someone to wash dishes."

"So you'll be doing that Thursday, at the grand opening, and then every weekend, Friday and Saturday evenings?"

"Yes, and I'm going to help him with ordering and hiring and things like that. He's lost when it comes to organization."

Henrie wisely didn't offer his opinion on that issue.

"And will you continue at Mo's Tap after this week?"

"Yes. Right now it won't be full time, because Cookie will still be there, but we're going to see how it goes. And George said there will always be opportunities for me to fill in either at the front or back at both the Tap and the Café."

"That is true. We help one another out. Which means that if I have a need at the Inn and you are so disposed – and available – that would bring another opportunity. There would also be opportunity at Sassy P's and Mr. Bean's."

"That's what George said. I'm going to be okay, Henrie! I'm going to be okay!"

While everyone at the table smiled, Martha, inwardly, was sad. Soon, she would lose this, probably her last guest, to an apartment somewhere in town.

Henrie once again became practical. "Have you arranged for JoJo through Saturday?"

"Yes. She's available, except for Friday night, and she has a friend that will come in her place."

"Now that I think about it," he said, "might it be easier for you to bring Fred to the Inn? You can call JoJo to arrange for the change in location. That way, the feline nannies will already be present and accounted for."

"If it won't be too much trouble?"

"It will be no trouble at all. We will be full, that is certain, but if the library is not available for JoJo, she will be welcome to use my apartment."

Henrie was finally able to coax the two big cats away from Fred with the promise that they would see her tomorrow. Henrie always had doubts they really understood what he said, but they seemed to cooperate if only he explained things fully.

Gema, Garry and Geraldine left the gem show, now closed, when Geraldine received a text. "The table we wanted at Mo's Tap is going to be free any minute now."

Hank waited for them at the door, opened it and followed as Geraldine led the way. They passed several people on the way by. By now, Gema had met many of these individuals and in particular knew Mem, Janet and Annie.

She knew Garry was trying to sell big ticket items to them, and he schmoozed them all as they walked out. She needed to make sure they paid more attention to her jewelry, but she was not quite the salesman Garry was.

And, frankly, she felt guilty about meeting here, now, with people that planned to purchase Annie's building. Up until now, she had seen no indication that Annie intended to sell and no indication that Annie was a friend to or partner with these people.

This was only the first day of the show. Now that the excitement had worn off, the serious shoppers would return. Gema had seen many women, enamored at first with Garry's bling, come to her before the shows were over. If only she could have some major sales this time.

As the people from the big table filed by, Geraldine picked up her phone to send a text. Within minutes, they were joined by a man introduced as "Howard, the man with the plan."

The server handed menus around, and while conversation centered around the food, the drink and the first day of the show, Gema looked around.

This was another very nice place. Mo's Tap was definitely upscale, and blues played softly in the background. Loud enough to hear, soft enough to allow for pleasant conversation.

Even in the dim nighttime lighting, she could tell the walls were a buttery yellow color with light taupe on the accent wall. The tables were burnished oak with comfortable oak chairs. The booths were also oak with dark taupe cushions. On the other side of the room she saw several private areas with overstuffed chairs and accent tables. A few areas had oaken barrel tables. The lighting over each table was unique, pendant lights at some places and Tiffany lamps at others. Candles were lit at each table.

She noticed the candles were unusual in that they had roof-shaped lids with holes.

When the server got to her order, she asked about them. The server laughed. "Well, after a long time of dealing with Mo, our cat, someone finally got smart and put the tops on. Now he can dance around them all he wants, and his tail won't catch on fire."

Gema smiled. She noticed that Geraldine, Hank and Howard grimaced.

When the server left, Geraldine spoke. "Gema saw the yoga studio, and she thinks the storefront would be appropriate."

Howard smiled. "That would make a perfect mix on this street. Keep the café, this place, the bakery, the winery, and add fine jewelry. Yes. A much better mix."

Gema looked at Howard. "Please fill me in on the ownership of this building. I haven't seen any indication that it is for sale."

"Well, it isn't right now, but it will be, and probably within the month."

"How do you know?"

"Now, can I assume we are business partners? Are you going to keep this to yourselves?" He looked pointedly at Garry and Gema.

"Well, yes. But we can't guarantee the silence of the people who work here."

"That's why we're sitting in the back, and that's why I'm watching for our server at all times. We just need to keep our voices low. And for now, let's stop talking."

A new server was headed in their direction. Candice placed drinks around the table. "Good evening. It's nice to see you Howard. And you Geraldine, Hank. She looked at Gema and Garry. I'm Candice. I'll be your server this evening. Your first server turned your orders in; they'll be right up."

As she left, Gema turned back to Howard. "So?"

"Well, the fact is, Annie is having problems with the Inn. She's not a natural manager, and the Inn is going under. I've been watching the situation, and I've been building up some capital. The three of us have formed a partnership to purchase the Inn, this building and all the businesses."

Geraldine and Hank smiled and looked intently at Gema and Garry, neither meeting Howard's eyes during his exchange. The longer he remained in the dark about their true financial positions, the better.

Gema and Garry turned to look at one another. Garry spoke first, addressing Gema. "Did you get the impression the Inn was in trouble?"

"No, not at all. It's a lovely place, clean, and the manager said they would be full this week. They aren't now, but I gather others are coming tomorrow to fill it up."

"Yeah, I heard someone at the show saying even the carriage house would be full."

They turned back to the partnership. "But she's in trouble?"

Howard waved his hand dismissively. "She can't handle money, and frankly she made some very bad business decisions, took guests she should never have allowed. There were, um, incidents."

"Incidents?"

Geraldine and Hank smiled sheepishly. Geraldine leaned in and patted her hand on the table next to Gema. "Now don't let this scare you off. Everything happened as a result of some guests at the KaliKo Inn. There were a couple of murders."

Howard added, "And kidnappings. There were a couple of those."

Gema and Garry, eyes wide, leaned back and looked at one another.

Candice returned with food orders. "Here you go. I think I have these in the correct order." She handed around burgers, ahi tuna tacos, and stuffed portabella mushrooms.

As the food was placed, Gema found her footing again. Something was wrong with this picture. She wanted a storefront. This town would be perfect. The yoga studio would be perfect. But she didn't want to get any of it through fraudulent means.

When Candice left, she said, "So you're going to capitalize on the crimes committed by her guests?"

Howard blustered a little bit. "Well, no, not exactly. When you combine that with her very poor management skills, it's a recipe for disaster."

Hank had to add, "And she hires the lowest sort. Take that bartender, for example. He is the biggest womanizer in town."

Gema looked around. If he were the biggest womanizer, he was very good at it. There were men in groups, women in groups, couples of every variety, and he seemed to be on good terms with them all. And pretty servers. None of them acted, well, like he was womanizing them. As a matter of fact, he and the server from their table seemed to have a top notch professional relationship.

Hank seemed to sense her observation. He said, "Trust me. When you have your store, he'll be the first one to come around and make a pass."

Gema smiled. "Well, as long as he's in the store making a pass, I'll make sure to sell him something nice."

Howard wanted to make sure he had this couple in his pocket. He needed their rent money as part of the package. But he realized he needed to back off a bit.

"Just keep in mind that I know she's going to lose everything if she doesn't accept our offer. I don't want to give you a hard sell. I want you to look around while you're here and make up your own mind. We'll talk later."

Candice returned to the table. "Can I get more drinks? Anything?"

Gema turned and smiled. "I'll take my check please." She looked back at Howard. "Thanks so much for a wonderful evening. It's been a long day. I need to turn in."

Candice returned to the bar following her first trip to Geraldine's table, a little smile on her face. She had succeeded in getting under the skin of three of her least favorite people in town.

At the bar, as she pretended to turn in additional orders, she and George leaned in to talk to one another. "Annie was right. I think these two from the gem show are interested in one of our storefronts. Probably the yoga studio."

"Why do you say that?"

"Diana said she came in early this morning, and she spent more time looking around the room than concentrating on the class. Add that to the rumors, Howard's involvement, and of course the fine touch of our leading citizens, it's not hard to figure out."

"Do they think we're that stupid? Do they think Annie's that stupid, or that she doesn't have a natural pipeline?"

"They never were the brightest people in town."

"Yeah. Coming here or going to Sassy P's to make their plans. Not bright at all."

Candice laughed. She did enjoy talking to George. If only he weren't such a schmuck.

George said, "Well, I'm glad Annie asked you to take that table over. They'll probably stop talking as soon as you walk over there, but you might catch something."

After Candice delivered the food, she updated George. "It seems they've told the gem folks something that surprised them."

"Must have unloaded about the murders and kidnappings."

"Would be my guess."

Earlier than she would have thought, Candice was back at the bar, preparing tickets for the table. George found a reason to need to be at that end of the bar.

"They're leaving?"

"I think that woman from the gem show is not an idiot. She asked for her check before anyone else was ready."

"Good to know."

Annie was in bed. She was tired, she was a little worried about Howard, she was a lot worried about Chris. Had she done or said something, or was his week just as bad as hers?

Oh, well. Nothing she could do about it tonight. She finally dropped off to sleep, surrounded by cats. When sleep came, they quietly slipped away.

In the dining room, sitting in a row on the windowsill, they couldn't see one another's faces, but they didn't have to talk in loud cat voices. Their cat ears were very good.

Tiger Lily was happy Mommy liked fresh air. The upper part of the windows were open to let in the air. Street sounds filtered in as well.

Tiger Lily watched as Dwight walked to the Inn from Mo's Tap. He met three men coming from the public parking lot. She noticed them on The Avenue earlier in the day, but she didn't know who they were. They all stopped in front of Sassy P's under the light. One of the men carried a case.

Dwight said, "Let's see what you got."

The man held the case so another man could open it, showing some sparkly things.

Dwight picked up a piece and inspected it, picked up another piece, and another. "This is good stuff. Good stuff. Have you found a place for tomorrow?"

Someone came out of Sassy P's; the man with the case closed it and put it back down at his side.

When the couple that left the winery was out of earshot, the man said, "There are two more places in that neighborhood where everyone is gone during the day. We've got tomorrow only. After that, everyone will have beefed up their security."

Dwight laughed. "We should get into the security business."

The men smiled. The case was given to Dwight and he handed something to the man in return. It was cash. The man counted it and gave some to each of his companions.

"Thanks. See you tomorrow night." Dwight walked to the Inn; the three men walked back to the public parking lot.

Tiger Lily turned to Little Socks. *"Did you see that?"*

"Yeah."

"Think you can be a cat burglar tonight and find out what's in that case?"

"Sure. I hope he leaves it open."

"Find out what you can. We probably need to tell Cyril about him."

"I'll go when I think he's had time to go to sleep."

The cats lapsed into silence. Then Tiger Lily said, *"Have you heard anything at the yoga studio about Mommy selling the building?"*

Now she had everyone's attention. *"What?" "Selling?" "Wot you talk about?" "Trill!"*

Little Socks stood up straight and looked Tiger Lily square in the eyes. *"Not the yoga studio. Not that. What would I do? Why would Mommy do that to me?"*

"I don't know that she is; I was just asking if you heard anything about it. Geraldine was talking about it with that woman that's staying here."

"That woman was leaving my place when I got there this morning. I thought she just took a class."

"I think she was checking it out, to see if she wanted it."

"I'll scratch her eyes out!"

"No you won't. You're going to keep your ears open."

"When did you hear about it?"

"At lunch today. I was really upset, but after talking to Cyril and Jock, I can consider the source. Geraldine told her that Mommy was going to sell the building. That woman wants the yoga studio for a jewelry store."

Sassy Pants, indignant, said, *"Dat Geraldine is a ravin' – wot duz Mommy calls it? A ravin' witch wif a bee."*

Little Socks pushed her forehead into the cool window, hoping to ease the pain of listening to Sassy Pants talk and the fear that she might lose her livelihood.

Mo said, *"Trill."*

Kali and Ko said together, *"He said Geraldine always has idiot plans." "He said Geraldine can't plan her way out of a paper bag."*

Tiger Lily looked at her siblings in the reflection of the glass. They all looked back the same way. *"We need to stay on top of it. It probably has to do with that Howard mess Mommy and Henrie have talked about."*

Kali and Ko looked up sharply. Kali spoke. *"Who's Howard and what's Henrie got to do with it?"*

Tiger Lily rolled her eyes. *"If the two of you were not so involved with that baby, you might pick up on what's going on around here. Howard is one of the B&B owners, and he's trying to make trouble for Mommy and Henrie. And that woman talking to Geraldine is staying here. I bet you don't know the first thing about any of the guests. And you need to help Henrie with everything, not just that baby."*

The two big girls looked at one another in the window reflection, then looked down.

"You need to start paying attention. You know what happens when we don't stay on top of things. Mommy gets herself into trouble!"

Ko said, *"But Fred needs us. She'll still be here while her mommy works, and we have to take care of her."*

Kali added, *"You should have heard her crying until we got there. She really needs us!"*

Tiger Lily said, *"You're going to have to, you know, do something. Maybe take turns being with her and nosing around."*

Kali and Ko looked at one another again through the reflection. They took turns talking.

"It's hard, taking care of a baby."

"Yeah, she needs us all the time."

"We'll have to think of some way she can get along without us."

"Maybe Georgia can get a cat."

"How are we going to make her do that?"

Tiger Lily had the answer. *"Every day, once a day, we all have to send a message out to the universe to ask for a cat for Fred."*

The group nodded to one another through the reflection of the window.

"What else is going on?"

Mo said, *"Trill, trill, trill, trill, trill."*

Tiger Lily was startled at the long recitation. She looked at the window reflection to her normal translators, Kali, Ko and Sassy Pants.

Sassy Pants was ready, *"He sez dat Georgia was at Mo's an she wented to da kichen an helpted Cookie get da meals out, an den George and Cookie and Georgia – dat's funny, George and Georgia – dey decided she wood work dere and wif Cookie in his new place."*

Mr. Bean beamed into the window reflection. *"That's great! That means she'll be staying in town, and we'll all get to see Fred lots and lots."*

Kali and Ko added, with a little chagrin and at the same time, *"We were busy with Fred, we didn't hear that." "We knew she had a job but we were too busy to listen."*

"That's okay, girls. I know you're going to pay more attention. And yes, I know, Fred needs you." Tiger Lily shook her head and rolled her eyes. She sighed and turned to Mr. Bean.

"What's happening at the Confectionary?"

Mr. Bean sat up, feeling important. He looked over the backs of the other cats at Tiger Lily. *"Tillie and I met that Fiamma today. She's a big, pretty dog."*

"She was at the Café, too. Did anyone see where all she and her human went?"

Mr. Bean continued. *"I did. They walked around and stuff most of the day, and they went in and out of several places, but at the end of the day, they went into Clara's place, and then she closed up. They didn't come out."*

"So he's a friend of Clara. That's nice. He seemed like a nice man."

"Yeah. He bought Fiamma some treats before they went out to the lighthouse. That's real nice."

Tiger Lily laughed. *"The boys are going to be fighting over her."*

"Cyril and Jock?"

"Yes. They're both in love."

"Oh, boy. That'll be fun to watch."

They all chuckled to themselves and watched the street again.

Sassy Pants saw him first. *"Look! Dat Dwight is out dere!"*

They looked. There was Dwight, without the bag, walking toward the median. He put something in one of the concrete pots, pushing it underneath the shrubbery. He got up, turned back toward the Inn, looked both ways and returned.

A few minutes later, another man came from Sassy P's. He walked to the same pot, reached in, felt around, picked up the package and put it into his jacket pocket. He then went to a bench on the median. He sat.

The cats watched for a while but were bored with the inactivity. Most of them started to doze, until Little Socks said, *"Hey, look. There's that guy coming out of the campground. He's been here before."*

"That's Adam."

"What's he doing?"

"He's gonna sit at dat bench with dat udder guy!"

The cats watched while the two met. They put their heads down while they talked. The men spoke in low tones and the cats couldn't pick out any words until Adam's voice raised. "Martin, I can't afford to do this for the rest of my life!"

Instantly, the two men looked around, apparently saw no one, but still quieted their voices. Eventually they went their separate ways, Adam angry, the man he called Martin smug.

Mo said, *"Trill."*

Even Tiger Lily understood. *"Yes, Mo. I'll tell Cyril when I see him tomorrow. You know, there is a lot going on at the show. We should go. Let's plan on going when we get off work tomorrow."*

She received nods from everyone.

Little Socks said, *"I'm going to see if I can get into that case."* She looked at Kali and Ko. *"With the bang-up job you've been doing this week, do you even know which room he's in?"*

Kali thought quickly. She and Ko had seen where the other three went, so by process of elimination, she had the answer. *"He's in the front room, right underneath us."*

Tiger Lily said, *"You all stay here. I'll follow Little Socks to the room."*

The two slipped quietly out the door onto the third floor landing, listened intently and crept down the stairs to the second floor. Once again, they listened intently.

Tiger Lily stayed at the base of the stairs while Little Socks slipped silently down the hallway. She put her ear to the cat door, opened it slowly and silently, took a quick look around and slipped inside.

The case was open and lying on the side of the bed that Dwight wasn't sleeping in. At least she thought he was asleep. She listened and heard only rhythmic breathing.

With the stealth of a panther, she jumped to the foot of the bed. She stayed as still as she could. The breathing continued. Gently, she took one step forward, then two, keeping an eye on Dwight and her ears trained to his breathing.

One more step and she could look into the case. There were several pieces of jewelry. Concentrating on the case, she saw a ring. She could carry that.

She reached a paw into the case and moved it toward the edge of the case. Slowly, slowly, so as not to make noise.

The ring was within her grasp. She put her head in and gently picked the ring up with her teeth.

Dwight snorted! She started, dropped the ring, then stayed still. He remained asleep.

She put her head in again, got the ring, sat up and stayed in place. He still slept.

She jumped down as quietly as she could and once again sat in place. He didn't make a sound.

Little Socks crept out the cat door. Once it shut behind her, she ran to the stairs and up. Tiger Lily took a quick look behind then followed her.

Once inside the apartment, Little Socks put the ring on the kitchen floor. The cats gathered around.

Mr. Bean beamed. *"You got a clue!"*

"Yes, she got a clue," said Tiger Lily. *"Now what should we do with it?"*

Mo said, *"Trill!"*

Sassy Pants translated. *"He sez hide it till you can tell Cyril."*

"Good idea, Mo. Where can we hide it?"

"Where does Mommy never look?"

"The cleaning closet!"

"Hilly looks in there."

They thought about it some more. Little Socks finally said, *"Behind the refrigerator. I can put it on the floor there, and we can find something to push it back."*

"What?"

"I know!" said Mr. Bean. He ran into the bedroom and came back with what they called a twirly stick. It was a stick with a colorful ribbon attached.

"Good job, Mr. Bean!"

Little Socks put the ring on the floor between the refrigerator and the wall, and Tiger Lily took the stick, positioning the tip of it at the ring. Then she pushed, slowly.

"We can't put it too far back. We have to be able to get it out."

"Mommy never looks there. It will be safe."

"Well," said Tiger Lily, *"We have a lot going on, and I have a lot to tell Cyril tomorrow."*

Mr. Bean said, *"Tillie told me that Fiamma taught her human some sign language. Maybe we can teach Mommy."*

"How long did it take?"

"Apparently months and months."

Tiger Lily sighed. *"We'll have to talk about it. But for now, let's go to bed."*

Seven tired cats went to the bedroom to get back into bed with their mommy.

13

Henrie, relying on the information given him when the gem show folks checked in, had breakfast ready by 7:00. Breakfast ready in the dining room, he sat at the kitchen table with a cup of coffee, safe in the knowledge that would not show. At least, not at the stated time. Annie joined him.

As she poured coffee, Henrie got two plates from the cabinet. "Allow me to serve."

"I will allow."

Soon, they sat together with helpings of egg casserole – this morning it was bacon, mushroom and Swiss – French toast stuffed with strawberries and cream cheese, oat groats with walnuts and kale, and glasses of cranberry juice.

"Henrie, I will ask you again. Will you marry me?"

"I believe there is someone in line for that honor already. However, I may be convinced to be a kept man."

They laughed, and they told one another everything they knew about what was going on around town, paying particular attention to Howard and his shenanigans.

Annie mused, "I wonder if Howard knows that Geraldine and Hank haven't got a penny to their names?"

"Well, they do own homes. Perhaps they could leverage those assets."

"From what I hear, those assets are leveraged to the hilt already."

"As we know their plans can come to naught, we should concentrate on ways we can mitigate their intrusions."

"I wonder how they will intrude? They could make complaints to the licensing agencies, but they would have to have a reason to do so."

"They could possibly get word to the other B&B associations in the region, even statewide, and ask them to, well, I do not know what they would ask them."

"If they're smart enough, they could get into the system and put fake reviews in."

"They would have to intrude somehow into our system."

"There have to be other ways of getting things out on the web."

"I will investigate."

"Tell me what you can about Gema and Garry, since they seem to be involved somehow."

"When they are together, they are either arguing or scheming. I do not know how else to say it. She seems pleasant enough; he is rude and obnoxious. Using physical characteristics, they seem compatible. However, their personalities seem to be on a collision course."

"Maybe they wouldn't be best of friends but good business partners."

"That could be a possibility."

They heard footsteps from the stairway. Henrie rose, went to the dining room and stood ready with the coffee pot. "Good morning, Gema. Did you sleep well?"

"Yes, Henrie. Thank you. I'm going to have some of this oatmeal, then head for the yoga studio."

"Would you like coffee?"

"No, thanks. I'll just have water."

"Certainly. Let me know if I can be of assistance."

"Thanks."

Henrie went to the kitchen and raised his eyebrows to Annie. She took his cue and carried her cup to the dining room.

"Good morning, Gema. I plan to concentrate on your jewelry today."

"Wonderful. I have some pieces you would love."

"Do you mind if I join you?"

"Please do."

Gema put some brown sugar on her oatmeal as Annie sat down.

"Tell me about your business, Gema. Do you design your own pieces?"

"I do. I have a workshop at my home, and I make my pieces right there. I work mostly with silver and precious stones, but I also have semi-precious and some synthetic pieces. A few pieces in gold and platinum."

"Do you enjoy going to shows like this one?"

"I do several a year, the typical circuit. There are some larger shows, of course, but most of them are small, like this, and no, I have to say I'm getting tired of the life."

"Is this your only sales outlet?"

"No. I have a website and sell from there, and I'm connected to a few other online opportunities, like Etsy. The shows do help get my name and designs out, and I often have sales after the shows, people who saw me at a venue and then looked online."

"Have you ever considered having a storefront?"

"Funny you should mention it. Yes. I've considered it, and I have the opportunity to partner with a colleague – Garry, he's staying here – in starting one or more storefronts. Garry loves the life of traveling around. I would like to stay in one place."

"It sounds like you're planning it."

"Yes." Gema took a drink of water and a couple of bites of oatmeal. "Annie, you're a smart, connected woman. At least, that's what I believe, after seeing you several times in the last couple of days."

"I think so, yes."

"Then I think you may know that I've been approached about a place here in town."

"I have heard the rumors."

"It's funny about small towns. People think they can act in complete privacy. They tell you no one knows anything, and in the same conversation, they tell the person they're with about everything that everyone else is doing."

"It sounds as if you speak from experience."

"I do."

"Perhaps we should get together again."

"We should."

"I look forward to it."

Annie smiled and went back to the kitchen just as Dwight, Nelson and Garry came into the dining room.

Gema said, "Good morning boys. I'll see you at the show." And she left.

This morning, unlike the day before, the three men dug into breakfast with a vengeance, even asking for to-go containers as they left for the show. Henrie was happy to oblige. He wondered where the freeloader from yesterday was. Perhaps he figured he could get by with it once, but not twice.

Dwight hung back as the others left. "Henrie, try this card, see if you can get enough credit on it for me to charge meals and things like that."

"What amount would you desire?"

"Try two hundred dollars. I'll let everyone pay their own way from now on."

"Certainly."

Henrie ran the card and gave the paperwork to Dwight to sign. "I shall inform the managers to allow you to charge."

"Thanks, Henrie. Sorry about the trouble before. It was, well, I was distracted." Dwight left.

Henrie sent a text to all the managers and sat at the computer, turning on his Skype capabilities. He had plans to make.

Today was going to be a good day. It was Wednesday. The moon was full. If they could hang in for a few more days, all would be well.

Henrie was cleaning the dining room when the front door opened. He heard, "Hello! Anybody home?"

He went to the foyer and saw a tall, slim man dressed in business casual attire. "Yes. How may I help you?"

"I'm Fred. Fred Calendar. I have a reservation."

"Oh, yes, Mr. Calendar. My name is Henrie. I will be your host. I am so sorry to be in the middle of something. I expected you later."

"Check-in time is in the afternoon, I know, but I'm kind of anxious to get going with the business I've got in town, and I was hoping that, at the very least, I could drop off my luggage."

"Please do not misunderstand me. Your room is ready. The last occupant left yesterday. By the way, the room was occupied by another Fred. It seems serendipitous."

"At this point, I'll take all the serendipity I can get."

Henrie smiled. "Please, allow me to take your bags. I am not prepared to show you the amenities of the Inn; I hope you will allow me to do so at a later time today."

"Certainly, and thanks, Henrie."

Henrie placed the bags in the back room and escorted Mr. Calendar to the sign-in desk. As he ran the credit card, he asked, "Is there anything I can do to assist as you conduct your business?"

"Well, I don't know. I'm looking for someone, you see, and I don't really know where to start. I'm certain she's here. Or at least she stopped off here. I can start at the police department, but they probably wouldn't know anything about her. Is there a place I can get a list of all the hotels and places to stay?"

"Certainly. I have a brochure right here, and it is up-to-date. Who is it, may I ask, that you seek?"

"My daughter. I don't know if she's using her maiden name or her married name. She's used both as I've followed her movements from one place to another."

"I gather her maiden name is Calendar?"

"Yes."

"And her married name?"

"Jones. Georgia Jones."

Henrie was glad his head was down tending to paperwork. He gathered his thoughts and looked up. "I see. I can tell you are anxious to find her. Have you been looking for a long time?"

Mr. Calendar hung his head. "Not nearly long enough. What do you do when they grow up? You know, they're adults. You can't keep 'em on a leash."

"No, you cannot."

"I've been looking for a couple of months. I finally decided that maybe she was never going to come home, and I don't know what I did, you know, to send her away. So I decided to find her to see if I could make it up to her, whatever it was. I started where I could. I started at the bus station, tracking all the places she coulda gone, and eventually, I found her. Or, you know, I found where she'd been stayin' at a shelter, then an apartment, and then she left. So I started at the bus station again."

"And why here, Mr. Calendar? Why Chelsea?"

"Well, I figured she'd choose a town on the lake. She always liked the lake. So I contacted the bus stations up and down the coast, and I sent pictures. It took a few weeks, but finally the Marsh Haven place called me back. Said a driver saw her picture hanging in the office and remembered her. He said she said something about coming here. I made my reservation here that very same day. It took me a couple days to get things in order where's I could leave."

"Well. Here is that brochure of hotels, motels and bed and breakfast facilities. If I think of anything that would be helpful, I will let you know."

"Thanks. Thanks so much. Oh, there's a map in this brochure. Show me where we are."

Henrie pointed out the location of the Inn. Mr. Calendar took a pen, crossed off the marker for the Inn and said, "Okay. I'll just follow this map. Thanks again."

Henrie waited until he had gone. He then called Martha and said, "Is Georgia ready to go? I thought I would pick her up on her first day."

"Come on over. I'll tell her you're coming."

Once there, Henrie took note of the cries in the background and took Martha aside. "Martha, a man, perhaps Georgia's father, will be coming around asking about her. Until I investigate further, I will not know if he is her father, and if he is, I do not know if she wants to see him. Please lie like the proverbial rug if he knocks on your door."

"I sure will. I'll let you know if he stops, and you tell me if you hear anything."

Georgia came to the kitchen dressed for work with a diaper bag over one shoulder, a cooler bag with breast milk over another, and a screaming Fred kind of all over the place. "I can't wait to get her over to those cats. Lord help me if I have to steal Kali and Ko from you and Annie."

"We will work something out," said Henrie. "Come. We have things to discuss."

Gema slipped off her caftan. She was always prepared for a yoga class. As she went through the poses, led again this morning by Diana, she looked around.

Yes, she liked this place. It was a clean, empty space. One wall was totally windows, from knee to almost ceiling, and the ceiling was tall. It appeared to be the original tin, or a good reproduction. The opposite wall was completely mirrored. The entryway and the trim around both the windows and the mirrors were bright orange. The other walls were painted eggshell. In primary colors were silhouettes of yoga poses. In front of the windows was a row of backless benches, each painted a different color of the rainbow. The windowsills were deep. She had not noticed them the day before. Each sill had a black pillow, but one pillow was a little lumpier than the others.

As she looked, the lump seemed to sigh, deep breath in, deep breath out. She laughed to herself. Of course. This was the Lil' Socks of Lil' Socks' Virasana. Not in her signature pose, but in her signature stance. Asleep in the sun, all white parts hidden.

If she had this space, she would keep the rainbow colors. Instead of yoga poses, she would mimic some of her own designs. The main counter would be close to the mirrored wall, making the display, even the store itself, seem twice the size. She assumed the office area would be appropriate for her, and the dressing rooms that she saw yesterday could easily be made over into storage. She might keep one shower, for emergencies.

But then, who was she kidding? Annie had no reason to sell this building, and she had no reason to change out the yoga studio for jewelry. The studio seemed to do a good business. Every time she walked past, there was a class in session, none with fewer than ten members and many even larger.

It was just her luck to find the perfect place and for that place to be out of her reach. This was her lot in life. If only she had made different decisions when she was younger.

If only.

If only. What was that saying? If wishes were fishes...oh, yes. If wishes were fishes, we'd all swim in riches.

Well, what if she turned that around? What if she stopped hanging out with what could possibly be the upper-crust riffraff in town and started hanging out with real people? What if she threw her lot in with Annie, in whatever form that might take?

She probably wouldn't get this place. This place was taken. But maybe there was a similar place in town that could be had for a song. And Garry? She didn't need him. Any fool could see he was a fraud in many ways. Sure, he had a couple of pieces that he could have possibly designed, but, really.

She heard the Indian or Pakistani woman say she'd seen those pearls on Etsy. Garry wasn't on Etsy. At least, not as a dealer. Honestly, thought Gema. I need to spend more time looking through other jewelry items on Etsy to see if I can find Garry's "originals."

Gema barely heard Diana, but with the little she did hear, and seeing from the side what others were doing, she performed the poses effortlessly. Soon the class was over.

Gema went to the bench where she had folded her caftan. It happened to be in front of the black cat. She sat down as she put the caftan over her shoulders. She leaned back and whispered to the cat, "If you have a way to tell your mommy, tell her I'm on her side. I'll help her stick it to those folks, and maybe, just maybe, I can land on my feet. But you tell her."

Gema sat up and looked back. The cat hadn't moved while she was speaking, but now, her face came up and bright green eyes peered into Gema's own. Gema was graced with one slow blink. Then the cat licked a paw and curled into a ball again.

Gema thought, message sent. But I probably still have to talk to Annie.

To thank the rock and gem show vendors for all the business this week, the Café sent up a mid-morning snack. A table around the corner of the elevator held various caffeinated and decaffeinated coffees and teas, fruit salad, homemade power bars, tea sandwiches and chocolate covered strawberries.

Felicity, the owner and manager of the Café, was bright, inquisitive, creative and the best chef in Chelsea. Up here, though, she was out of her depth. After setting up the table, she wandered the room. She stood at Martin's exhibit, looking at a selection of what she could only describe as three dimensional Stars of David.

She read the labels. They were all called merkabah. Some were made of a stone called shungite. Others were made of amethyst, fluorite, adventurine, and varieties of jasper and quartz.

Martin approached her. "Can I help you with these?"

"These just called me to the table. What are they?"

"They are called merkabah. They are divine light vehicles. You can use them to connect with beings in a higher realm."

"What?"

"Mer means light. Ka means spirit. Ba means body. MER-Ka-Ba means the spirit/body surrounded by counter-rotating fields of light, wheels within wheels, spirals of energy that transport the spirit from one dimension to another."

"Do you have an English version of that explanation?"

Martin laughed, and Felicity was immediately attracted to him.

"You said they called you here?"

"Yes, like a rod reeling me in."

"That is the power of the merkabah. Hold your hand over them, move it slowly, slowly, stop when you feel one in particular pulling you, but keep going, until you feel the strongest one."

Felicity's hand moved from one to the other. On occasion, her hand was pulled down slightly. In one instance, she had to fight to keep it up. She did this for all the stones, then went back to the one that pulled the strongest. It still had power for her.

"This one."

"This one is made of shungite. Many people think shungite merkabahs have the most power, and it certainly does for you. Shungite is from Russia. It's an ancient stone, said to be around two billion years old. It is the only natural material known to contain fullerenes. Those are powerful anti-oxidants."

"And anti-oxidants are important in a stone?"

"Well, the energy from this stone, which includes the fullerenes, is said to absorb and eliminate anything that is a health hazard. It has powerful metaphysical properties, strong healing powers. It's found only in the Karella area of Russia. Czar Peter was known to have come to the region to use water infused with shungite."

"So what would I do with this?"

"Lots of things. For one, consider meditation. Pick it up, close your eyes, breathe deeply, and cradle it in both hands next to your heart. What are you feeling?"

"I feel dizzy."

Martin laughed again. "Then it's working. I can't give you an entire metaphysical lesson, but I can point you to some resources. This particular stone is powerful for you, and if you decide to go further in your personal life than you've gone before, this is what you need."

Felicity continued to hold the stone next to her heart. She was still dizzy and realized she was staring at Martin like a love-sick puppy dog. She shook her head to come out of the semi-trance and put the stone down.

"I may have to come back for this. Right now I should get back downstairs."

"So, you work at the Café?"

"I'm the chef. The manager. The…whatever."

Martin smiled. "Are you open for dinner?"

"Um, no. We close in the mid-afternoon."

"Is there a good place to get dinner here in town?"

"Yeah. Mo's Tap or the winery."

"Will you be eating dinner tonight?"

"Probably."

"Would you care to eat it with me?"

"Oh. Um. Yeah. That would be nice."

"Why don't I meet you at the winery when the show closes. Say, about 7:30?"

"Sure. Love it."

"Oh, I'm Martin, by the way. You are?"

"Felicity. I'll see you tonight."

That smile turned up even higher and Felicity thought she would swoon. She turned to leave but was drawn to the messiest exhibit in the room. The man behind the tables had a filthy rag and picked up first one stone and then another to, maybe, clean them.

Adam looked up. "Help ya?"

Yes. Do you have any merkabah?

Adam looked around his tables, got up, walked around, picked up pieces of dirty plastic to look underneath, opened freezer containers, pulled out larger plastic containers to look inside. "Well dang it. I was extra careful to put some of those in a container just like this." He waved a quart freezer container. "Give me a minute."

He looked underneath his tables, pulled out crates, looked everywhere he had looked before. "Are you gonna be here for a while?"

"I have to get downstairs to work, but I can come back."

"I'll look around. Stop back and I will have found them."

Felicity turned to wave at Martin, who had watched with amusement, and returned to the Café.

Mem and Janet were at the ticket table, and what a busy table it was today. Dwight was cordial, even friendly. He said nothing more about the money Mem had taken the day before. Mem saw the three men mentioned by Gema. They looked out of place, coming into the show. But they had come up once the day before, and again, today, here they were.

They were careful to look only briefly at Dwight's booth. They wandered around, looked at each booth, but never got closer than a couple of feet to any of them. Mem noticed, when she had time to look, that all of the vendors seemed to recognize them. No one spoke to them. They spoke to no one.

She turned to Janet. "I wonder how many of them actually know them, and how many just know who they are?"

"Seems mysterious to me," Janet replied. "Or just weird."

They paid in cash both days. They could have purchased a multi-day pass, which would allow them in every day of the show, but they paid each day for one ticket. As if they wouldn't be recognized.

Janet had her laptop. "There were times yesterday when time stood still, so I brought my toy. Also, I wanted to show you what I found."

She brought up YouTube and searched for Bergamasco. There they were. A jazz fusion band, and sure enough, Ramon was on the saxophone. Janet plugged in earphones and passed one earpiece to Mem.

They listened. They liked. Mem gave a deep sigh. "This is going to be great. I forgot to tell Diana. I'll text her right now."

She did, and about fifteen minutes later, Diana texted back. "Did u c YT? WOW!"

"I guess we did okay, for old folks."

Candice stopped at the table to buy a multi-day ticket. "I want to buy stuff, so, as long as I can get here before work, I'll be back more than one day. Where do you suggest I start?"

"Go by Gema's booth, over there, her stuff is unique."

Candice looked, and at the same time, Gema looked her way. She smiled and nodded in recognition.

"Okay. Any other booth?"

"Just walk around. See what catches your eye."

Candice did just that. She stopped first at Gema's booth and found the perfect necklace and earrings, out of her price range. Not for the first time, she wished she hadn't broken off with George. He might be willing to buy this for her. Gema seemed to read her mind.

"Is there someone in your life that might buy this for you?"

Candice shook her head. "No. Not now. Maybe a few weeks ago."

"Someone I might run into while I'm here?"

"I doubt he'll come in here, but he's the bartender at Mo's."

Oh. So maybe Hank was right. She took a stab, intentionally digging a little deep. "Oh. He's the love 'em and leave 'em kind?"

Candice was evasive. "We had something going on and, well, we just kind of ended it. Recently."

"Well, he must be a great guy. The two of you work well together. I noticed."

Candice smiled. "He is a great guy. I kind of wish we were still together."

"What's his name?"

"George."

"George. Well, Candice, I might find my way into the bar today and, well, just roll with it if you see me, okay? We girls can use all the help we can get."

Candice smiled and moved on. She had to be careful with this woman. She walked around, not particularly drawn to anything, until getting to Martin's booth. She saw some pyramid-shaped stones in rainbow colors. They ranged from two inches high to maybe eight inches high, and the colors were evenly dispersed. She picked up several, holding one at a time, looking closely, moving on to another.

She was so intent on her observation that she started when the man spoke. "Those are made of fluorite. It can clear your mind of confusion, cluttered thoughts, negativity."

"They're beautiful."

"They're made of several different types of fluorite." He picked up a pyramid and pointed to each color, from the bottom to the top. "Pink cleanses and heals your emotions, the high heart chakra; yellow enhances your intellectual ability; green will cleanse and heal the heart chakra; blue is good for the throat chakra and will improve your ability to communicate; black is the ultimate astral cleanser; and on top, purple will purify your mind, give you access to the spirit world."

"Well, I don't know about the spirit world, but I could sure use help with the rest of it. What do I do with it?" Candice looked up at the man for the first time. He was gorgeous. That smile could melt a glacier.

"Keep it close. Put it by your bed at night, keep it near you at work. Pick it up every now and then and do some deep breathing, holding it close, or hold it when you meditate."

Candice thought she might like to hold him close. "I think I'll get this one."

"Let me wrap it for you." His hands grazed hers as he took it. He put it in a cloth bag, wrote up a receipt and handed it to her.

As he gave it to her, he asked, "Would you be free for a drink sometime later this evening?"

"Um, no. I work at the bar here on The Avenue. I work really late."

"Do you work over the lunch hour?"

"Yeah, mostly. But, well, I could meet you for breakfast?"

"Tomorrow?"

"Sure. What time?"

"I have to be here by 9:00. Do you want to meet at 7:00? 7:30?"

"I think 7:30 will be great. How about the Café downstairs?"

"I was thinking about the Confectionary. They serve breakfast items, right?"

"Yeah, they do, and it might be more, um, private than the Café."

"Well, then. 7:30 tomorrow morning. I look forward to it. I'm Martin."

"Candice. See you then."

Candice walked past Mem and Janet and didn't hear them when they asked what she had purchased.

Janet said to Mem, "Have you been watching?"

"Well, I haven't seen everything, but I'm thinking Felicity and Candice are getting ready for some heartbreak."

"Well, let's hope they'll look at it as good, healthy fun. I just hope they don't end up crosswise of one another."

"We could tell them."

"We absolutely will not get involved."

"Absolutely. But just because it's quiet now, I'm going to look at that selenite tower."

Janet laughed as Mem got up to go to Martin's booth.

Martin saw her coming. By the time she reached the booth, he had the tower in his hand. It was oddly shaped, obviously a natural stone that did not require polish. The tower was about six inches tall, with a base that was just a little smaller than a baseball, narrowing to a pencil thin point.

Mem knew how to test for personal fit. She closed her eyes, held the tower with both hands and felt the power course through her body.

"Not only is it exquisite, but it calls to me. I'll take it."

Martin started to wrap it, but Mem stopped him. "I'm going to leave it on the ticket table. I figure having a positive stone such as this at the entry can only be a good thing."

While Mem looked at the selenite tower, Chris stepped up to the ticket table. Janet was listening to Bergamasco, and his appearance startled her.

"Ma'am, I have a multi-day ticket. Do I need to show it to you?"

"Chris! My goodness! You scared me! No, I remember getting it for you yesterday. Don't tell me you're here to look at that ring!"

"She liked it."

"She did not. She is absolutely convinced it is a fake."

"But…"

Janet knew right away what the problem was. "You're concerned she doesn't like the ring you picked for her."

"It's semi-precious."

"You have been listening to poppycock, pure and simple. She loves that ring. I can't tell you how many times I've caught her looking at it on her finger. And other people, too, have remarked about it."

"You're sure?"

"Chris, what you need to do, if you want to buy something for Annie, is go for the good stuff. See that booth over there?"

"The artsy one?"

"Yes. You go over there and tell Gema about the stones in that ring and the setting, and see if she can show you something that is worthy of Annie."

"You're sure?"

"Yes. Get a necklace or a bracelet. Not another ring. She has the ring she loves."

Chris smiled his thanks and walked to Gema's booth. Gema recognized him immediately. What luck! The man that was most important to Annie. She greeted him warmly. "I'm Gema. I saw you as you left the bar last night."

Chris looked at her again. "Oh, yes. You came in with Geraldine and Hank. You're staying at the Inn, right?"

"Yes. It looked as if you and Annie are friends?"

"Well, I guess you could call it that." He knew he had to be careful with this woman, but he was on a mission. "I'm looking for something for Annie, a necklace or bracelet to match a ring that I gave her."

"Did you bring the ring?"

"Well, that's a long story. But to make it short, first, this would be a surprise. Second, we can't get to it. It's in a police evidence locker."

"That sounds like a story waiting to be told, but we'll save that for another time. Can you describe it?"

"I'll try. The setting is platinum. Do you work with that?"

"I do. I'm sorry to say my selections here are limited in platinum, but we could look at settings you like and I can craft something. What is the stone?"

"The largest stone is a deep purple amethyst. It's surrounded by white topaz and garnets of various colors."

"Oh, I love it already. We can match one or all of them."

"Do you have something here with those stones?"

"We don't have to look for items with the correct stones now. As long as I plan to craft it in platinum, we can change the stones at that time. And I have to be honest with you. I came prepared."

"How's that?"

"I knew I would be staying at the KaliKo Inn; I knew the show would be upstairs of Tiger Lily's Café. I read about all of the places on The Avenue. I knew who one of my prominent customers might be."

Chris followed her as she walked to a display case at the end of her table. She opened a drawer and pulled out a medium-sized box. Inside were finely crafted necklaces and earrings. All were in silver, and all featured cats.

"I didn't put these out. I was waiting for Annie to stop by, and I was going to show them to her. If you order something, I'll keep them hidden. We don't want to ruin your surprise, and we don't want anyone else in town to wear something similar."

Chris looked at the box. One setting in particular intrigued him, but he picked up and looked at each piece before settling finally on the perfect one. He leaned with his elbows onto the display case, picking up and looking closely at the setting.

The ring he planned to match had swirls of garnets and white topaz set in platinum. The pendant setting he now held had a profusion of silver swirls making up an avant-garde heart.

In the upper right corner of the heart was a sleeping cat, head and shoulders tight into the curve of the heart. Its underneath leg and paw stretched into the rest of the curve, ending at the intersection of one heart half with the other; the overhand leg and paw curled into its chest. The legs drooped lazily down the inside of the heart, and the tail curled up, making a half-heart that met at the overhand paw.

The upper left corner of the heart was filled with a profusion of stones in what could be interpreted as a flower. Draping down from the flower, to the bottom of the heart, were similar but smaller arrangements.

At the bottom of the heart were four sets of dangling stones, each a different shape and length. One set had just one major stone, oval in shape; another had two round stones; another had an oval and a round; the last had one round stone.

Gema knew she had made a sale. This man would not even ask how much. She would remain silent until he spoke again.

Chris finally looked up. "I don't know how to tell you to make this, what stones to use where."

"Do you like my work?"

"Yes, very much."

"Would you trust me to make you an outstanding piece that will match the ring?"

Chris looked at her. He didn't know how to answer that question. He trusted her to do good work; he didn't know if he could trust her as far as Annie was concerned.

Gema leaned into the display case with her elbows, mirroring Chris's stance. In a low voice, she said, "I'm not a fool. I want a storefront, and I like Chelsea. I was approached by people who knew what I wanted, and they told me to look at the yoga studio. I had no reason to believe they were anything but honest business people. Last night, I got a different feeling. I'm pretty sure Annie has no interest in selling the buildings and the businesses. In fact, I'm pretty sure no one has talked to her about it. I'm also pretty sure that she knows what they are up to, and that she is at the very least twice as smart as the fine upstanding citizens wanting to do business with me."

Chris looked her full in the eyes but said nothing.

Gema stood up. "Work with me here. Pretend to be looking at some other options while we talk."

Chris stood up, too. "Okay. Show me what you have."

As they talked, they moved from one part of the exhibit to the other. Gema picked up pieces, showed them to Chris and appeared to describe their attributes as she continued to talk.

"I'll be honest. I like the yoga studio. I know it's not available. The Avenue is the best place in town to have a business, but it's not the only place. I may find myself a realtor and look around on my own. But…."

"But, what?"

"I'm a little ticked at being drawn into a scheme. It seems like they think they can get Annie over a barrel, and they like the business make-up with the exception of the yoga studio. Probably not enough of a money-maker for them. So they heard I was looking and thought they could co-opt me into being part of their financial plan."

"And?"

"And if there is anything I can do to help Annie in this situation, I would be happy to do it."

Chris didn't respond right away.

Gema asked, "Did I step into something criminal?"

Chris seemed to be mulling something over. Finally, he said, "I'll tell you what. I'm pretty sure there is nothing criminal, but the people you are dealing with have dipped that far in the past. I have to be honest with you. I don't know how far I can trust you."

"Tell me this. Do you think there might be an opportunity for me? Here in Chelsea?"

"Probably. It's a town that supports and celebrates small businesses."

"Do you know people that can help me?"

"Yes."

"Do you think Annie would understand if you told her my plan, and I continued to pretend to work with these folks? To find out what they're up to?"

"I think Annie would understand if you talked to her."

"I don't know that I'll have the opportunity."

"You're staying at the Inn."

"So is Garry."

"I see your point. Let me think."

"Let's go back to the one you've chosen. We can make some decisions and then I'll have some cover."

"Good idea. And I'll have to get back with you on when and how to talk with Annie."

Looking at the heart again, Chris said, "Make the bulk of the flowers out of the amethyst, use the white topaz in the center of the flowers, and pepper the garnets throughout. Use a combination of all of them in the parts that dangle."

"My thoughts exactly. Any chance I can get a look at that ring?"

At that moment, Garry walked over. "So, did you find something different for Annie? I know she liked that ring."

"Well, I think I found something more her style. We're working on something like this." He held the heart and showed it to Garry.

"Working on?"

"Well, yeah. It's taken me quite a while to make a decision. I must have looked at twenty pieces, but I keep coming back to this. Gema was just telling me she can make something similar with the stones I want."

"And speaking of that again, is there any way I can get a look at that ring?"

"I don't know. I'll ask. Do you have a card? I assume you can't make this until after this show is over."

"You're right. Here's a card, and please put your contact information in this notebook."

Garry looked to the entrance, then looked back and Chris and Gema. With mock fear in his voice, he said, "Here comes the law!"

Chris looked. Pete and Cyril had stopped to talk to Janet and Mem. Janet pointed to Chris. He looked up, waved and headed over.

When he arrived, Chris said, "Pete, you showed up just in time."

"Really? Got a crime for me?"

"An old one. I'm going to have Gema make a necklace for Annie, and I want it to have the same stones that are in her ring. Is there any chance Gema can see it?"

Garry asked, "Why do you have to ask him?"

Pete turned to him with a laugh. "It's in evidence. Annie was mugged and the ring stolen. It's the only evidence we have tying the guy to the crime, so we're holding onto it for a while." He turned to Gema. "I could take a picture of it for you."

"That will help, but it won't really show me what I need to know about the color and clarity of the stones."

"Well, I can show it to you. I can't let you touch it, can't even let you take it out of the plastic bag."

"I want to do a great job on this and even that would really help me."

As Pete and Gema made arrangements to meet at the police station, Chris walked with Garry back to his exhibit. "If you see Annie, please don't say anything to her. If she wants to buy the ring, she'll buy it. Or anything else that might strike her fancy."

14

Annie spent the morning moving from one place to the other. She started at the Café, then went to the yoga studio, the bakery and finally the winery. She would go to the bar for a late lunch.

At each place, she checked in with managers, making lists of things she could do to help them get through the week, then talked with the staff on hand, thanking them for taking care of their guests in a truly busy week.

Everywhere she went, she found Howard. As she entered the Café, he was at a back table, engaging the server in an animated conversation. He stopped the conversation and asked for his check as soon as he saw her.

At the yoga studio, he stood at the counter talking to Diana. As Annie entered, he picked up a brochure with the schedule, tipped the schedule to his head in a greeting and walked out the door.

At the Confectionary, he stood at the counter with an array of "tastes" in front of him. It was rare for customers to ask to taste a bakery product, because most people know one taste meant the entire item was unusable. Typically, even if asked, Carlos and Jerry politely refused.

Today, Carlos was bending over backwards to be nice.

This time, Howard was not in a position to leave right away, so Annie spoke to him. "What are you trying, Howard?"

"Well, I wanted to try the spelt cinnamon rolls, so I'm testing them against the originals. There's a spelt poppy seed cake, too, and even a cookie. So I'm trying all against the originals."

"Planning to change your diet?"

"Maybe," he said, with a noncommittal air.

"Enjoy. Carlos, while you're helping Howard, I'll go to the back and talk to Jerry."

She and Jerry talked until Annie was sure Howard was gone, then they both went to the front.

Carlos finished with another customer, then turned to them with a smile.

"Spill."

"He wants to know how much you pay your staff, what kind of benefits we have, what the deal is with our apartments, of course what we think of you, and what kind of profit we make."

Annie's jaw nearly dropped to the basement. Except there wasn't a basement.

"What did you tell him?"

"Henrie got us together on Skype this morning, and we came up with a plan. If asked, answer, but lie. Howard is talking to just about everyone, managers, servers, cooks, anyone he can catch. And he started doing this, as you know, on Monday night with Candice."

"And he's been doing it ever since?"

"As far as we know, with the exception of Candice, he didn't really get started until this morning. And we started it."

"What?"

"After our meeting, Candice called him to alter what she said the other night. She made a point to tell Howard she was trying to be polite, but now, she's frankly worried about her job and she wondered if he was working on something that would save it. If so, she's all in, and the rest of us would probably be grateful for any changes he might have in mind."

"Oh, my."

"Henrie called Boone and Hilly, too, just in case Howard digs that deep."

"What kind of lies are you all telling?"

"Annie, Jerry and I both appreciate our pay and benefits, as does everyone who works for you at every level. But when we talk to Howard, we claim you are a slave-driving miser."

Annie pulled a chair over from one of the tables to sit down. Mr. Bean came to sit with her, jumping into her lap. Tillie stood at her feet, looking up at her with an anxious face.

Carlos continued. "We figured that most people in town have heard you give us benefits, so of course we tell him that we're forced to go with your plan, which is too expensive and has minimal coverage, and we might be able to get better in the market."

Annie put her head in her hands. Mr. Bean nuzzled her cheek.

"Those of us who have apartments pay top dollar, and we have to pay all our own utilities, which, of course, you manage. So we have to trust you when you tell us what we owe."

Annie wanted to melt into the chair. Mr. Bean touched his nose to hers. "Anything else?"

"You micro-manage, and the only reason the managers have stuck with you is that we haven't been able to find other jobs. You lose your temper at the drop of a hat, order us around, blame us for all of your bad business decisions."

"Bad business decisions?" Mr. Bean looked at Carlos as if he would jump and bite.

"Well, things like letting repairs and maintenance go, filthy kitchens and bar areas, the serving areas are despicable, bugs in the flour, meats stored over fresh produce, meats and other foods used past the expiration date, cleaning supplies stored with and over food, improper food handling techniques, hiring illegal immigrants, you don't pay our withholding taxes, your anger when people want to take the time to make it right. Oh, and you eat all your meals at our places, and you never pay and probably never account for them on your personal taxes."

Annie thought she actually was melting into the chair. Mr. Bean shifted, putting one paw to her face and turning it to him so he could kiss her with little licks.

Holding his face in her hands so she could talk, she said, "That isn't all, is it." It was a statement, not a question.

"A little more. With the pay we receive, the bottom dollar inventory you force us to carry, and the income we know the businesses produce, we should be making a profit. But you control the books, and according to you, we barely break even. That is, we barely break even on the months we haven't lost our shirts."

"Is that really all?" Mr. Bean sat back down and looked at Carlos.

"That's all."

Annie couldn't look up. She pulled the chair back to the table, put her back to Carlos and put her elbows on the table, burying her face in her hands. Mr. Bean jumped to the table as she made the shift and wrapped himself around her arms.

Carlos moved to the table to sit beside her. "Now, let me tell you what you're feeling," said Carlos. "You're angry that we are reduced to this. You're sad that someone is trying to take advantage of you. You're scared that the rest of the community will believe what we've been saying about you."

"Yes. Yes. Yes." Mr. Bean squirmed on the table, fighting for the best place to put his legs around Annie's arms.

"Believe me. This is the best way to do it. Howard is going to try to ruin you, and he's going to do it quickly. He's going to start making calls to regulatory agencies, if he hasn't already. He'll call Labor, Health, state revenue, the IRS, every agency he can think of. And he'll have what he believes is documentation. It will be bad enough that they will be in here quickly. It will be massive enough that the papers will get hold of it. You will be exonerated quickly and in the most public manner possible. And he will be outed as a rat."

"What if my cats get thrown out of the businesses as a result of all this?" Mr. Bean sat up, surprised.

"We've done our groundwork there, also. Jesus paid a visit to Joan of Chelsea."

Annie perked up. This was the nickname they had given to Joan, the president of the town council. It was by the grace of the council that cats and dogs were allowed to be inside businesses on both sides of The Avenue, as long as they stayed out of kitchen and prep areas.

"Joan knows that Geraldine and Hank are involved in the little scheme, and she has called on every council member that she can trust, which, as far as I know, is all but one."

"Who's the one?"

"A relative of Hank. An in-law of some variety, like a son-in-law or the stepson of a sister. I'm not clear on that."

"And they'll protect the cats? And dogs?"

"Yes." Mr. Bean gave an audible sigh. Annie and Carlos looked at him, surprised that he seemed to be taking it all in.

At the winery, Annie took a piece of cheese offered by Minnie. "Thanks. I needed this. Wish it was infused with zinfandel."

"I could get a glass for you."

Annie looked at the window. "The sun hasn't cleared the top of the sky yet."

"It's five o'clock somewhere."

Annie laughed. "Tempting, but not today. So, have you been visited by Howard?"

"Oh, yes. Along with everything else I spilled, I told him you were livid about Jesus and me."

Sassy Pants, on top of the bar with her underside exposed to Annie for rubs, jumped up. She looked at Minnie, then at Annie, both of whom were laughing. She fell to her back again, inviting Annie's attention.

15

This very hard week just kept rolling. Georgia was at work at Mo's Tap, happy to be there, but worried about the news Henrie had given her. Her dad was here. In Chelsea.

Georgia loved her dad. Her mom died when Georgia was ten. Her dad raised her at the restaurant. The school bus picked her up and dropped her off at the restaurant. She did her homework in a back booth, getting up to help him during slams from the age of twelve.

It was a small town. People talked. People had prejudices. Georgia's dad had many of those same prejudices, including a low opinion of single mothers. She left town to spare him the misery. She was surprised he was looking for her, but maybe he didn't know about Fred. He said nothing to Henrie about a baby.

She pushed that to the back of her mind and concentrated on the lunch rush. She couldn't worry about her dad now. She and Henrie had a plan.

She looked through the window when she saw Annie at the bar. Annie smiled and waved. Georgia smiled and gave the universal upward motion with her head that said, hey there, how are you, I'm too busy to say a proper hello.

She watched as Annie ordered and ate a sandwich, talking with George or Candice whenever one of them was able to spend a minute or two with her.

The big gray long-haired cat sat on the bar with her the entire time. Sometimes he sat, for all the world listening to the conversations, looking back and forth from Annie to George or Candice. Sometimes he moved to his back, exposing his stomach to Annie for strokes. Sometimes he wrapped himself around whatever body part was close to the bar.

One time he climbed from the bar to her shoulder, wrapping himself around the back of her neck. When he did that, Annie absently pulled on his tail with one hand and scratched his cheek with another.

As Georgia watched, she saw Annie speak to every server. When she finished her sandwich, Annie stuck her head into the kitchen door to say thank you to everyone for their hard work this week. She particularly thanked Georgia for joining the staff.

Annie walked to her place at the bar to pick up her phone. Georgia was surprised to see Annie leave a tip.

She didn't know that Annie did that at each and every place she went, whenever she was served by a staff member. She also didn't know that Annie, even though she didn't pay for her meals, accounted for every meal and drink in her books. The computer system registered each expenditure.

Just before Annie left, Georgia noticed Cookie leave the kitchen. He and Annie had a brief conversation, nodded to one another, and went their separate ways. The conversation was quick, to the point, friendly.

She had heard staff talking to a man called Howard. They said awful things about Annie, but to watch them communicate, and from what she knew of Annie during her stay at the Inn, she couldn't put the two pictures together. Perhaps she was some kind of Jekyll and Hyde.

Georgia was smart. She knew when to keep her mouth shut.

Henrie was in his element. He had way too much on his hands. Just the way he liked it. But now, he had too much on his hands without having to worry about cleaning and laundry. Thank goodness he had relented and allowed Annie to hire Hilly.

Hilly came up from the laundry room, lugging a laundry basket full of sheets and towels.

"You know we do have an elevator."

"I need the exercise, Henrie."

"As if you do not get enough."

Hilly laughed. "You know, Henrie, this is just about my favorite place to be in all the world. There is always something going on." Her head gestured to the foyer, where JoJo sat reading, a sleeping baby on the floor in front of her.

"You do not know the half of it."

"Oh, I think I do. You have Annie's folks coming in for the month this afternoon; tomorrow you have another big group coming in. Those two groups will fill the carriage house. The upstairs is full, and you have a new guest in the back room. And I know how to keep my ears open. Each and every guest has a back story, and it generally comes out here. It's the ultimate in people-watching pleasure."

Henrie laughed. "And you know we rely on your discretion."

"Sometimes it's hard. By the way, that man, Howard, stopped Boone and the boys this morning. Boone just called to tell me."

"How did it go?"

"Boone was appropriately hateful toward Annie, you and all of the other managers we deal with. He told Howard I wasn't allowed in the kitchens. I'm only supposed to keep the dining and service areas clean. You know, to keep up appearances. He told him about that time I tried to clean the kitchen at the Café and she almost fired me. She didn't want to pay for my time where people couldn't see."

Henrie gave a formal Henrie smile. "I remember that time well. And what was Boone's major complaint?"

"She's a little dictator. Talks to him badly in front of the boys."

"And the boys?"

"They're always embarrassed for their dad when Annie is around. They're using it as a learning tool, something never to do when they have their own small business."

"I am amazed you still come to work every day."

"I am, too."

They heard the door open, and a female voice called, "Henrie? Annie?" Then they heard, "Oh, I'm sorry! Did I wake the little dear up?"

It could only be Nancy and Sam, Annie's mother and step-father. They rented the lower level of the carriage house for a few weeks at a time throughout the year. Many of their friends owned or rented vacation homes in the south or west, leaving their homes for four to six months. Nancy and Sam stayed in their Midwestern home and visited their daughter whenever they chose, without the expense of a second home. The arrangement was simple. They paid a room fee, less than most, because they did not use the ancillary services, like daily cleaning and laundry. They ate breakfast most days, but Henrie would have made enough regardless.

Staying in the carriage house allowed them and Annie to maintain privacy. The parents-are-too-close syndrome didn't pop up. Usually. And the room was very nice.

The downstairs accessible room had every amenity of the main rooms plus a walk-out deck with a hot tub large enough for four people. The deck was enclosed by a six-foot fence for privacy. This was the room usually reserved for honeymooners.

Hilly went to the foyer to say hello and offer her services. As Henrie arrived, Sam was saying, "I'll just get one of those carts and take care of it myself."

Henrie had a platter of sandwiches and a pitcher of lemonade. "When you have taken care of that, Sam, please join Nancy and me. We will be on the porch."

Nancy put her arm around Henrie's back for a quick hug and followed him to the porch. "I'm starved! How did you know we didn't stop for lunch?"

She stopped quickly and said, "Oh! Excuse me, Henrie!" She turned back to the foyer. "Sam! Sam!"

Sam stuck his head back in the door, halfway in and halfway out.

"Please take the baby with you. I don't want to have to go around locking all the cat doors in the Inn."

"Sure thing, dear." He picked up a pet carrier and placed it on the luggage cart, receiving a low growl in reply. He thought "the baby" was growling at him, but he was growling at the two cats on the other side of the sofa. Kali and Ko remained hidden and sent low growls only "the baby" could hear.

Hilly called after him, "I locked all the cat doors over there as Annie requested. You should just be able to open the carrier and let him go."

Sam waved behind his head as he pushed the luggage cart down the ramp of the porch.

The other baby, Fred, remained calm through all the activity, holding a tail with each hand.

JoJo continued to read, marveling at this wonderful babysitting job that allowed her so much time to put the work off on, of all things, cats.

She soon heard voices on the porch. It was Annie and her step-father. As they entered, Annie said hello to JoJo and asked if she had met Sam.

"We weren't introduced, but I gather he's your dad. Hi. I'm just here to babysit."

"I see. Did our loud entrance bother the little tyke?"

He walked around the sofa and noticed Kali and Ko for the first time. "Well hello, girls! Your grandpa is here!"

Kali and Ko meowed polite hellos but didn't leave the baby's side.

"So, are they babysitting, too?"

JoJo answered, "You wouldn't believe me if I told you how good they are with her."

"Oh, I've seen these cats do amazing things, so I'd believe it. It's good to see you, girls. Now I'm going to the porch for some lunch." He turned to Annie. "Coming?"

"I'll come back to say hello to Mom, but I have things to do this afternoon. Can we have dinner tonight?"

"We've got plans with Frank and Mem. I imagine if we don't see you later on, we'll have breakfast with you."

"That's a plan. Come on, I'm sure Henrie has a great lunch for you."

As they walked toward the porch, JoJo heard Sam say, "I saw sandwiches. And lemonade."

The cats and Fred settled down again, Fred cooing and pulling on two tails. The cats were on their backs, wiggling in pleasure.

A man came in. JoJo wondered if this was "him."

"Oh, hello," he said. "I didn't realize there was a baby in residence."

"Well, she's not really a resident. I'm babysitting, and this is just a good place for us to be during the day."

"Let me see. Oh, she's a beauty. How old is she?"

"You know, I'm not sure. A few months, maybe? She's still on a bottle but she eats some baby food."

"Are these cats okay to be around her?" Both Kali and Ko were on the alert. They were on their feet next to Fred, surrounding her, ready to take out eyes if necessary.

"They're great. And the baby loves them."

"What's her name?"

JoJo hesitated for just a moment. "Fred."

"Fred? Well, that's my name. Henrie said there had been another Fred in that room before I came. Was it her?"

JoJo nodded.

"Well, it's good to know that Fred's parents have made friends. I assume the folks here are friends, or goodness, who knows why Fred was living here, or her parents, or whatever. Excuse me. I'm babbling."

"Don't worry. I babble sometimes myself."

The man, yes, it was "him," laughed. It was a good laugh.

A rude sound could be heard from the vicinity of the baby, followed quickly by a rude smell. JoJo got up, putting a diaper bag over her shoulder. "Excuse me. I haven't been able to teach the cats to take care of that."

As she left with the baby, Fred the elder went to his room, sat on the bed, put his face in his hands and started to cry.

16

Chris got to the Café for a late lunch, having convinced Ray he had to get away from The Escape. Jock ran ahead of them, hoping to find Fiamma.

Jock waited impatiently at the door, half a block ahead of his human, until someone walked out. He took the opportunity to dash into the open door and took a quick lap through the dining room, checking it out.

Seeing no Fiamma, he dropped to the floor behind Tiger Lily, dejected.

Tiger Lily turned her head to look at him. *"She's not here. I could have told you."*

Jock sighed. *"I suppose Cyril has had lots of opportunity to flirt with her."*

"I don't know. Not in front of me."

Jock looked around the room. *"Lots of people here today."*

"It's been busy all week. We have lots of things going on, lots of things we have to tell Mommy and Pete about, but you know how that goes."

"Yeah. For as nice as they are, they're sure stupid."

"Fiamma has taught her human some sign language."

Jock perked up. *"Really? How long did that take?"*

"According to Tillie, it took months and months."

Jock slumped back. Then he sat up. Fiamma was on The Avenue with her human and Clara! They were headed this way!

Chris and Ray stopped at the door, having noticed Clara coming across The Avenue. When Clara and Ramon got to the door, Chris introduced Ray to Ramon and

Fiamma. They didn't notice Jock on the other side of the door, jumping for joy, begging them to come in.

Fiamma noticed. She gave Jock a sexy smile, and he stopped, standing entranced as he looked into her eyes.

"Oh, brother!" said Tiger Lily. She turned back to the business of greeting guests and looked around the room to see if all was well. It was.

Jock and Fiamma were well away from the front window, choosing to sit under the table of their humans, so they did not see Cyril and Pete.

Pete invited Gema to lunch after they looked at the ring. Pete decided to ditch the very busy Café in favor of a slightly less busy Confectionary.

"Carlos, what kind of sandwiches do you have on special?"

"We have Virginia ham and Swiss on a pretzel bun, and if you're a little more adventurous, we've got a grilled cheddar, bacon, tomato, onion and avocado on a whole wheat croissant."

Gema said, "That second one sounds good."

"That sounds good to me, too. And a couple of treats for Cyril. You choose them."

As Pete and Gema made their order, Cyril sat near the window watching Mr. Bean and Tillie compete for attention. Their dances were, well, silly. Cyril finally snorted a laugh of derision. *"Do you have no pride?"*

The little ones sat down suddenly, looking at one another, then at Cyril.

Tillie spoke first. *"I guess we do kind of get carried away."*

"Yeah," said Mr. Bean. *"We probably need to get over it. We're probably going to be together a long, long time."*

"I get that it's your place, Mr. Bean. I just like people. I have to say hello when I see them."

Cyril knew he had not been asked for his opinion, but he decided to give it anyway. *"Why don't you take turns?"*

"What?"

"Take turns. One of you goes somewhere to play or sleep, like over in that far window, while the other one draws in the crowd. Tillie, I hate to tell you this, but it is Mr. Bean's place. Maybe he gets first choice, like maybe he goes first every day unless it's a day that he comes in late."

"Or maybe," said Mr. Bean, *"we both stay in this window, but just one of us does the dance."* He looked at Tillie. *"And we take turns."*

Tillie and Mr. Bean considered this while they considered one another.

"That will work," said Tillie.

"Yep. That will work," answered Mr. Bean.

Tillie then got excited. *"Hey, Cyril, have you talked to Tiger Lily yet today?"*

"No. What's up?"

"Well, it won't hurt if we tell you. It's stuff you need to know." Tillie's chest puffed up. Mr. Bean told her everything. It was just as if she had been there with them last night, spying from the window. He and Mr. Bean took turns talking.

They told Cyril about the three mystery men, their talk about "two places" for today, the clue stolen from Dwight and hidden behind the refrigerator, the package Dwight left and that Martin picked up, the curious behavior of Adam and Martin, and the possibility that Geraldine and Hank were going to try to get Mommy in trouble again.

"Sounds like another busy week for us. And no way to tell our humans what they need to know. Tell me a little more about this clue."

Mr. Bean sat forward. *"It was a ring, like the one Mommy got from Chris, but more sparkly. It had lots of stones in it, pretty clear ones and others with bright colors."*

"I'll bet it was from those burglaries we had yesterday."

"Really? If so, then there will be two more today!"

"They've probably already happened. Pete was going to have the reserve police officers tell everyone to improve their security. They would have done that last night, and if the people were going to do anything, they would have started calling this morning."

"Well, that's good, I guess, but what about the ones that already happened? How can we get that clue to Pete and will he know what to do with it?"

"That's a pickle, alright."

"Hey!" said Mr. Bean. *"I have an idea. We're going to go the show this afternoon."*

"Who?" asked Cyril.

"All of us. Tiger Lily and all of us, except probably Kali and Ko. They might stay with the baby." He looked at Tillie. *"You can come, too."*

The three friends looked sharply at the door when they heard a struggle at the cat door. The commotion was caused by two heads. The heads of Simon Finnegan and Oscar McMurphy. They struggled to get through the door. Finally, Oscar McMurphy pulled her head out and let Simon Finnegan go first.

Simon Finnegan said, *"Where are you going?"*

"We're going to the rock show. There's a thief up there, and a couple of other guys that are acting real weird, and we're going to do some detecting."

"We'll go, too. We're good at detecting."

"Yeah, you are. We're going after work."

"What time is that?"

"Well, I don't know. Whatever time it is that my place and the Café close."

"Oh, we know when that is. We'll go over to the Café and wait for you when it's almost time."

Pete and Gema sat at the table nearest the counter with their order. As they ate, Gema looked around. This was the first time she'd been at Mr. Bean's for an extended time.

The décor was bright. Most of the walls were painted lime green with the exception of a bright white accent wall behind the counters. The accent wall was strewn with lime green and sunburst orange shapes. The glass counter was trimmed in bright white. The natural light from the front windows was augmented with pendant lights similar to the ones everywhere else on The Avenue, each one colorful and unique.

Pete had been prepared not to like Gema, because she seemed chummy with Geraldine, but it was hard to resist her charm. When she laughed, it was like the tinkle of a bell.

"So," he said, never one to mince words, "you've got friends here in town. Geraldine and Hank."

Gema rolled her eyes. "I don't know why I let myself get tangled up with them. I saw you with Annie, so I know you're a friend. Just know that I'm going to string them along for the rest of the week, but I have no intention of becoming a part of their smarmy little plan."

"What's the plan?"

"Not sure. I just know they're going to do something underhanded and try to force Annie to sell. And then they'll offer to lease the yoga space to me, because I might make more of a profit for them."

"Interesting. But you don't know what the plan is?"

"No. They just go on about what a poor manager she is, what poor decisions she makes."

Pete laughed. "That would be like the pot calling the kettle black, but the only ones seeing that kettle as black are those fools."

"Well, I hope she'll understand that I have no part in whatever play they're going to make."

"She'll understand."

They finished, and Gema excused herself. "That jewelry doesn't sell itself."

"It ought to. It's pretty enough."

"Well, you ought to come take a look yourself. You might find something for that pretty wife of yours."

As Gema left, Pete got his phone out of his pocket. He had received a long email in reply to an inquiry about Ramon. Ramon was his number one suspect in the burglary.

What he read was intriguing.

He returned to the counter. "Carlos, give me three cat treats and another dog treat. It would be rude of me to hand something to Cyril without sharing."

Gema didn't go immediately upstairs. Instead, she went to Mo's Tap. She had a box in her purse, and she intended to try to make a sale.

She sat at the bar and watched as the girl from the Inn, Georgia, triaged tickets. She smiled and waved when she caught Georgia's eye, then gave a thumbs up.

She put the box on the bar and opened it. George came up. "Can I get something for you?"

"Oh, no. I just want to sit here and talk to Candice when she has a minute to spare."

"That might be a while."

"I can wait, at least for a while, then I have to get back to the show."

George looked at the creations in the box.

"Wow. Those are pretty. Is Candice going to buy them?"

"I was hoping she would, but I don't think she can afford them. I hoped to give her a better deal, and I didn't know if she would come back up. Won't this be pretty on her?"

"Outstanding. With her long neck, this would be perfect. What are the stones?"

"Black opals and diamonds."

"Black opals? Are they a poor relation to the other kind?"

"No, quite the opposite. These are the most rare and precious of the opal family. See how the blues and greens sparkle?"

George looked at a necklace with three rough ovals, a large one about six inches in diameter and two smaller ones, between three and four inches, one on each side. He took it out of the box to get a closer look.

They were the outline of the ovals only, to allow the woman's skin to show through. Inside the outlines were blue and green opals interspersed with diamonds. The earrings were a smaller version of the necklace, dangling from a post of one large opal each.

Gema continued to talk. "You can tell this is rustic work on the gold. I pride myself on having one-of-a-kind pieces, and hammering out the gold to make a statement is part of my signature. This necklace and earring set have a total of seventy-six carats of Australian black opals and eight carats of round brilliant cut diamonds. They're set in eighteen karat gold."

George leaned into the bar on his elbows while he held the necklace, mesmerized, and perhaps visualizing Candice's neck inside it, Gema caught Candice's eye and gave her a hand signal to come over.

Candice came to the bar and leaned on her elbows as well to look once again at the necklace set. She sighed and said to Gema, "I just can't do it. The set is so pretty, but, well, look at me. I'm a server. I don't have the kind of salary to support this purchase." A tiny tear trickled down her cheek and she wiped it off quickly.

Gema thought she could have won an Oscar.

"This would be so lovely on you, with your complexion and your long neck, and that head of hair would only help to show it off. I was afraid I wouldn't see you again, and, well, I wanted to make you an offer. I'll take another five hundred dollars off the price."

Candice sighed, reached in and picked up an earring. George still held the necklace.

"Thanks, Gema. I can't. I just hope you don't sell it to anyone else in town. I don't think I could bear to see it being worn by another woman."

Candice and George continued to lean on the bar as Gema put the earrings back into the box. She held out a hand to take the necklace from George. She was not aggressive about it. She just, well, pretended to be ready to get back to the show, sale not made. "I hope I didn't keep you from your work. I knew you loved it, and, well, I just had to try."

Candice stood. Gema stood. George stood. He finally realized Gema was going to leave. "Oh! So sorry. Here. It's quite the necklace."

He gave it back with regret. Gema pretended to regretfully put it away. On her way out the door, she winked at Candice.

Tiger Lily waited at the elevator for everyone to arrive. Oscar McMurphy and Simon Finnegan were the first. They didn't want to be left behind. Little Socks came next.

"That woman gave me a message for Mommy, but I don't know how to give it to her."

"What woman?"

"That woman that's staying at the Inn."

"That one? She can give Mommy a message all by herself. Did she think you could talk to her?"

"I don't know. Maybe she was just playing a game."

"What was the message?"

"She said if I have a way to tell Mommy to tell her she's on Mommy's side and she'll help stick it to those folks."

"Do you trust her?"

"Yeah, I think so."

By then, Mr. Bean, Tillie, Mo and Sassy Pants were present and ready to go.

Mr. Bean told Tiger Lily about their conversation with Cyril. *"I hope you don't mind that we told him."*

"No, you did the right thing. Cyril didn't come into the Café today, so I didn't get a chance to talk to him."

She looked around. *"We probably don't have to wait for Kali and Ko, so let's go on up."*

Seven cats and a Jack Russell Terrier ran up the stairs, through the cat door and into the exhibit area. Some people thought they were cute. Some were perturbed. Some crouched or got down on their knees to get closer. The kids didn't seem to notice.

Between them, they hit every exhibit, several of them by more than one "detective." Tiger Lily, Little Socks and Sassy Pants made sure to go through the exhibits of Dwight, Adam, Martin, Garry, Nelson and Gema. They went at different times and looked at different things. Little Socks took time to jump to the counter and give Gema a slow blink. Tiger Lily did the same.

Gema thought, huh, what's up with that.

Mo went to Gema's booth, then Pattie's, then Kristina's, then to the booths of all of the minor exhibitors that happened to be women. Then, all his energy exhausted, he went to the ticket table to sit with Mem and Janet. For reasons he could not fathom, he wrapped himself around a tall white stone instead of a woman's body part. He was a little dizzy....

Mr. Bean and Tillie, partners at work and partners now in detecting, got up close and personal with Martin and Adam. They stayed with the two, crawling around the product, getting into the product, listening to them talk to customers. They took turns, practicing, no doubt, for the window dancing starting tomorrow morning. First Mr. Bean was with Martin while Tillie was with Adam, then they switched.

Oscar McMurphy and Simon Finnegan, not sure what to look for, investigated the fine work they had done on the tables and chairs, crawling around, standing tall to look and sniff, until finally all of the tables had been pronounced perfectly repaired. They didn't realize until later how much they had heard during their wandering.

Tiger Lily couldn't help but think about her friends by the names she gave them. Before they had a fur-ever home and real names. She watched them make their way around the room, and by the time Fat Cat and Scaredy Cat had gone completely around the circle, she called to everyone.

"Time to go!"

The room had gotten used to the cats and dog, so when they all jumped up to run for the elevator en masse, once again people buzzed with excitement.

The cats and dog didn't care. They hit the stairway and went down. They nearly knocked George over. He held onto the railing and got as close to the wall as he could. Mo stopped for just a few seconds. George looked at him and said, "Really? This is what you do in your spare time?"

At the bottom of the stairwell, Tiger Lily said, *"Tillie, Fat Cat, Scaredy Cat, come over after supper. We'll talk about what we learned."*

On the sidewalk, they watched as Pete and Cyril got into a police vehicle and sped off, sirens blaring. Tiger Lily said, *"They must have burgled those other houses today."*

Little Socks answered. *"Yep. Folks would be home from work by now. They'd find out and call the police."*

"We need to find a way to talk to Cyril about that clue. We'll talk about it this evening."

High school students, ready to take tickets until the show closed, got off the elevator just as the cats and dog entered the stairwell. Mem laughed to see all the activity. "Janet, I guess this is our cue to go!"

George staggered out of the stairwell. "What were they all doing here?"

"You know they have to know everything that's going on."

"Well, let's hope they're done with it for the week. Hey, what's this?"

George picked up the selenite tower, holding the base in his hand. "Nice. I used to pitch with something this size, but it didn't have a spear on the end."

Mem said, "This is my selenite tower. It's supposed to bring positive energy to whatever it is near. I'm hoping it can work its magic on everyone in the room. If it doesn't," she took the tower from George, held it by the base and made a menacing gesture toward George, "I'll stab them with it!"

"I'm positive! I'm positive!!"

The students laughed and asked, "What do you want us to do with it when we close up?"

"Just leave it here. I'm sure no one will take it."

17

The Avenue was busy Wednesday evening. There was evidence of a full moon in every building.

Mo's Tap played host to several people. Annie, Felicity and Cookie had dinner at the back table. Gema and Garry had dinner again with Geraldine, Hank and Howard. They wanted the back table but had to settle for one of the private areas set up with overstuffed chairs and accent tables. Dwight held court – separate tickets, please – at another large table with several vendors.

At Sassy P's, Frank and Mem had dinner with Sam and Nancy in the front room. Chris met Pete and Ray at the back, where the boys – Cyril and Jock – vied for the attentions of the lovely Fiamma. Ramon and Clara sat at a private table for two near the back tasting bar, which was not in use this evening. Martin sat at another private table at the other end of the bar and was eventually joined by Felicity.

At the Inn, quite another supper gathering was happening. Henrie set a private table in his apartment for three adults and a baby. He would be joined by Fred Calendar, Georgia Jones and Little Fred.

Upstairs at the Inn, another dining table was set. Well, not set, exactly. Nine cats and a Jack Russell Terrier, aided in getting up by the use of chairs, sat in a loose circle, watching over The Avenue while they had their important conversation.

Annie, who generally allowed her managers to run their businesses, felt the need for some hands-on supervision of the fine dining venture.

"You both know I'm a hands-off manager, but Cookie, I'll want to keep a closer eye on this new venture."

Cookie immediately bristled until Annie continued. "When I moved to Chelsea, all of these businesses, everything I own, was up and running. My dad hired everyone that is a manager today. The businesses were ongoing. This is my first venture into something new. So you see, Cookie, this has nothing to do with you."

Felicity took over. "Annie knows everything, Cookie. From the food orders and menu, decorating, staffing…she knows everything. I've kept her informed."

"I've always felt, Cookie, that you didn't want to talk to me, or you were afraid of me, or something, but that ends today. I've stayed in the background while you and Felicity made plans, but after this weekend, your primary conversations are going to have to be with me."

Cookie seemed to consider this. "Yeah. I can see that. Felicity helped me get started, but after this weekend, she has to get back to her own stuff."

Felicity nodded. "That's right. I've spent a lot of time with you – and I'm glad I did – so you could have a success. But now I have to get back to my catering. Summer is just around the corner. Orders are pouring in, and I still have to get ready for Ray."

"Were you able to restock?"

"Yeah. My best vendor filled everything, even though we were off schedule."

"Good. Now, let's get back to tomorrow evening. What needs to happen?"

Cookie said, "I think we're set. The menu and inventory are good, I have a great triage expert now, and she can help me in the kitchen. George Two said he would wash dishes this weekend."

"Trudie and I are going to serve as combination hostesses and servers, which should work, and a couple of my part-timers agreed to work all weekend."

"What about staff moving forward? We can't expect current staff to take up the slack, and we certainly can't afford to pay overtime to everyone working at a new restaurant."

Cookie had the good grace to apologize. "I'm really sorry, Annie. I put Felicity off, hoping she would cover my back, but I didn't even consider the overtime part of it."

"That's okay for this weekend, but what's the plan?"

"An ad is running right now, and Ben volunteered to take some flyers around. He took some to the community college in Marsh Haven, too."

"Are you going to do the interviewing?"

"I'm going to have Georgia help. She's got a lot of experience for as young as she is. She'll be my right hand person. And I have a hostess, too, after the first of the month. Actually, she's going to manage the floor as well."

"Who is it?"

"Isabel. Carlos said she wanted a part-time job. For now, this will work out for her, and I met her before, the last time she was here."

"She'll be great! Oh, I put out a press release about the grand opening, and I expect to have a couple of newspapers and two or three television stations on hand for grand opening night."

Cookie went pale.

"Oh, no," said Annie. "Don't go gutless on me now. You wanted this, you've got it. But it takes marketing and advertising, and this will be a start."

Felicity looked at her watch. "Oh! I have to go! Cookie, I know we've had some bumps this week, but I'm really excited for you. This is going to be great!"

With that, she left. Annie and Cookie, who had never been alone together, settled into what would become their new relationship over the last of their burgers and fries.

Gema and Garry arrived first. They looked at the back table, already occupied, and settled on the next best option, one of the private areas with furniture more suited to a living room. They sat close together and talked in low tones.

Garry was, well, Garry was ticked. "You're taking all my best customers of the week, Gema. We used to work so well together, and now, you're stealing my customers!"

"It's usually the other way around, Garry. I show people my things, then you blind them with your promises of 'the most exotic gemstones' – that are really fake ninety percent of the time – let me finish! I need to make a splash in this town if I want to open a store. You know that. You need to back off."

Garry sat back, looking at her. He leaned forward again. "Are you still 'in,' Gema? Are you still planning to get the storefront?"

"Why wouldn't I be?"

"I just see you getting chummy with everyone."

"That's called marketing, Garry. Marketing. I have to imprint my brand, so when I have a store, people will not only come, but they'll send their families, friends, old school chums and bitter enemies."

Garry seemed appeased. For the moment.

Geraldine and Hank arrived.

Geraldine wailed, "Why are we sitting here?"

"The other table is in use," replied Gema. She could tell Annie was almost finished, but she had no need to move.

"Oh, well. These chairs wrinkle my skirt, but just this once."

Candice came back to get their order. She nodded at Garry and Gema. "Can I take a drink order?" She took the orders but before leaving asked, "Would you like menus tonight?"

Hank replied, "I know what I want. I want your tenderloin, breaded, everything, heavy on the onions."

Geraldine made a face at Hank and turned to Candice. "Do you still have the portabella mushroom sandwich?"

"Yes."

"That will do for me."

Garry ordered a burger and Gema ordered the salad special, spinach, strawberries and walnuts. As she gave her order, she winked at Candice, who smiled back, understanding. Candice left to put the order in.

Garry said, "Really, Gema? Strawberries and spinach?"

"Yes. And gorgonzola cheese, red onions and a raspberry vinaigrette dressing if they make it correctly."

"You'll fit in perfectly here, that's for sure."

"Speaking of which," Gema turned to Geraldine and Hank, "do you have any new information?"

"We'll have to wait for Howard. I wonder where he is…." Geraldine looked around the room, as if to see him sitting at another table, having not found them in the back. It was Karma. Howard came in, spied them, and walked toward the back of the room.

"Did you think to order a drink for me, Geraldine?"

"I did. It will be here shortly. What news do you have?"

Howard looked around, spied Annie getting ready to leave, gave her a quick wave – well, only because she made eye contact – and turned back to his companions. In a low voice, since Annie was so near, he said, "Strap in. Tomorrow's going to be a great day!"

Geraldine and Hank smiled in glee. Garry joined in a small laugh with Howard.

Gema gave a perfunctory smile. "What will be great about it, Howard?"

"I've been talking to just about everybody that works for Annie, and they tell me horror stories, absolute horror stories. I have a contact. I got enough stuff my contact was able to assure me they're coming tomorrow. The health department, wage and hour, the IRS, probably the alcohol folks. She won't know what hit her, and by the time those reports start hitting the papers she will have come to me to make me an offer."

Gema couldn't help it. She let out a small gasp and sat back, horrified.

Garry looked at her. "You told me you were in."

"I didn't know it would come to this."

"Do you want a chance at the gold ring or not? These people are going to own the prime real estate in the state in just a few weeks. Don't blow it for yourself. Don't blow it for me!"

"I'm not blowing anything, Garry. I was just caught off guard. Certainly, I want my chance. I'm in. You can count on me."

At the largest table in the middle of the main room, Dwight sat with several vendors. He had asked for separate tickets, which was unusual for him. This caused a few of the minor exhibitors to leave before giving an order. Others ordered regular drinks or beer rather than the top shelf drinks they had when Dwight paid. An immediate damper was placed on the table. Dwight, who normally felt the love of his peers when drinking, suddenly realized how life could be if he had to make friends on his merits rather than his money.

That would never be the case, however. He had plenty of assets, but he had been so busy the past four months, he had not had time to convert them – his stolen goods – to cash. He was running low, having to pay his partners first. And his blackmail. The blackmail money was never going to stop flowing. He had to put that to the back of his mind.

He was drinking. He didn't want to slip up and say something he shouldn't.

Candice didn't wait on this table, but she heard snippets of conversation as she walked by them throughout the evening.

"He asked out that manager of the Café. They're on a date right now over at the winery."

"His stuff is so fake. Fine gems, indeed. Do you know he tried to sell fake rubies to the wife of the police chief? The wife of the police chief!"

"He keeps telling people my stuff is fake, but his?"

She heard Dwight say, "I'm going to call it a night, folks. See you all tomorrow." She watched as he rose to go without leaving a tip.

Then, the conversation turned on him.

"Dirty, rotten weasel. He bought a third of his stuff from me and just marked up the prices."

"He always gives himself the first and best booth. Some people spend all their money with him and never see what the rest of us have."

"What does he do with the money we give him for exhibit space? He didn't have a dime on him when he got here, and the expenses were piling up."

"Did you know he has a thing for Gema?"

"No!"

"Oh, yeah, for a long time. He wanted Gema before Martin had her."

"No, that long ago?"

"She wasn't good enough for him. He was well out of that relationship."

"She wasn't good enough for Dwight?"

"No, you twit. I thought we were talking about Martin now."

"You're just jealous. You wanted him yourself, but he got tired of you."

"Yeah, well now he just finds a skank in each town. I hear he's got two here."

"Well, I'd rather talk about Dwight. Why do you all think he tries to keep those three men secret from us?"

"Do you really think that he thinks they're still a secret?"

"Well, yeah. He never talks about 'em, and if you ever see 'em, like today they were up at the show for a few minutes, he never looks at 'em. Even if they stop at his booth. Some stranger walks up, and he's all over 'em, tryin' to sell somethin'. But these guys, he ignores."

"They come in and set him up when no one is there. They take him down after all of us have left. What else do they do?"

"I'll bet…."

Candice, who had tried to keep up with the conversations, finding reasons to walk by every chance she got, was called to the back room. Geraldine and her friends were ready for their tickets.

At Sassy P's, Sam and Nancy met Frank and Mem for an early dinner. Well, actually, they didn't meet at Sassy P's. Frank and Mem went to the carriage house to pick them up, first dropping off a special visitor, Frank's beautiful Claire, a blue point Himalayan.

Claire loved people and hated cats. Except for Honey Bear. Unless he wasn't in town. Then she loved Mo. But Honey Bear was in town.

Nancy, Honey Bear's human, was, of course, Annie's mother. This made the large, golden long-haired mutt of a cat an uncle to Annie's brood. They referred to him often as The Dreaded Uncle Honey Bear and were happy he was confined to the carriage house.

The four friends walked to Sassy P's, marveled at the good spring weather, and caught up with one another. Sam said, "Well, I've got a few body parts acting up these days, but Nancy's doing great!"

"Yes, Sam keeps me on my medicine and makes sure I eat right. I've not gotten dizzy or forgetful in, well, I forget how long it's been!"

Nancy and Sam greeted several people they knew from their extended visits to town and enjoyed their first night in Chelsea. They ate, drank, talked, and finally realized there was a line of people waiting to sit down. Still, it took another fifteen minutes before they forced their way from the table.

As they left, they met three men and two dogs. Sam and Nancy received nudges and licks on the hand, and Nancy and received brief hugs from Pete and Ray. Chris took Nancy in for a long, deep hug.

"It's good to see you. I know it's been a long day, you're already on your way out, but I've been invited for breakfast tomorrow. I'll see you then."

Sam shook his hand, grabbed Chris's left hand, held it and turned it slightly, looking at the watch. "So that's it, huh?"

"It's a beauty, isn't it?"

Annie gave Chris an expensive vintage watch on Leap Day. She got it for a song with the help of Frank. He found it at an antique sale and was able to purchase it before the current owner realized its worth.

Nancy said, "I understand I can't see the ring yet. Henrie said it's still in evidence?"

"Yes, I don't know how long it will be there. It might be the end of the year before she gets it back."

"So sad. Oh, well, at least it will help to convict that monster."

The men and dogs settled in the back, until Cyril and Jock spied Fiamma. They ran to her, and she to them. They met in the middle, stopping suddenly before anyone touched anyone, and headed for the furthest potted plant, there to spend the evening getting to know one another.

The activity caused the two tables to look at one another. Waves all around, but no one interrupted anyone else. Pete allowed his eyes to linger on Ramon's back for a time.

Ray ordered "your best viognier, my good man!" from Jesus. Chris and Pete stuck with something dry and red.

"Tell us about the boat."

Ray told them about the boat. In a perfect world, he would have taken a private test run today. Well, in a perfect world, he wouldn't need the repairs in the first place.

It would probably be finished in time for a short run by the crew tomorrow, late in the afternoon. It would not be finished, actually, it would be sea-worthy but would look like a patchwork quilt with a lot of unfinished parts. No paint, no stain.

"Aren't you taking a chance, taking it out for the first time with your crew on board?"

"You think I don't know that?"

Pete and Chris looked at one another but said nothing.

The wine came. Pete and Chris hoisted theirs like beer steins. "He knows that!" The three settled in for a short evening of good friendship.

Pete, sitting in the best position to see, waved at Felicity when she came in, but she didn't see him. Her eyes roamed the room in the way people look over everyone else until they find the one person they seek. She found Martin and went to his table.

"Who's that?" asked Ray.

"One of the gem show people," answered Chris. "Handsome guy."

"Too handsome," said Pete. "I don't like people comin' into my town makin' off with my town's women."

"Okay. Who was that? John Wayne? Gary Cooper?"

"Pete the poe-lease-man, that's who."

"Well, Pete the poe-lease-man, did I hear sirens today?"

"You did, indeed. A couple of houses got hit again today, burglary, just like the day before. Folks got home from work and found they'd been broken into. Again, all they could find missing was jewelry. Good stuff."

"So Chelsea is in the middle of a crime wave."

"Looks like."

"Any suspects?"

"I have a fellow to look at, but that's about all."

"Come on, tell us."

"Can't talk about it."

"Well then, you need to get some rest. Tomorrow isn't that far away."

The men prepared to leave, but it took several minutes and the help of Ramon to get the dogs headed in the right direction.

Pete liked the way Ramon handled his dog. You had to like people that were good to dogs. Too bad he was probably a burglar.

At the Inn, Henrie set his private dining room table with a meal prepared by Felicity earlier that afternoon. He knew nothing of Fred Calendar's tastes, but he knew the man ran a local restaurant that served typical Midwestern fare from breakfast through dinner.

He asked for something along those lines and received meatloaf, mashed potatoes and gravy, steamed vegetables and apple cobbler, all prepared to serve family style. Of course, Felicity couldn't help but put her personal style into the preparation, but she went light on the rosemary.

Henrie issued the invitation to Fred in the afternoon, offering to provide dinner in a private setting so he could talk about his day. Perhaps Henrie could provide assistance. Fred agreed, and they set the time for Fred to come to the apartment.

Henrie drove to the Snuggle Inn to pick up Georgia and, as he had now begun to think of her, Little Fred. They waited together in the apartment for the appointed hour. When they heard the knock, Henrie touched her arm and gave her a reassuring smile.

He let Fred in, and the first thing Fred saw was his daughter. They ran to one another and embraced. When they parted, Fred noticed the car seat. "Is this the baby I met today? Fred?"

"Named after you, Dad. Frederica. Fred for short."

"Fred for short. Oh, my. You did this all by yourself?"

"I didn't want to put you through it, Dad. You know, single mothers and all that."

Henrie left the apartment, picking up his current book on the way. He would sit in the library until they had finished this long-left-undone conversation.

On the third floor, nine cats and a dog watched over The Avenue as they discussed their detecting. Tiger Lily coordinated the information, receiving surprising tidbits from everyone, including Simon Finnegan and Oscar McMurphy.

They learned that Gema really was on Mommy's side, and Geraldine had some kind of an awful plan. Martin was a womanizer. He flirted with and tried to ask out several women in the short time the cats were there. Adam was mean. He talked in a nice way to everyone, well, almost everyone, at least when there were customers in the room, but he kicked at cats. Everyone knows that someone who kicks at cats is bad. Pattie talked to several people about

Martin, saying unpleasant things about him. But that was only because she liked him so much. None of them could understand the attraction, but there it was.

Mo said, *"Trill."* Kali translated, *"Unrequited love."*

Little Socks said, *"He writes one poem, and now he thinks he's Shakespeare."* Of course, she was referring to the poem Mo recited to them on Leap Day. The one about his romantic tail.

Kristina and Nelson liked to argue with one another, but it seemed they had a little something going on the side. And maybe it wasn't so secret when they weren't on the road. Dwight was on the phone with some people a few times. He was talking about "the job" and "the take." He didn't seem to know much about his products. He could tell people the names of the stones, but he didn't know their properties. At least Adam and Martin could tell people how the stones were typically used.

Little Socks had the best information. *"I know where to put the clue. If we can get it in there, we can put it inside a paper sack where Dwight keeps all the copies of his receipts."*

"How do we get it there without being seen?"

"Does anyone think they can carry it in their mouth from here to the second floor of the Café without being seen?"

"And not urp up? Who are you kidding?"

"I know! We have a toy that will work!"

"A toy?"

"Yeah. Remember when Mommy got some earrings from Clara, they came in a little purple bag? Mommy gave that to us a toy. Who knows where it is?"

There was a flurry of activity as some of the cats and Tillie ran from room to room, looking into toy baskets, under chairs, under the bed. Mo, Simon Finnegan and Oscar McMurphy supervised from the table top. They watched as Sassy Pants struggled to get her body out from under the dining room buffet. In her mouth was a small purple jewelry bag covered in cat hair.

"Founded it!"

"Now all we have to do is get the clue, get it into the bag, and then carry that bag to the room."

"This is only slightly less visible than the ring itself."

"No one will notice."

"Right."

They went to the kitchen. Mr. Bean picked up the twirly stick on the way. Tiger Lily carefully reached in with the stick and snagged the ring. She pulled it out to a chorus of *"Careful!" "Don't push it under!"* and *"Trill!"*

The ring came out from behind the refrigerator with a clump of cat hair. That wasn't the problem, though. Without opposing thumbs, they didn't know how they would get the ring into the bag.

Mr. Bean was the bag man. He worked and worked until he had the bag open. Then Sassy Pants figured out how to get the ring inside. All she had to do was put one paw inside the bag to hold it open while she pulled the ring toward it with the other paw. Eventually, the ring went into the bag, cat hair and all.

Tiger Lily said, *"I'll take it to work with me tomorrow. I'll go really early and take it upstairs before anyone comes in."*

The cats were finished and napping innocently by the time Annie got home for the evening.

Garry and Gema returned to their rooms at the Inn, saying a quiet good-night in the hallway. After several minutes had passed, Gema went to her door, opened it quietly and looked around. She went downstairs, through the dining room, through the kitchen and knocked on the apartment door.

Henrie, cleaning up from the meal he served, opened it, wide awake and still fully dressed. "Is something the matter?"

"Oh, yes, Henrie. Something is really the matter. I need to talk to you and Annie. Tonight."

18

Annie didn't sleep at all the night before. Well, maybe two or three hours. After talking with Gema, she and Henrie stayed in his apartment and got on the phone. No texting in the middle of the night. They needed everyone to wake up and get moving.

Annie called Gwen, her accountant, first. That had to be a message. She left the message on Gwen's phone at work, then sent a text that Gwen would see in the morning. The text said, "nine-one-one listen to message on office phone." The next message, sent in similar fashion, went to Jenny Howard.

Between them, Henrie and Annie talked to all of the managers. After a long argument with herself, she also called Cookie.

Cookie took the news with surprising calm. "So this is what it's like to work for you, right? Phone calls in the middle of the night to tell of imminent disaster?"

"Pretty much."

"Alrighty, then. We'll rock and roll."

At some point during the long evening, they went out the back, to the beach side of the Inn. Annie looked up. "That moon is beautiful."

"Yes, it certainly is."

"Tell me, Henrie, why does the full moon wreak such havoc?"

"Do you want the scientific explanation? That seventy percent of our bodies are made of water and respond to the gravitational pull of the moon?"

Annie looked at Henrie. "No, I guess not."

Annie dragged herself out of bed to help Henrie with breakfast. That was the least she could do. After a short time of Annie's "help," Henrie assured her it was, in fact, the least she could do, and could she find some other place in which to be helpful. Please and thank you.

Kali and Ko, concerned that Mommy felt the need to help with breakfast, followed her into the library and curled their large bodies into her lap as she took a power nap.

Felicity was at work earlier than usual, not because of Annie's call, but because she was cooking and freezing meals for Ray's cruise this morning. Trudie arrived to help, and Felicity filled her in. Trudie checked the coffee bar, not because she needed to, but because she wanted to assure herself no one had booby-trapped the place.

Secure in the knowledge that all was well, she and Felicity continued to work on Ray's meals. While they worked, they talked.

"I thought you might be late coming in last night, or that you might bring company. I was surprised to hear the door as early as I did. And no company. I listened."

Felicity laughed. "It's good to know I have a chaperone."

"No, really, he's a hunk. What happened?"

"I just got a bad feeling. I think picking up women at the towns they hit is what he does for fun. Anyway, I'm glad I was home early and could take Annie's call."

Tiger Lily, arriving early on her mission, heard this last statement. Mommy's call? Why had Mommy called Felicity last night? Oh, well. She would find out sooner or later.

She slipped up the stairs and went to Dwight's booth. There was the paper sack, right where Little Socks said it would be. Tiger Lily dropped her small jewelry bag into the sack and used her front paw to fluff up the pieces of paper until the purple bag could not be seen.

She crouched down when she heard someone come up the stairs. The person coming up didn't have a key and couldn't open the door. There were benefits to having cat doors all over The Avenue. She could get into places that humans could not. But until this person left, she couldn't get out without being seen.

Tiger Lily decided to get closer to the stairway. She went to the ticket table and crouched behind the waste basket. Before too long, she heard the elevator key downstairs. Someone had unlocked the elevator and was coming to the second floor. It was Dwight. He opened the stairway door and Adam came in as well.

They said gruff good mornings to one another and Tiger Lily skedaddled. Downstairs, she jumped to her place at the hostess stand and curled up to take a nap. The first customers wouldn't arrive for another fifteen minutes.

Diana ran the first class of the day, again, and as Gema came in, she gave her a warm welcome. Little Socks followed Gema through the door. She jumped to a pillow and gave Gema the warmest welcome she knew how to give, a long, slow blink. She then curled up to go to sleep, keeping, as always, an ear open for information.

Candice arrived at Mr. Bean's before Martin. She had decided she did not want to meet him, even for breakfast, but she had no way of contacting him.

Carlos was surprised to see her sit down at a table, as if nothing was happening.

"Did George call you last night?"

"About what?"

"This is an all hands on deck day, that's what."

"What? What's going on?"

Customers came into the store right then, so they could not continue the conversation. Candice picked up her phone to call George, to find out why he hadn't told her there was an issue, and then she remembered. Her phone was set to reject calls from him. He would have heard nothing but ringing.

Her back was to the door, as she worked with her phone to undo the block. Trouble was, she couldn't remember how to do that. She could tell George tried to call several times.

Martin came in and sat at her table, facing the window. "You look lovely this morning."

Candice looked up, distracted. "Oh, thanks. Say, I'm sorry, but I'm going to have to go. Sorry you got up for this, but Carlos has great breads. You'll enjoy breakfast."

She got up to leave, and as she turned to go to the door, she saw George. He was standing still, looking in at her, at her sitting with Martin, for breakfast, and he couldn't reach her the night before. He had a package in his hand and thunder on his handsome face.

Candice hurried out and ran to Mo's Tap. The door was already closing behind him.

Mr. Bean saw George. It was his turn, and he danced for George, inviting him to come in, but George wasn't looking at him. George didn't look happy.

When George turned to go to the bar, and when Candice followed, Mr. Bean and Tillie stuck their heads out the cat door to follow their progress.

Mr. Bean, his head on the bottom, turned his head a little bit and said, *"That didn't look good."*

Tillie agreed.

Jesus and Minnie got to Sassy P's early as well and found the girl herself ready to go to work.

Sassy Pants pranced around their legs as they checked out the bar area, the dining room and the coolers. When Minnie went to the kitchen, Sassy Pants politely waited at the door.

Minnie came back out, picked her up and said, "That was the right thing to do. Just always do the right thing, no matter what."

Cookie went first to the Café. He went to the kitchen to see if Felicity needed any help. Hearing she didn't, he went on to the Tap. There he walked into a full-blown argument between George and Candice.

Everyone knew about George and Candice, but they didn't carry on their relationship, the good times or the bad, in front of people. Cookie almost backed out of the bar, then thought better of it. He pressed forward and went to the kitchen. He took a quick look to make sure everything was as it should be, then pulled out one item at a time to prep for the day.

Because he was human, he listened to the conversation out front. Their voices, if anything, had gotten louder.

George said something about earrings. He said he could afford those, so he got them and put a deposit on a necklace.

Candice said she didn't know he was doing it, she didn't know she wasn't supposed to see other people.

George said something about calling her over and over.

She said his calls were blocked. She was home all night, and it wasn't his business anyway.

George said she was having breakfast with him! So she was home all night, what? Entertaining?

Then Cookie heard something crash and break. Then silence. Candice ran into the kitchen and back to the supply area. She came out with a broom and dustpan and ran back to the dining room. There were no voices now, so Cookie went to the servers' window.

Candice and George were cleaning up a glass, thrown in anger, certainly, and shattered along the bar and the floor. George was cleaning one side of the bar, where the glasses and other serving items were. Candice had brushed glass off the bar and was now cleaning the floor. Tears streamed down her face. George no longer looked angry; he looked, well, he looked scared.

He took an inordinately long period of time checking for broken glass. He moved everything out of the way, shook things, turned them to and fro, got out a flashlight and searched for small pieces.

Cookie found a sliver on the servers' window. "Hey, George, when you finish with that light, give it to me. I found some here."

George saw him first. Mo was on the floor under the servers' window, a shard of glass sticking out of his neck surrounded by thick, red blood.

19

Annie ran to Mo's Tap. The little guy was in pain, he was bleeding, he either couldn't or wouldn't move, and they couldn't take the piece of glass out. All of Annie's people had to be at their stations, today of all days, but Annie didn't trust herself to drive.

George called Henrie, who called Nancy, who threw on an exercise jacket and ran to the car. She drove to Mo's Tap and went in to find Annie, George and Candice on their knees around the little guy.

Nancy called to Cookie, "Get me two large towels and two small ones."

Cookie got them right away. Nancy put the two large towels together and laid them on the floor next to Mo.

"All of you get out of the way. You're far too nervous."

They did, and Nancy picked Mo up carefully, placing him on the towels without moving his neck. She and Candice picked up the towels with Mo inside and carried him slowly to the car. Nancy directed Annie to sit in the back seat, and they handed Mo in carefully.

"Now dear, you hold these towels just like this for as long as it takes. He can't be moved."

Annie nodded, and Nancy gently placed the two smaller towels around Mo to keep him warm, careful not to touch the glass. Nancy started the car. She started up gently but gradually increased speed, up The Avenue, around the police department and up to the highway.

Doctor Ralph didn't answer any of Annie's questions, just ordered her to stay in the waiting area. Nancy, knowing her daughter as well as she knew herself, wisely said nothing.

Chris arrived for breakfast at the Inn, surprised to find Henrie in a semi-coherent state. Kali and Ko wandered from kitchen to dining room over and over, crying incessantly. They had two things to worry about. Mo and Little Fred. They would not be consoled.

Henrie, over the clamor of the big girls, told Chris about Mo. Chris immediately called Annie. She answered, a little dull of voice. He said, "Talk to me."

"He's in with the doctor now. They won't let me in. All the way there, I held his paw with one hand, and he just kept kneading it. Over and over. He knew I was taking him to get help."

Chris didn't know what to say. They had never, in all of the ups and downs that happen in relationships, resorted to platitudes. The "he'll be alright" or the "you'll get through this" comments that took up so much of everyone else's conversations. With the two of them, if there was nothing to be said, then nothing was said.

Breakfast was typical for the week. The rock and gem show people showed up, eating quickly or getting something to go. They complained about the noisy cats, but neither Henrie nor Chris offered an explanation.

Fred came in for breakfast, but Henrie couldn't find the energy to talk to him. Chris introduced himself and told Fred there had been a family emergency, and would he like coffee with his breakfast. Chris tripped over Kali and Ko, who seemed to concentrate their pacing around his feet.

Fred replied, "Let me take care of myself. I'm going to have a quick breakfast and then go over to the Snuggle Inn."

Chris looked confused. "Moving?"

"Oh, no, my daughter and granddaughter are staying there. I'll visit for a while, then bring my granddaughter over here for the babysitter. That will quiet these cats down."

Fred didn't know the crying was for Mo.

Chris wondered what else he had missed. Had Henrie installed a nursery? Why would the baby quiet down the cats?

Kali and Ko, weakened with thirst, took a break from prowling the kitchen and dining room. No one would talk to them. No one would tell them what was happening with Mo. They knew he had been hurt, but that was all.

At the water dishes, they drank voraciously. Suddenly, Kali looked at Ko.

"We need to let Tiger Lily know Mo got hurt."

"How are we going to do that? We need to wait here for Fred."

"Remember, she told us we had to take turns, so we can do other things that need to be done."

"Well, okay. I'll wait for Fred. You go."

"No, I'll wait for Fred. You go."

The fight quickly escalated to a hissing, spitting and slapping match, in the kitchen, by their water dish, in front of Henrie and Chris. Fred leaned back in his chair to look in as well.

The girls realized they had an audience and ran to the foyer.

Kali said, *"Okay. I'll go, lazybutt."*

"I'm not a lazybutt! You're a big bossy banana!"

"I'm not a banana!"

"You're bossy!"

"Lazybutt!"

"Hiss!!!!!!!!!!"

Two investigators from the IRS arrived first. Chris opened the door, not having been informed of the expected visits of the day.

One man spoke. He said, "We're from the regional IRS office. We're here to see Mrs. Mack."

Chris replied, "Certainly, please come in and I'll get Henrie."

They stepped into the foyer and were nearly run over by two hissing and spitting cats who chased one another out the door.

They recovered, and the man spoke again. "It's Ms. Mack we want to see."

"Ms. Mack is not here at the moment. I'll get Henrie."

Seeing their upturned noses, Chris declined to invite them to sit. He went to the kitchen, passing Fred in the dining room. "Henrie, some folks from the IRS are here."

"And so it begins."

"What?"

"Sit down, get a cup of coffee, I will tell you all about it after I have disposed of them."

Chris couldn't just sit. He followed Henrie to the doorway of the foyer and listened as Henrie first asked for identification, then told them, politely, where to go. Fred listened as well. He couldn't help but hear.

"You will find all of Ms. Mack's financial records at the office of her accountant. The business name is Beancounters, just around the corner on Main Street. She is expecting you."

"This is a surprise visit. How could she be expecting us?"

"We heard of the surprise last night. Ms. Mack called her accountant to inform her of the pending…surprise…and Gwen – that would be the accountant – called this morning to confirm she would be ready. She cancelled all other appointments for the day."

"We prefer to make surprise visits."

"I am certain you do. Believe me, we learned of this less than twelve hours ago. It is still a surprise."

The IRS agents dispatched, Henrie walked to the dining room doorway, turned Chris around and pushed him to the kitchen, walking him past Fred. There, he poured coffee. He told Chris of the late evening visit by Gema and her news. Annie could expect to see the IRS, the health department, wage and hour and possibly alcohol officials before the day was over.

Fred sat still, listening intently to the conversation in the other room.

As Henrie and Chris finished their first cups of coffee, the doorbell rang again. Henrie walked through the dining room past Fred and answered it, finding two wage and hour investigators on the doorstep. He asked for identification, then directed them to Beancounters.

"We have to see the timecards at the businesses themselves."

"I will show you timecards for the Inn. On your way to the accountant, you can go into each business to view timecards. The formal payroll records, including pay and all deductibles, federal, state and local taxes, FICA, benefit deductions and the like, are kept with the accountant."

Henrie took them through the dining room and past Fred, to the kitchen where a corner served as the office. He opened a file drawer and pulled out a file with timecards. There were cards for each part-time employee. Hilly worked by contract and he, Henrie, was exempt from timecard usage.

"You don't keep these locked up?"

Henrie's gaze was steady. "These carry no private information, only the first name of the employee and the date and time the employee arrived and left. The private information is with the accountant."

When they had taken custody of the timecards – Henrie demanded a receipt – he escorted them through the dining room, past Fred, into the foyer and out the door.

As Henrie walked back through the dining room, Fred decided to tell him what he knew.

"Georgia heard several people at work talking to a man and being pretty negative about Annie. She didn't say anything at work, didn't want to ask about it, but she wondered if Annie was some sort of Jekyll and Hyde character. Do these visits have anything to do with that? Are you all in trouble?"

Chris stepped into the dining room to hear Henrie's response. Henrie, believing Fred to be an ally, told them everything, including the staff roles in the façade to bring Howard and his cohorts into the open. And, hopefully, to see the disgrace actually land on them.

Fred decided he had better get to the Snuggle Inn. "I have to go, Henrie. I wish you the best of luck today, and if it's alright with you, I'm sure Georgia and Martha would want to know what's happening."

"That would be a good idea. Georgia would hear about it at any rate when she arrives at work. Best she know before. I fear Kali and Ko have left the house, but they should return soon. I expect they will want to tend to Little Fred."

Fred smiled. "I'm going to stop at the shelter and get another cat. I'll bring Little Fred and the new sitter here so your girls can train her."

Chris, more confused about the girls training a cat to sit a baby than the rest of it, left for the Coast Guard Station. He sent a quick prayer up, asking for, well, he didn't know what to ask for. He figured the message would get through.

Kali and Ko saved their energy for running. By the time they got to the Café, they were breathing hard and no longer fighting with one another.

Tiger Lily, surprised, jumped down from the hostess stand. She knew the girls would not leave the Inn without a good reason. *"What's wrong?"*

Kali spoke for both of them. *"It's Mo. Something happened at the Tap, and they had to take him to the cat emergency room."*

"What happened?"

"No one is saying anything. Mommy ran out of the house, and Henrie called Grandmommy, and we tried to ask people to tell us, but they didn't. We asked and asked."

"Go on back to the Inn. If you hear anything, let me know. Stop in and let the others know on your way back. Tell them to keep their ears open."

Tiger Lily was scared now. It was really bad if no one was talking about it.

Two inspectors from the health department arrived at the Café at the peak of the breakfast rush hour. They marched in and demanded to be allowed into the kitchen. Trudie asked for their identification, then led them to the kitchen. All staff had been alerted in advance; they continued to do their jobs while paying no attention to the investigators.

Having cats in the businesses was against their rules, but in this town, the Town Council had decided cats and dogs could be inside, as long as they did not go into the kitchen or prep areas. Trudie was incensed to see an investigator try to entice Tiger Lily into the kitchen with a sliver of cheese.

Tiger Lily went as far as the doorway, then she stopped. No matter what the investigator did, the girl did not enter the kitchen.

Felicity was whipping up a sauce when Trudie sent her a text. Whisk still in hand, she turned and stormed over to the investigator, took the cheese out of his hand and walked to the door. There, she kneeled down and offered the cheese to her, saying, "You are absolutely the best, Tiger Lily. Do you want this?"

Tiger Lily looked at the cheese, looked up at the investigator, looked into Felicity's face, and turned to walk to her hostess stand, little behind wiggling and tail waving in the air.

Felicity stood up with hands on her hips and glared at the investigators. Then she stabbed the air with the whisk in her hand, emphasizing every sentence until she got to the last one. Then she emphasized every word.

"You look around all you want. Open every cooler. Open every freezer. Open every cupboard. Open every container. Check our temperatures. Check our rotation dates. Give us the white glove treatment. Get in our way. Spill drinks. Knock over meals so we have to start over. You can do anything you want. But leave our cat alone!"

Felicity was not perky.

Eventually, finding not even a warning to write up, they finished their paperwork for Felicity to sign. She initialed each line and signed at the bottom.

"Why did you do that?"

"I just want to be sure that the paperwork that goes to wherever it goes is the paperwork I've been given."

"Huh. That's never happened before."

They went next to Mr. Bean's Confectionary. Mo's Tap was next in line, but they preferred to get to places during a rush. It was too early for a rush at Mo's; unfortunately Mr. Bean's rush was over for the day, so they had nothing to lose by going there now.

Inside, Mr. Bean and Tillie greeted them together. Before even introducing themselves to Carlos and Jerry, the men tried to entice the cat and the dog to go to the kitchen.

"Come on, come on, let's go to the kitchen."

"Don't you want to go to the kitchen?"

"Come on, now."

Finally, one man reached down to pick Mr. Bean up. He started to walk into the kitchen. Mr. Bean squirmed in fright and caught the man's neck with a back claw.

"Ow! He's dangerous!"

"No one comes in here and picks him up, and no one tries to take him to the kitchen. He knows he doesn't belong there."

Carlos had stood by, watching. His face told the men he was not being friendly, however.

Mr. Bean scurried to a corner of the dining area, followed by Tillie, who turned and growled, daring the men to follow.

The men looked at Carlos, said, "So, you know who we are."

"I do, but show me your identification, nonetheless."

They did, and Carlos gestured with his hand for them to go back to the kitchen.

Jerry went back to his chocolates, and they worked around him, opening everything, placing thermometers, testing for dust.

Again, they couldn't find anything worthy even of a warning. Handing their paperwork to Carlos, he initialed every line and signed at the bottom.

They backtracked to Mo's, just beginning to get a lunch rush, and looked around for the cat. They didn't see him. One of the men said, "Maybe he's in the kitchen."

"We should be so lucky."

The man at the bar was friendly enough, but he looked a little grim. The server who appeared to manage the dining room had a grim expression as well. They assumed the expressions were for their visit.

The dining room was half full and people were piling through the door.

"We're here to do an inspection."

George came to the end of the bar where they stood. "Identification, please."

They handed it over. They had not been ID'd so often in one day…well, in ever…as today.

Once again, they looked at everything, starting with the bar. They made sure to keep George from making drinks, getting beer, even pouring water, until they were darned good and ready to allow it.

George said nothing and kept to the end of the bar until they were finished. When they left the bar to go to the kitchen, he got drink orders more quickly than he remembered doing in a long time. But he got Candice and the only other server working up to date with their orders.

In the kitchen, Georgia held forth at the window and chopped vegetables and garnishes, as usual. George Two had the dishes under control, John had the grill and fry stations under control, and Cookie made the more complicated dishes.

The investigators were as intrusive as possible, but with all of their opening, temperature checking, white glove handling and under-the-sink poking, they could find nothing worthy of a warning.

On their way out the door, they handed the paperwork to George, who initialed every line and signed at the bottom.

"Where's your cat?"

"He had to step out."

The men stared at George for a while and he stared back. They left, on their way to Sassy P's.

They fared no better at the winery. Sassy Pants followed them gleefully wherever they went. Except the kitchen. She stopped at the threshold and no amount of enticing would get her to enter. When they came out of the kitchen, she dropped to her back and offered her tummy to be rubbed.

Neither man complied. Minnie looked at the little girl with sympathy.

Once again, they handed paperwork over, this time to Jesus, who initialed every line and signed at the bottom.

When they got to the sidewalk, they looked at one another. "This was a witch hunt," said one.

The other one said, "They couldn't have known we were coming before we did. They didn't have time to fix everything. This is the way they operate. They're clean as a whistle."

"We have one more place. The boss said this is the place that's really bad."

"What, that B&B? Bad?"

"That's what the boss said."

"How does she know?"

"Apparently, the complaint was specific."

"Well, if it was specific, we should have seen something in these other places. Oh, well. Let's finish it."

They walked to the Inn, and Henrie, once again, opened the door to a pair of investigators intent on finding "something wrong." He asked for identification.

When they had completed their inspection of the kitchen, dining room, coffee area, restrooms and guestrooms, they handed the papers to Henrie. He initialed every line and signed at the bottom.

"Why do all of you do that? Initial every line?"

Henrie's answer was to turn and walk them to the door.

The health department investigators were followed that afternoon by investigators from the agency that regulated alcohol sales. They went first to Mo's Tap. The first thing they asked to see was the bar log. They found daily entries of items of note that occurred. They focused on people who had too much to drink. Sometimes guests were cut off and provided with food at no charge. In other instances, guests were just cut off and there would be a notation that someone else had promised to drive the guest home, or the guest wasn't driving and would walk home. They checked bottles in storage, to see they still contained tape signifying they had not been opened, checked the wells for types of alcohol, and noted the daily calendar, which stated in tall, bold letters, "you may not be in this business or order alcohol unless you were born on…" and the date was correct. They asked for and were shown up-to-date licenses for George and all the servers on duty.

They handed paperwork to George, who initialed every line and signed at the bottom.

20

Nancy and Annie waited for the doctor. It seemed like days, but it had only been a couple of hours. Annie was getting a little punchy. Random thoughts flew through her mind; she verbalized some of them.

"What do you think about people and their pets looking alike?"

"What, dear?"

"People and their pets. Clara has a boyfriend, and he has dreadlocks. His dog has dreadlocks, too."

"Really?"

"Yeah. It got me to wondering, which of my cats do I most resemble?"

"I'd have to say Little Socks, because of your dark hair, and the gray, you know, matches her tuxedo look."

"Maybe. You know, I always wondered why I didn't look like you or Dad. Patti looks like you, mostly, but she has Sam's eyes." Patti was Annie's half-sister. "I don't look like either of you. I have dark hair, both your hair and dad's were fair; I have a body type unlike either of yours. My skin tone is darker. I have high cheekbones. How many generations does a thing like that skip?"

Nancy didn't respond.

Annie, who had been sitting in a chair, legs crossed, right leg swinging, face pointed toward a picture she could now paint by heart, stopped swinging her leg and looked at her mother.

"Mom? Are you okay?"

"Yes, dear, I'm fine."

"Anyway," Annie took up her leg-swinging stance again, "how many generations did that skip? Which of you had Indian blood, you or dad?"

Nancy didn't respond.

Now Annie put both feet on the floor and turned in the chair facing her mother.

"Mom?"

"Neither."

"What?"

"Neither your father nor I have, or had, as the case may be, Indian blood."

"So where did I get my cheekbones?"

Nancy didn't respond.

"Mom? Where did I get my cheekbones?"

"From your real father, dear."

Annie sat back, stunned. Doctor Ralph came out holding a very still Mo. She jumped up, hand over her mouth.

"Now don't get excited. He's sedated. It was a delicate surgery, and we didn't want to say anything to you until we had observed him for a while. He'll be fine, but you'll have to keep him quiet for several days. I've got a prescription for some special food and some medicine. They're taking care of the paperwork now, and then you can go."

Annie took Mo in her arms like a baby, rocking back and forth.

Doctor Ralph continued, "Whoever had the idea to make that sling for him saved his life. If he had come in here any other way, that glass would have severed an artery."

Neither Annie nor Nancy said a word on the way home. Annie sat in the passenger seat, still holding Mo like a baby. Her mother had helped with the seatbelt, but beyond that, they had no interaction.

21

Early on Thursday afternoon, Henrie greeted Ray's crew. They were referred to as "the crew" because all of Ray's passengers for multiple day cruises became the crew for the duration of the cruise. They would get a crash course in the operation of engine controls this afternoon and take off in the morning. All-in-all, it was an easy situation for Henrie. Book them in, feed them breakfast, and move on.

Henrie sent a text to Ray to let him know the crew was on deck, so to speak.

Annie put one of Mo's favorite cat cushions inside a tent made for cats to play outdoors. There was room for a small litter pan, placed on one side, and water and food dishes, placed on the other. This way, Mo would not have to travel far to get to either.

Kali and Ko, who spent a few hours breaking in a new babysitter for Little Fred, went upstairs to tend to Mo. They couldn't get to him, but they could stay near the tent, ready to protect him from whatever it was that hurt him this morning. For now, Mo was still asleep.

She got a text from Gwen and knew she had to leave. Henrie was busy. Everyone was busy. Her mind cast around and finally lighted on JoJo, downstairs in the library with Little Fred. Annie went downstairs and saw, for the first time, a tortoise shell kitten, actually, a small cat, orange speckles rampant on her body. Fred had its tail in one little hand. The cat was on her stomach, paws in the

I'm-getting-ready-to-run pose. She looked up at Annie with a terrified expression.

Annie wondered if this really was beginning to be her new normal, or if she was just too tired and dejected to react. "JoJo, can I pay you to babysit someone else? You can bring Fred upstairs, and, um, the cat."

"You need me to watch Mo? Thank goodness! Kali and Ko are up there! Speckles is still in training. I'll get Little Fred's bags and go right up."

Annie wondered if she should consider turning the Inn into an animal shelter. Or a nursery. Or both. She wondered what the Health Department would say about that. She wondered if her mind had gone off the rails.

When she arrived at Beancounters, Gwen, Jenny and the wage and hour and IRS investigators sat at the conference table, some of Gwen's awful coffee in front of them. The lead investigator for the IRS briefed her on their progress.

"We had information that you were not paying taxes as you should, including withholding taxes, FICA, your personal taxes for use of business resources, for example, the meals you eat, either there or for take-out. We had planned to do a cursory review today and come back later for a more in-depth investigation."

Annie looked at him, holding her breath. She realized her error and forced herself to breathe, so she could think if necessary. Fortunately for her, Gwen was her accountant, so she had no fears about the legitimacy of her books.

The investigator continued. "From our cursory review, we find no reason to come back. Everything seems to be in order. I would like to apologize for the inconvenience, and for the costs I'm sure you incurred for today's investigation. As you know, we have to respond to information such as we received."

One of the wage and hour investigators concurred. "The same is true from our investigation. It appears that if people work overtime, they are adequately compensated. Also, everyone is paid a reasonable rate for the job they were hired to do. Frankly, more than reasonable for the industry. We found nothing that will call for a further investigation."

Annie took another deep breath and asked, "How is it that you were all here so quickly? The information I have is that the complaints were made only yesterday. Calls to you, the health department, the alcohol people…how did you get here so quickly?"

The four men looked at one another, then the first man to speak decided to answer. "You deserve to know. From our perspective, and I venture to say from the perspective of every other agency involved, our bosses received a call from the Governor's office."

"The Governor?"

"No, the Governor's office. The particular person from that office called out the dogs, so to speak."

"Can you give me the name of the person who called out the dogs?"

"No. I'm sorry."

The four men nodded to Gwen, then Jenny, then Annie, and left. As they walked out, the man who had spoken held the door for the other men. He then turned back to shake

Annie's hand. As he left, she looked down at the piece of paper he had given her. It held the name of a man.

Annie, still in a daze, handed the paper to Jenny, thanked both women for staying with the investigators all day, and left. She walked to Mo's, feeling a combination of sadness and anger, plus scare that was being released. What was the name of that feeling, she wondered.

Candice saw her through the window before she arrived. She ran to the sidewalk to embrace Annie, crying, saying how sorry she was. Annie held on, murmuring that it was okay. It would be okay. Mo would be fine. When Candice finally let her go, the two women stood looking at one another.

Annie said, "Candice, there is a full moon sending all kinds of power to us this week. Let's move on. Just promise me one thing."

"Anything."

"I want you and George to use some vacation time as soon as possible. I don't care that you don't like to be gone at the same time. You have to do it. Go. Go together. Work it out. Come back a couple or not a couple. But no matter what, I hope you can continue to work together. For me."

George had pulled another server behind the bar, and he heard this promise that Annie wanted to extract. He said, "We can go next week, if Candice agrees."

Candice looked at him and nodded.

"Then start calling your replacements. Take at least a week. Longer if you think you can."

"Yes, ma'am."

22

Tiger Lily was to accompany Mommy and Chris to the grand opening of the Bon Vivant Grille. Her siblings were confined to the apartment. Mommy locked the cat doors from the inside so Tillie would not be able to get to them. Mommy was on to their greatest secret. Darn.

Tiger Lily was upset she had not heard any more about Mo until she got home. Everyone was so up in the air with all the investigators that no one talked about the big accident.

She checked for herself that Mo was still living. He seemed to be sleeping quietly. His neck had a big bandage around it, and his paws were wrapped up so he couldn't try to take the bandage off. She heard Mommy tell Henrie they couldn't put something called a collar on him because of where the injury was.

Mommy also told Henrie that Grandmommy saved Mo's life by making a sling out of a towel. Tiger Lily was having trouble coming up with a visual on that one, but apparently Grandmommy was a hero.

Mommy was probably sorry that it was Grandmommy and not herself, because Mommy didn't seem to be very happy with Grandmommy. What was up with that?

And what was that thing Mommy was putting on? When Chris came to pick her up, he made all sorts of compliments, and Mommy's face got red. What was up with that?

And what was the new cat smell in the apartment?

Attendance at the grand opening of the Bon Vivant Grille was by invitation only. Gema was ecstatic to have received an invitation. She would be seated at a table for six that included Garry, Dwight, Adam, Martin and Pattie. It was a black-tie optional event; most had opted in. Even Annie, practical, no-nonsense Annie, stood at the hostess stand in a strapless, shimmery, low cut, tight-fitting dress in tones of rose and lilac. The necklace would have looked perfect with this dress. No matter. It would be in her hands soon enough.

Gema looked down. Annie had new shoes. They matched the dress. Strappy, glitzy sandals, purple, with a two inch heel.

Chris dazzled in a very dark blue tuxedo with a cravat and bowtie to match Annie's dress. They were lilac with rose polka dots. He sat with an older couple. Gema recognized them as Annie's parents, Nancy and Sam, also guests of the Inn and dressed to the nines.

Annie handed a menu card to everyone as they entered and explained, "Just choose an item for each course. Your server will pick up the card before dinner. Tonight only, feel free to order wine or beer at no additional charge."

Gema, who worried all day about the investigations, finally began to relax. It looked as if the restaurant was fine. No one put a "closed for business" sign on the door, and all the staff seemed to be happy and relaxed. Except for Annie. But she was probably nervous about the evening, stressed about the inspections, and on edge about her cat. Everyone had been talking about the cat. And the accident.

Gema and her tablemates ordered a bottle of chilled chardonnay over Pattie's objections. "We need to wait for Martin. I don't think he likes white wine."

"Then he can order a glass of something else when he gets here. Where is he? It's almost time to be served."

"I don't know. He's probably on a date with some floozy. Something more exciting than this."

Gema couldn't think of anything more exciting than this. Most of the tables were filled with gowned women and tuxedoed men, and even more were in line on the sidewalk, waiting to be greeted and seated.

She looked around. The Café had a different look tonight. Linens in every color of the rainbow covered the enamel table tops. They were hemmed to allow Tiger Lily's ledges to stay visible. The napkins were also in rainbow colors. At her table of six, they had a red tablecloth and napkins of blue, red, green, yellow, orange and purple. This evening, the lights were turned on, showcasing each unique design. They were kept low, to provide ambiance. Seeing them lighted provided a different experience from daytime dining, when the café used primarily natural lighting from the windows.

The flowers were also different. She had noticed the pretty purple bouquet in a crystal vase every day. Today, the vase was filled with flowers of every color. The arrangement was elegantly eclectic. Adding to the ambiance were the three big dogs – an English setter, a Portuguese water dog, and that dog with the beautiful mass of dreadlocks – and Tiger Lily herself, sitting proudly with Annie at the hostess stand.

When the tables were filled, Annie greeted everyone using a microphone at the hostess stand, thanked them for coming and then sat, with a smile somewhat to the west side of ecstatic. Who could blame her? She had to be tired.

The first course was delivered to every table. Between the five of them, they had ordered four of the options. Gema had chosen a mixed green salad with brown butter walnut vinaigrette. Others had parsley salad with lemon and almonds toasted in olive oil, roasted shrimp with a signature cocktail sauce, and an aged cheddar fondue made with grilled tomatoes and bacon with crusty pieces of French bread for dipping.

The next course was soup, served with pretzel bread croissants. Gema had the creamed pea and leek. Others had minestrone vegetable, broccoli with miso and mushrooms, and spicy tomato with yogurt and pistachio dumplings.

Gema glanced at Annie's table several times during the evening. She noticed tension at the table between Annie and her mother. In the middle of the soup course, the cat, Tiger Lily, hopped to the table to sit in between Chris and Annie. She stayed there for the rest of the meal.

The next course was vegetables and starch. Gema's table ordered a combination of steamed or grilled peapods or asparagus, and four unique starch choices came to the table. Gemma had the whole new potatoes sautéed in curry; others tried cilantro lime basmati rice, quinoa onion bites, and vegan lemon and garlic angel hair pasta.

Gema ordered a vegan dish for the entrée, eggplant meatballs served with a peppery marinara sauce. Others had roasted pork loin with rosemary, Japanese spiced New York strip steak, and salmon sautéed in garlic butter.

For dessert, Gema and Pattie ordered the Bavarian wild berry fruit-tea sorbet. Dwight had the mixed berry and apple pot pie, while Garry and Adam tried a decadent chocolate pretzel cake. Gema's table had just been served when disaster struck.

A loud noise and the sounds of men and women screaming came from the kitchen. Gema froze as she watched Annie and Chris jump up to see what the problem was. She recognized the police chief. He and some other men were right behind them.

They didn't make it to the kitchen, however, because a cook and a server ran out, screaming "Fire! Fire! The grill's on fire!"

Annie immediately turned to crowd control. She rushed to the hostess stand and turned on the microphone. "Don't panic. By now, the fire is already out. If you heard that big "whoosh" coming from the kitchen, it was the fire suppression system. You are in no danger, but if you want to leave, please leave in an orderly fashion." No one left.

Chris and Pete came to the kitchen door. Chris nodded. The fire was out. Cookie stood behind them at the door, a combination of mortification and anger on his face. Annie, at the podium and still using the microphone, said, "Felicity, are the rest of the desserts alright? Can they be served?"

Felicity nodded. She and the servers hurried to get the desserts out of the kitchen before the ambulance arrived. Trudie returned to the coffee bar and came out with carafes to continue serving coffee. There was no question that the wine and beer would stop flowing, but they would salvage the rest of the evening as best they could.

Annie went to the kitchen to sit with John until the ambulance arrived. Jennifer was there, too, doing what she could to ascertain John's vital signs; Marie had run for the ambulance. In a haze, Annie heard Cookie say, "I don't know how this happened. The grill had been off for a half hour. It was cool enough to clean…and John…."

Annie was careful to touch nothing while they waited for the ambulance. Another cook had doused John's uniform with a fire extinguisher. The uniform and John were now one.

When the ambulance left, John inside, Annie called his mother and told her to go to the hospital. The crowd stayed, almost excited to be at the scene of another of Annie's crises.

Annie walked slowly to the table where Nancy and Sam still sat. She had just taken a bite of decadent chocolate pretzel cake when she heard another scream. This was a high-pitched and awful scream, and it got louder and louder as the screamer ran down the back stairs, hit the stairwell door and stood. Still screaming.

Thinking back in the days to come, Annie would marvel that her first thought was, does she ever come up for air?

Hilly rose from her table and rushed to the woman, one of her own staff, who had been cleaning the second floor. Annie rose to help her to a chair, but sat back down when the woman screamed, "Murder!"

Mem had watched from a distance as Annie and Nancy seemed to grow further apart. They didn't move their chairs apart. However, it was apparent that Annie talked to Chris and Sam and that Nancy talked to Chris and Sam. Chris and Sam seemed to be withering under the tension as well. Even Tiger Lily, sitting at the table since the soup course, couldn't seem to help.

Annie looked so pretty tonight. And Chris! He dazzled in a tuxedo! Mem turned her attention back to her own handsome date, Frank, and was waiting for dessert to be delivered when the fire broke out. Thank goodness the Chief of the Fire Department and a couple of his officers were on hand. And Jennifer and Marie. As that crisis wound to a close – well, she thought, it won't close until an investigation is conducted – another crisis came to a head. A screaming woman made it to the bottom of the steps and cried, "Murder!"

Mem watched as Marco and Pete split their duties. Both dressed in tuxedos, Marco stood outside the kitchen, probably preserving it for evidence, while Pete went upstairs. Chris and Ray made for splendid-looking crowd control, keeping others from following.

Mem's table was close to the stairwell. She heard Pete when he returned. "We have a murder. I called the state police; they'll bring forensic investigators. I don't know how the guy died for sure, but there's a big hunk of white stone in his chest."

She put her face in her hands and tried to think peaceful thoughts. Going through her mind was one phrase: "There's a full moon. There's a full moon. There's a full moon."

No one paid attention to the cat and three dogs. Tiger Lily, smaller and less noticeable, had managed to get into the kitchen to see what had happened and to listen to what was being said. She also followed Pete up the stairs to see the dead body. She was able to figure out who it was, and before Pete shooed her away, she got a sniff of the object in his chest.

When Pete went back downstairs, she followed and went directly to the dogs. She looked at Cyril and said, *"I know you'll want to investigate the murder, but now's your chance to show Pete the clue. Make sure he looks in the paper sack under Dwight's table. The clue is in there."*

Cyril nodded as he and Jock rose, each one assuming an air of importance for Fiamma's benefit. They walked majestically to their humans to stand by until needed.

Pete had a hand in both investigations, but he left Marco in charge of the grill fire, working with the fire department, and he concentrated on the murder.

Funny thing about that murder. Cyril didn't seem the least bit interested in the dead man. He planted himself by another exhibit and refused to move, snuffling and sniffing under the tables at a paper sack.

It was late. Well, it was actually early. It was very early Friday morning. Pete was ready to turn everything over to the state police. He would get back into it after a few hours of sleep. But Cyril wouldn't move.

Pete finally went to him and he backed up, giving Pete a clear shot at the sack. Pete, gloves already on, picked up the sack and looked into it. He didn't see anything but paper. He shook it a little bit, and it felt like there was more than paper inside it. He used a pencil to push the paper around and found a purple jewelry bag. Using the pencil to snag the loop of the enclosure, he picked it up carefully. The loop had obviously not been pulled tight, and he didn't want to lose what was inside.

When he had the jewelry bag safely out, he put the paper sack on the floor and used both hands to look at the bag. It was covered in what looked to be cat hair. He opened it.

Inside was a ring. An expensive ring. A ring that could possibly be on an inventory of stolen items. And more cat hair. He was certain the tangle of hairs, most of them gray, were from one cat. Or maybe seven.

Pete looked at Cyril and asked, "Did Tiger Lily tell you where to get this?"

Cyril, going back to a trick Pete taught him months before, lifted a paw and tapped Pete's right hand.

Pete, closing his eyes, shaking his head and praying no other investigator was watching, squatted down. He put the bag, now in a plastic evidence baggie, into his pocket.

He looked at Cyril, both fists out, and asked again, "Did Tiger Lily tell you where to look for this?"

Paw to right hand.

"Does she know who took it?"

Paw to right hand.

"Is it the man whose booth we're next to?"

Paw to right hand.

Pete threw in a trick question.

Is that man the dead man over here?"

Cyril looked at Pete as if he were being chastised, then he put his paw to Pete's left hand.

Pete shook his head again, sighed, gave Cyril a stroke and stood. When he turned, five men and women, state troopers and coroner's investigators, were staring at him.

Pete shook his head again. "Just don't ask."

What Pete didn't tell them was that he had stepped back into the burglary investigation, and his number one suspect, Ramon, may not be the guy.

When Pete finally got home, Janet waited up for him. Mem was with her. A fresh pot of coffee waited.

"We have to talk."

Pete was glad to hear from Mem and Janet that the stone belonged to Mem. It would be a benefit to Mem when the fingerprint analysis came back. Mem's fingerprints would be on file because she did forensic computer work on occasion for the department.

Mem was concerned about George as well. When she realized fingerprints were important, she told Pete that George had handled the stone. George's prints would be on file as well, and his name would come up as someone who had cause to be angry with Martin.

But the real benefit to Pete was the relationship chart that Janet kept in her purse. Every day she had added to it when she heard a significant snippet of conversation. She couldn't explain why she had done it, except Mem introduced her to the concept and she was fascinated with it.

She noticed particular looks at Martin when his back was turned from Garry, Adam and Dwight. She had darkened the "dislike" lines from them to Martin. Pattie seemed to have a love/hate relationship with him, and that line, the "something" line, had been darkened as well. For no particular reason, but because of Pattie's comment about Gema, she had also darkened the "something" line between Gema and Martin.

Janet looked at Pete, who struggled to stay awake. "Is this evidence you can use?"

Pete yawned, signaling the end of the conversation. "It's not evidence, but it will narrow the initial focus of the investigation. It's helpful."

23

It was Friday morning. The moon would not start waning gibbous until tomorrow. Annie prayed she would make it that long. She made an early morning – before the break of dawn – run to a twenty-four hour grocery in Marsh Haven, taking the supplies to Mo's Tap and Sassy P's. No one ever said you couldn't get a great breakfast in a bar or a winery. Right?

All of the open food venues made banner sales that morning. Everyone wanted to be the first to know "the real story." Of course, Annie's staff could not talk about it, leaving the naysayers to think the worst. Felicity, Trudie and the morning staff were spread out all over Annie's businesses, trying to keep breakfast going with the Café closed for investigation. She thought they could get in by early afternoon, in time for Cookie to set up for his first night of business.

What a disaster. Rumors were flying all over town about the cleanliness of Annie's kitchens, and didn't we just know this was going to happen. There was a reason for all those investigations.

And Henrie, at the Inn, served all of his guests. Fred Calendar was the only guest that didn't eat breakfast. He went to Martha's to eat with Georgia and talk through what could happen next in her life.

Henrie cooked early to have breakfast ready by 6:00 for Ray's crew, his only responsibility to this group of six young adults. This group ate heartily. On the one hand, Henrie was pleased. On the other, he mentally counted the eggs, slices of bacon, pieces of sausage, loaves of bread and trays of cinnamon rolls on hand.

The rock and gem show exhibitors were down two hours later. They, for once, stayed to eat. They wanted to be ready to go the minute the police cleared the show venue. They would be allowed to check their exhibits sometime this afternoon, but the show would not open again until Saturday. They stayed right there and ate. And ate. And ate. When Henrie thought he would have to call Laila to bring more eggs, they finally had enough.

Would this week never end? Would the moon never turn?

Pete started the day by interviewing the kitchen and serving staff of the Grille. Or the Café. No, last night, it was the Grille. Pete was punchy from lack of sleep.

Annie's accountant had delivered the personnel files to the police department that morning. The file box sat on his desk as he questioned everyone. To keep Annie's businesses going, he interviewed Felicity and Trudie quickly, then took his time with the rest.

He called Cookie into his office. Pete went through Cookie's personnel file, asked every question he could think to ask. Finally, he asked, "Did everyone come in to be interviewed?"

"No. I was thinking about that before you called me in here. He might be late, but the last cook that I hired wasn't out there. His name is Ed. He came into Mo's Tuesday or Wednesday this week, looking for work, and I hired him to cook."

"Did you see him during the incident last night?"

"Yeah. Well, not when it happened. I didn't see it happen. There was a scream, and when I turned to look, Ed had the fire extinguisher out, and he was hosing John down."

Pete excused Cookie and looked in the office at the rag-tag, tired looking bunch of people waiting to be interviewed. He turned to Cookie. "Is Ed here?"

"No, sir."

Pete pulled Ed's file from the stack and handed it to Marco. "See if you can find this young man."

He then called the Fire Department. "Do you have a cause of fire yet?"

"Yes, we do. It was arson, alright. The accelerant was kerosene, and the lighting devise was a pack of matches. Looks like they were all set aflame and thrown on the kerosene."

"How fast is that?"

"Pretty fast. What's your real question?"

"If the head cook had his back turned, could someone have started it, someone else come into contact with it, and then a fire extinguisher be in use as soon as the head cook heard it and turned?"

"Well……" This was a long, drawn-out word. "It coulda happened like that, if the person was right on top of the extinguisher and knew it was there. But…"

"But?"

"That woulda been a big coincidence, that someone would be there so quick with a fire extinguisher, unless that someone knew it would be needed."

Annie kept all the kids inside for the day, again locking the cat doors from the inside. Before leaving she paid special attention to Mo, who wanted to walk around. He wanted that bandage off, as well.

Annie lectured him, knowing that even though he understood her, he was a cat. He would do what he wanted and she couldn't stop him.

She left him in the tent, though. No sense giving him ammunition to hurt himself further.

She went first to Mo's Tap. After telling George and Candice that Mo had spent a good night, she went to the kitchen to check on Cookie. She stood close to the door as he prepared breakfast and asked if he could handle the night to come.

Cookie turned to her, spatula in hand. "You know what? Now I'm mad. I had a killer grand opening. Those people loved it. And what did the papers and television report? Did you see?"

Annie closed her eyes and nodded. They had not reported at all on the unique dishes, the daring combination of foods, the atmosphere. Not one word about the perfectly cooked entrees or the tour de force soups. Nothing said about the outstanding service or the smooth movement from one course to the next. And they didn't mention her dress! Every report had been on the explosion and injury and the murder on the second floor. Annie strikes again.

Annie snapped out of her reverie. She needed to concentrate. "So, Cookie, anger is good?"

Cookie's back was to her again as he finished a plate of plain old bacon and eggs. He spoke, continuing to look at his work. "Anger is good. Bring it on. We'll kill again tonight."

Annie didn't tell him that was probably a poor choice of words.

"And we'll be down two cooks. How's that going to work out?"

"Georgia worked with some people in a restaurant in the city. She called, and a couple who have the weekend off are going to work it. Already on their way here."

"Do they have a place to stay?"

"I'll work it out. We're gonna kill tonight."

She went from Mo's Tap to the hospital. John was in intensive care and the medication kept him in a semi-comatose state. His injuries were not life threatening, but the burns to his hands and arms were second and third degree.

Annie assured John's mother that his insurance would cover anything not covered by Workers' Compensation, but that route would have to be explored first. She offered the services of her attorney, Jenny Howard, to deal with Workers' Comp, notorious for trying to get out of paying claims. John's job would be waiting for him as well, if he wanted it.

She stopped into the police department next and told the receptionist Pete wanted to see her. He was in the middle of an interview, but Annie was offered a seat. She decided to wait, not wanting to go home. Her mother was there.

24

Mem and Janet didn't have to struggle to get out of bed to get to the ticket table for this, the last full day of the rock and gem show. No, this, the last full day of the show, would be a nothing day. The show would certainly go on tomorrow but would close by noon.

Mem got up at a reasonable time and went downstairs to her own store, where she checked on stock, made notes to replace inventory and did a little cleaning. The young people she hired didn't seem to see everything that needed to be done, but their hearts were in the right place.

Her part-time helper unlocked the front door and was startled to see Mem. "Hey. Do you need me today?"

"Yes, please stay. I need to do some other things. You've heard about the show, right? That it won't be open today?"

"Wow. What a night. That Annie knows how to throw a party!"

Mem gave a half smile and walked out the door on her way to the Inn.

She knew Annie and Henrie would be busy. She wanted to check on Nancy. Nancy answered her knock right away.

"Oh, it's you, Mem. I thought it might be Annie. Come in. Tea?"

"Certainly. You haven't seen Annie yet today?"

"No, I'm sure she's busy, and we didn't want to add to Henrie's burden today, so we made breakfast here."

Sam came to the kitchenette. "Mem, it's good to see you. What's Frank up to today?"

"He's probably taking advantage of the boaters not having a gem show to go to today. I think he called Ben to come help, expecting more business than usual."

"Well, then, I'll go help, too. Unless he kicks me out."

Sam left and the two friends sat down with a cup of tea. Mem looked at Nancy. "Usually, when two women are having a cup of tea and a serious conversation, it takes place at my tea shop. Today, we're here."

"Oh, are we having a serious conversation?"

"We are. Tell me what's going on between you and Annie."

Nancy said nothing.

"Nancy, please, let me help."

Nancy finally looked at her cup and sighed. "So, you've noticed something. I wonder how many other people have."

"I dare say I'm the only one, with the possible exception of Sam and Chris, but they may already know what it is."

"No. No one knows. I don't know how to fix it, Mem."

"Start at the beginning."

Nancy explained yesterday's conversation in the waiting room, how she had just told Annie that Victor Mack was not her father, and that Mo had been presented to them. They had not spoken since.

Mem digested the information. She sipped her tea and thought about all of the ramifications while her eyes roamed around the room. Wisdom, well, it wasn't really wisdom, it was common sense, but it came more easily to her if she multi-tasked. So she thought with her right brain and took in all the details of the carriage house suite with her left.

Nancy finally said, "So, you're not speaking to me either?"

Mem smiled and touched Nancy's hand. "I'm sorry, Nancy. I'm a little, well, tired this morning. I was up late and my thinker is a little slow. That's what I'm doing. I'm thinking. But I'm ready, I believe, to offer some insight."

"Please."

"Well, I'm sure a million things are going through Annie's mind. Let's start with the obvious ones. Why didn't you tell her much earlier in her life, did her father know, or perhaps was that the reason her father left. Who is her father, and what were the circumstances surrounding the, um, parentage."

Mem paused. "I'm remembering the few things Annie said about you and her father, Victor. She said that even though he was wealthy, you never asked for support, and that you and Annie, and later Sam and Annie's half-sister, lived frugally. She also said that when she spent those summers with her father, they never spoke of you. However, in those last few months of his life, he told her how much he loved you but he couldn't stay, and how Annie was the best thing that ever happened to him. I believe Annie struggled a bit over the thought that he loved you but he couldn't stay. He never gave a reason."

Nancy had started to cry, silently. She kept her eyes on the cup of tea and tears streamed quietly down her cheeks and into a tissue that had found its way to her hand.

"I'm trying to remember the circumstances in which she told me. I believe it was on the anniversary of his death, that first year, and we drank tea, just as you and I are doing now."

Mem reached over again to touch Nancy's hand. "You have to talk to her, Nancy. You have to answer those questions. And you have to do it without making her wait, or making her have to ask."

Nancy continued to cry and look at her tea. "What good could possibly come of my telling her after all this time?"

Mem sighed and gave the last piece of insight she could offer. "I would actually place a wager that Annie is also wondering if everything that she has, everything that she is, here, in Chelsea, is based on a lie. She may be worried her father was hoodwinked into giving her the family legacy."

Nancy's head snapped up at those last few words. "No! That's not so! Victor knew. He knew he was not Annie's father."

"Then you have to tell her. You have to tell her everything."

Martha was a good cook. Her breakfast was not lavish, but it was a hearty meal of corned beef hash, eggs scrambled with Monterey jack cheese, fresh fruit and rye toast.

Fred had gotten to know Martha well in a short period of time. He was comfortable being honest with her. Little Fred was asleep in the next room with Speckles, who was finally getting the hang of things. When Martha, Georgia and Fred were seated and eating, he decided to go for broke.

"Martha, I've noticed that you don't have the energy to do everything that needs doing around the house, and I've seen no evidence – pictures or anything else – that would tell me you have a family."

"Strange beginning of a conversation, Fred. But you're right. I'm feeling my age, I have a few issues. My husband died a long time ago, and we didn't have kids."

"Well, please listen to me, and if you need time to think about it, take all the time you need. But I have a proposition for you."

Martha said nothing. She and Georgia put down their forks and looked at Fred with questions in their eyes.

"I was thinking that maybe I could pay for some renovations here to your house, make a little suite out of the two guest rooms you have. And maybe Georgia could stay here, pay you rent, whatever you think is fair, and it be more of an apartment situation. You wouldn't have to make breakfast every morning like she was a guest."

He looked at Georgia. "And you would help out, you know, with all the things that need doing in a house, like shopping, cooking, laundry. I'd be willing to maybe pay for daycare or a nursery, or whatever you need for Little Fred, as long as you need it. And I have that old car sitting in the garage. It just needs a good tune-up. You could have it."

"Dad, how can you afford to do that?"

"What did I spend my money on? You didn't go to college, and I'd been saving for that since you were a baby.

That restaurant is a gold mine. Building was paid off years ago, and the folks in town are probably lined up outside the door these few days I've been closed. For whatever reason, they love that stuff I serve up every day."

They both looked at Martha. Martha had said nothing. Her mouth was open in a little "o," and her hand was stuck in the air with a glass of orange juice, midway between the table and her mouth.

She came to attention, put her glass down and looked at Georgia. "What do you think, Georgia? Would you want to stay here?"

"Oh, yes, Martha, I'd love it! If I didn't stay here, I'd be looking for an apartment, and we wouldn't have a yard for Fred to play in. And, well, I'd love to stay here with you, you've been so kind."

"Well, then," said Martha, sitting up straight and looking Fred in the eyes, "I think I know a man that can make a suite out of those two rooms. I'll call him today."

Pete escorted a woman from an interview room and was finally ready to see Annie. Cyril sat with her, bored, because he couldn't go into the interview rooms. Cyril stood up as Pete came in, ready to follow him to wherever the next place was. The next place was Pete's office.

Pete pulled out a plastic evidence bag and showed it to Annie. In it was a purple cloth jewelry bag, covered in cat hair. There was also a beautiful ring and another clump of cat hair. Gray. It looked similar to the wisps of hair that floated continually through her own apartment.

"What's this?"

"Do you recognize it?

"The ring? No. It looks expensive."

"It is. Do you recognize anything else?"

"Well, not that this is the one that I would have had, but I got a little bag like that from Clara, and I gave it to the kids as a toy. It looks like cat hair all over it, and that's kind of the look the toys get at my house. Gee, Pete, are you asking me if that's my bag?"

"I know it's a stretch, but what you're saying is that it could be, right?"

"Right. But who would come into my apartment, steal a hair-covered bag and put an expensive ring into it? That doesn't make any sense."

"I'll tell you what doesn't make any sense. You know we've had some burglaries in town, and a ring like this was on the inventory of stolen items. I've checked with the owner, and she said yes, that's her ring, but she doesn't know where the bag came from, and she doesn't have pets."

"So…a burglar stole the ring, put it into a bag with hair, you found it, and you wanted me to look at it because…"

"Because while we were investigating the murder at the gem show, Cyril insisted I look into a paper sack, wouldn't move until I had, and that's where I found this."

"And again, what does this have to do with me?"

"It was Dwight's booth. He's a guest at the Inn."

"But it doesn't mean that Dwight…"

"I have a fingerprint from the ring, and I took fingerprints from, well, never mind, but I have his fingerprints. Once we confirm the prints match we'll know for certain he's involved with the burglaries."

Annie looked at Pete. Pete looked at Annie.

"Pete, do you have any idea how many hours of sleep I haven't had?"

"Probably about the same number as me."

"What are you saying?"

"I'm saying…I'm saying that our kids are at it again. I think your cats found this ring, put it in the bag, got it to the gem show, put it in the sack, and got Cyril to tell me where it was."

Annie stared for a few seconds more. Then she started to laugh. She laughed so hard she couldn't breathe. Tears ran down her face, she covered her mouth, leaned back and forth in her chair, and she finally leaned forward, elbows on her knees and face in her hands, until she got it under control.

Pete sat back in his chair and watched.

Annie continued to choke up with a laugh every now and then while she wiped her eyes and blew her nose. It was a good thing Pete kept a box of tissues on his desk.

"Pete. Do you have any idea how hard this week has been on me? Do you know what I've been through? No, forget that. No one knows. Only me. Even Chris doesn't…oh, forget it."

Pete continued to lean back in his chair and looked at her. Finally, he cracked as well. He laughed as Annie had laughed, and she got going again.

In between bouts of laughter, he said, "I have to go home with you and collect evidence."

She responded when she could. "Evidence?"

Pete couldn't stop laughing. "Cat hair. We have to do a DNA test."

By now, Cyril was barking, and Marco stuck his head in to make sure everything was alright. Pete waved him off, and he and Annie tried to pull themselves together.

25

Gema spend the day exploring Chelsea. She started with the shops on the other side of The Avenue. She had seen and talked with all of the business owners in the last few days, as everyone had come to the show.

Gema's Creations carried the kind of jewelry admired by all the women on The Avenue. She found them easy to talk to and helpful when it came to finding possibilities for a storefront.

Most of them said the same thing. Talk to a realtor named Greg. He'll lead you in the right direction. Stay away from…and they listed realtors that would do everything to make a sale and nothing to help Gema.

And the jungle drums beat like wildfire up and down the street.

Mem, back in her shop for the afternoon, waved Gema in from the sidewalk. "I hear you're looking in earnest for a storefront."

"Yes. Everyone on The Avenue tells me I should talk to a realtor named Greg."

"And you should. If you were going to get a storefront of your own."

"What?"

"Sit down. Let's have tea."

Annie spent an hour in the apartment. She was tired. She was torn. She had to think about her life, where to go from here. Everything she thought she knew about herself was a lie. Everything she now owned, she owned because of a lie.

Maybe Howard was right. Maybe she should sell everything, move, start over again, some place where no one would know her. Except the cats.

Yes, the cats had to come. And Chris. Henrie. All her friends.

Well, this was getting her nowhere.

Tonight she wore a dress she had owned for a couple of years. It was black, slinky and short. She lay on the floor next to the tent, one hand inside the enclosure, holding Mo's paw. Mo slept, but he let her know he knew she was there by continually flexing his paw into her two fingers. She returned the flexes.

Mr. Bean lay on top of her chest, sound asleep.

Kali and Ko cuddled, one beside the other, in between Annie and Mo's tent.

Little Socks slept on top of one knee; Sassy Pants was on top of the other. And they didn't fight.

Tiger Lily curled into her shoulder, the one on the opposite side from the tent.

Tears ran from Annie's eyes to the floor on both sides of her face. Except for the tears that Tiger Lily caught on her paw.

This was how Chris found her. He wore a black suit with an open-collared lavender shirt. He lay down beside her on the floor and held the hand that wasn't in the tent. They stayed this way for several minutes, not saying a word.

Chris finally spoke. "We're going to be late. I think Cookie is counting on you."

"I know."

"Do you want to let the kids come tonight?"

"Maybe a few of them. I don't want Mo to wake up alone. Maybe Kali and Ko can stay with him."

"Okay."

He waited. She made no move to get up.

"I'm going to get up now. You?"

"Okay."

He waited a little more, then rolled to his feet. Standing, he reached down and took both her hands. She stood with him and they spent several minutes getting cat hair off one another.

Annie took a deep breath and said, "Okay. Everyone but Kali, Ko and Mo. Let's go."

Annie and Chris had a reserved table at the back of the room, where they could see everything. The restaurant was already buzzing. It appeared several tables had already turned at least one time.

The menu was the same today as yesterday, giving Cookie and staff time to settle in. It would not change until next week.

When Nancy and Sam came in, Chris started to wave them over, but Annie stopped him. He looked at her, confused, and then watched Nancy request a four-top table in another corner. She seated herself with her back to Annie and Chris

"Okay. This was going on last night. I don't know what it is, and I'm not sure when it started, but I'm beginning to wonder if you're ever going to tell me about it."

"Tell you about what?"

Chris rolled his eyes and concentrated on his menu card.

It wasn't long before Mem and Frank came in. They waved at Chris and Annie as they walked over to join Nancy and Sam.

Chris and Annie took their time with dinner. They saw and greeted many of the same people that had come for the grand opening. Annie figured they were either giving it a second chance, or they had actually liked it before mayhem and murder took place. Or maybe they hoped to get another show tonight.

Several of the boaters were here tonight, and lots of local folks that had not been present at the grand opening. Annie knew some of them, but not all.

Geraldine, her husband and Hank came in mid-evening. They were seated at the table next to Annie and Chris.

Geraldine slipped into her chair, using her right hand in an obvious gesture so Chris and Annie would see the sparkle and shine of a nearly six thousand dollar ring on her finger. Annie also noticed the matching necklace. Another six thousand or so.

She turned to Annie and said, "Oh, hello," as if she had just noticed them.

Annie, whose typical response would be a sweet one, pouring honey on all wounds, could barely smile tonight.

Geraldine turned back to her table, a little miffed that she was not granted the esteem she was due.

Chris was beginning to worry about Annie, but now, with Geraldine so close, was not the time to broach the subject.

Then he saw them. The media. The same newspapers and television stations from the night before. Cameras were setting up outside, and reporters were coming in, looking around, looking, looking, until they saw Annie.

They descended.

"Ms. Mack! Ms. Mack! Do you have a statement?"

"Can you give us a statement?"

"What do you have to say to the allegations?"

"Is it true your restaurants will be closing?"

"Will this restaurant be closing?"

"And the Inn? Will it close as well?"

Chris moved his chair to put himself in between Annie and the media hoard, and soon he was joined by Mem, Frank, Nancy and Sam. Nancy and Mem took Annie by the arms and escorted her to the back stairwell while Chris, Frank and Sam held the reporters at bay.

When they got to the second floor, Mem locked the stairwell door behind her and used her elevator key – given to her to use during the gem show – to shut down the elevator.

They were safe.

But they weren't alone. In seconds, they were joined by Tiger Lily, Little Socks, Sassy Pants and Mr. Bean.

Annie sank to the floor, surrounded by her cats, and cried like she had never cried before.

Mem and Nancy let her be. They stayed at the ticket table, still set up and ready for tomorrow morning, the last day of the gem show.

The cats stayed at Annie's side, cuddled into her body.

When the restaurant finally closed and the media left, assuming Annie had slipped away, Annie went downstairs to the kitchen.

Cookie's elbows were on the prep table and he stood, head in hands, slumped in defeat. Annie looked around. All of her managers were here. In the kitchen. They had been waiting for her.

"Cookie, I'm so sorry. I don't know what that was all about."

"Annie, everyone here knows you didn't have anything to do with it. I just don't know if I should open tomorrow."

"How did you do tonight?"

Felicity said, "I just ran the receipts. We did really well. Better than we planned for tonight, and we were full almost all night. Even after the media came, no one walked away."

"Did anyone hear what it was all about?"

"I did."

Chris, Sam and Frank had come into the kitchen, followed by Mem and Nancy. Bringing up the rear was Annie's attorney, Jenny Howe.

Unnoticed by everyone, which was a good thing, because they weren't supposed to be in the kitchen, were four cats.

Everyone turned to Sam, who had spoken. "I buttonholed one of those newspaper reporters. Well, I bribed one of them. He wouldn't talk, otherwise. He said some guy from the Governor's office sent a press release to every state media outlet with this story. He gave me a copy of the email."

Sam handed it to Chris, who read it out loud.

"Recently, prominent Chelsea business owner Annie Mack has come under fire for substandard business practices. On Thursday of this week, several state and federal agencies descended upon her businesses to investigate complaints of wrong-doing. Those investigations are not yet complete, but all indications are that Ms. Mack will be forced to close her businesses, as she will be unable to bring them into compliance within a reasonable time frame."

Jenny walked over to Chris. "Let me take this, Chris."

She read it, read the name of the sender, and looked at Annie. "It's the same name. This is the guy in the pocket of someone here in Chelsea, probably Howard. Are you ready to fight now?"

Annie looked up. She felt the weight of defeat. She looked at Cookie. "Are we open for business tomorrow night?"

Cookie stood to his full height.

"We're going to be on fire tomorrow night! I dare anyone to get in my way!"

Annie looked at Jenny. "I'm ready to fight."

Chris raised his eyebrows. "Really? You said the words, but it didn't sound as if you meant them."

Annie looked around the room, at this, her staff, who had stuck with her through every upheaval. She looked at her good friends Mem and Frank, at her Mom and Sam. Then she looked at Chris.

Her strength began to wax gibbous. She stood taller, squared her shoulders, raised her head, looked Jenny square in the face and said, "I'm ready."

26

Gema woke to a brand new day. It was Saturday. She and everyone else would leave this afternoon. They had been granted a late check-out time so they could pack up their products before leaving.

The moon was no longer full; it was waning gibbous. She had heard so much about the moon since arriving in this town, she rejoiced with everyone else about the end of this season of angst.

She entered the dining room to find Dwight, Garry and Nelson fawning over the breakfast. It was disgusting! Henrie, for some reason unbeknownst to mankind, served scrambled eggs with chopped hot dogs, white bread toast with strawberry jam, coffee and orange juice.

The men were digging in. "Henrie, great breakfast!"

Gema said, "Um, I'll grab a muffin at the bakery after yoga."

At the yoga studio, she thanked Diana for the great morning workouts.

"I don't often have the opportunity to take yoga classes during a show."

"Where are you going next?"

"Oh, you know. Tomorrow is another day. We'll be in another town. Somewhere. Gadzooks, I need to get out of this rat race!"

Gema went to the show to rack up one half day of sales, then pack it up and move on.

She said good morning to Mem and Janet, who seemed glad to be in the final hours of the show. She looked at Martin's booth every now and then. The tables were still set up but everything was covered with tarps, secured at the floor with a heavy rope tied around the section.

There was no evidence of a murder, but the elephant was still in the room. She tried, but she couldn't pull up any feelings of grief over the man or regret for his passing.

Adam and Dwight seemed to be in great spirits. They spent most of the morning ignoring customers and walking around, talking to other exhibitors. Dwight had boxes behind his exhibit, looking like he was ready to pack up. That was unusual. His three minions always took care of that. Maybe they couldn't stay for some reason.

Nelson and Kristina seemed to be getting along today, but they always did on the last day of a show. Curious. Or maybe not.

Pattie seemed to cry at the drop of a pin.

Gema floated on air. After her conversation with Mem the morning before, she had conversations with a few other people, and a plan was coming together. It wasn't time to tell anyone yet, most of all Garry. She didn't want him to think he could tag along.

Speaking of Garry, he was in high spirits, too. He seemed to know something Gema did not. It probably had to do with that sneaky media trick that was played on Annie last night. The coverage this morning was outrageous.

Gema packed as she had time. She put her orders for custom-made pieces and the few pieces she had sold on lay-away in the case that would go with her in the front seat of the car. Everything that was on paper and not already on her digital system went there as well, including receipts, new contacts and her journal.

She packed up the pieces that weren't showing as well in Chelsea and left the "good stuff" where last minute customers could see them clearly.

Gema watched as Geraldine entered and walked to Garry's display. She didn't even look at Gema. It appeared the partnership no longer trusted her. Just as well. She didn't want anything to do with any of them. But, she cautioned herself, perhaps she couldn't afford to make an enemy of Geraldine. Not if there was a chance she could return to Chelsea. And to her own store!

Gema did a double take. Geraldine had on that ring. If rumors were to be believed, she and her husband couldn't afford to pay their mortgage, much less buy that ring.

But there it was, on Geraldine's right hand. Funny. She had never noticed how Geraldine spoke using that right hand before. Now, it appeared every sentence was augmented by a wave to or fro of that highly ornamented hand.

Gema turned back to her work with a laugh. She had every reason to believe the ring was a fake. She looked up as Geraldine left, carrying a bag with several jewelry boxes.

Annie, amazed at Henrie's breakfast offering, reacted somewhat along the lines of Gema. "Um, I think I'll have breakfast out. Somewhere. Maybe Mr. Bean's."

Nancy entered the dining room. "Ugh. Henrie, what happened to you today?"

Henrie smiled. "The male members of the rock and gem show loved it." He went back to the kitchen.

Annie and Nancy looked at one another. Nancy sighed. "Come on, dear. Let's go out to breakfast and have a long-overdue conversation. My treat. As long as it's the Café. I need sustenance."

Annie touched her mother's hand. "Let's go."

Tiger Lily was at the hostess stand when they arrived. Annie thought she looked positively radiant. As radiant as a cat can be. The place was packed. Tiger Lily had lots of customers to greet. She was in her element.

It always seemed that bad publicity brought in a crowd. They came in looking for something. Turtles in the soup, dead bodies hanging from the ceiling, kidnappers getting ready to nab some unsuspecting yacht captain or cat.

Today was no exception.

And as always, whenever something bad happened, Geraldine was front and center. She sat with her husband, Hank and Howard. She talked with that right hand, waving it back and forth with that gauche ring.

Annie smiled to herself. They were a happy group this morning. They wouldn't be happy for long.

Annie and Nancy sat as far from that table as they could and ordered two breakfast specials: southwestern egg casserole with Texas toast and fresh strawberries on the side.

Tiger Lily, torn about doing her duty on this busy morning and listening in on Mommy's and Grandmommy's conversation, went for the important thing. She followed them and curled into a ball on top of the table. They would think she was asleep, but she wouldn't miss a word.

To this point, the women had not talked. Then Annie said, softly, "I want to thank you for what you did for Mo, and what you did for me last night."

"You're welcome." Nancy took a deep breath. "Now let's get to the hard part."

Nancy reached over to take Annie's hand.

"First of all, your father, Victor, knew he was not your biological father. He always knew."

"He knew?"

"Yes. Your biological father, his name was Darrell, was a college friend of your father. Actually, he introduced your father and me. Darrell and I had dated a while in our high school days, but we hadn't dated for a long time when your father came to town to visit, and, well, your father and I fell in love and married. He, Victor, always wanted to come back here, but I didn't want to leave my home town. Oh, the times I have regretted that. But there came a time that he had to come back here, because his father was ill, and he was gone for a couple of months. There was no reason I couldn't come with him, but I didn't. I can't tell you why. Maybe I thought I would like it and there would be no excuse not to move. I was a silly young woman. But he was gone, and I was young, and Darrell came around one night. One thing led to another, and, well, there you go."

Nancy was silent for a time. Annie didn't say anything, waiting for the story to pick up again.

Nancy took a deep breath and started again. "Well, as you know, there is no hiding the date of conception. When your father got back, I was a couple of weeks late, and I knew. I knew deep in my heart that my mistake would be known soon. So I told him. I told him right away. It was hard, those months, being pregnant, the two of us unable to talk to one another. And knowing it was his friend. Well, that didn't last very long. They never spoke again. I don't know if Darrell ever knew he had fathered a child. Shortly before you were born, he died in a car accident."

Annie's breath came quickly. She forced herself to breathe.

"That was a tragedy, frankly. Your father had not spoken to him in months, and there were things he would have liked to say to Darrell. And yes, your cheekbones are from him. He was one quarter Cherokee."

"Cherokee."

"Yes. But let's get back to your father. I think he was ambivalent during my pregnancy, but that stopped the moment he saw you. He loved you. And he still loved me. But he couldn't stay. There was a piece of him that could never forgive me for what I had done, and, well, you know the rest. He moved back here, took over the family business. You came here every summer. He and I never spoke, unless it regarded you."

"Why didn't you tell me?"

"This is something we discussed, your father and I. Neither of us saw the point. Victor loved you, he considered himself to be your father, the law viewed him as your father, and your biological father would never have an opportunity to interfere, if he would ever have wanted to. Now, of course, I realize it would be important for you to know if you were to ever have children, or if some medical emergency arose and it was expedient to know your background. I've thought a lot about it these last couple of days, and I wrote down everything I could remember about Darrell and his family. No one is left now. He was an only child and his parents are long gone. But, I wrote down what I know, and if you ever want to investigate, at least you'll have a starting point."

There. It was done. Nancy had said what needed to be said and Annie had the information she needed. The relationship between Annie and Nancy would still need time and attention, but at least they could move forward.

Pete had his hands full.

First, there were the burglaries. He had some information to go on, as well as some compelling evidence against Dwight, but nothing that could be used to get a warrant.

Pete had first suspected Ramon for the burglaries. He conducted a preliminary investigation, focusing on the towns Ramon's band had been booked and incidents of burglary similar to those in Chelsea. The email he received combining the two was interesting.

There were times that Ramon had been in towns where similar burglaries occurred. There were also incidents of burglary without Ramon's apparent presence and incidents of his presence without similar burglaries. In all, there was not enough to even question him.

Then Cyril pointed him to Dwight. Pete did a similar search linking the rock and gem show to similar burglaries. That lead was solid. In every town in which the show had been booked, residential burglaries focusing on expensive jewelry occurred on two or three days of the show.

Pete's problems were two-fold. One problem was that Dwight was accounted for during the time of the burglaries. The other was his inability to get a warrant based on a dog's instinct and cat hair.

Pete decided to solve this problem by turning his research over to the State Police. Pete would not be able to put anything together before Dwight left town. He held onto the ring, however. He didn't quite know how to explain that piece of evidence.

Second, the arson that caused injury from the grand opening was an open case. He had a missing suspect and, at the moment, no motive.

Marco had done some digging on the missing employee, Ed, who apparently threw kerosene and a packet of lighted matches onto the grill. He was from a town two counties east of Chelsea. He sometimes visited his uncle who owned a B&B in town, the Sunset Breeze. The uncle's name was Howard. The B&B was in a place where the sunset couldn't be seen and a breeze couldn't be found.

Marco interviewed Howard and learned nothing of substance. He thought Howard appeared nervous, but that could just mean he was worried about the family connection. In a throwaway note at the bottom of Marco's report, Pete learned that Howard was the president of Chelsea's B&B association.

Third. Murder. Pete was working his way through witnesses, but he wasn't sure he would be ready for an arrest before the gem show folks left town. He worked with Janet's relationship chart and focused on the individuals for whom she had made darker marks to and from Martin.

The first was Adam. Based on the time of death, Adam could have committed the murder then gone to the Bon Vivant Grille for the grand opening. Besides an obvious dislike, he could find no reason for murder. During his interview of Adam and the interviews he made about him, he learned the two had never gotten along.

Martin's exhibit was a polished one. His display cases were made of wood and glass; expensive items were locked behind the glass; and all of his pieces, individual stones, jewelry and carvings, were, using the same word, polished. His prices were higher than Adam's, but his efforts in maintaining his stock probably demanded it.

Adam's exhibit was sloppy, dirty and disheveled, like the man himself. He put no money into his displays. Even though his prices were lower, his profits were higher.

To look at the two men, however, Martin appeared to be more successful. Adam pretended not to care. He was confident in the quality of his products, even though his customers generally had to clean off their purchases once they got home.

Adam made no secret of his dislike for the man, but, as he said to Pete, "If I was gonna murder someone, don't ya think I would try to get myself an alibi? I didn't know I would need one. I'm not your man."

The second was Garry. Like Adam, there was no specific reason Pete could find for Garry to commit murder. He had an obvious dislike of Martin, but the two didn't compete for customers. Martin sold stones and marketed them using the properties they had for healing or connection with a higher spirit. Garry sold fine jewelry.

During the interview, Garry veered from answering the question to expounding on his elegant designs and the flawless gems used in their creation. "I had no reason to kill the man, Chief. The few pieces of jewelry he sold didn't hold a candle to mine!"

Garry's alibi was that he spent the earlier part of the evening with Dwight and Gema at the Inn, and they walked to the grand opening together. Even though Garry's alibi was solid, making a good one for Dwight and Gema as well, Pete continued his interviews.

He learned that Dwight, while he overtly did nothing to or against Martin, made sure to keep Martin's booth around a corner from his so he didn't have to look at the man. This came out in a variety of interviews.

Pete was careful to stay away from the burglaries when he interviewed Dwight, but he had to ask about the mysterious three men. The three men mentioned in the relationship chart that supposedly traveled with Dwight. They could have been involved in the burglaries or the murder.

Dwight said he didn't know anything about three men and that someone must be making this stuff up. Pete couldn't pin Dwight down, and he had an alibi, so he moved on to Gema.

Pete liked Gema, but he knew better than to allow his personal feelings to interfere in the process. Gema, of course, had an alibi, but he wanted to find out about her prior relationship with Martin.

He pushed. Gema demurred. He pushed harder. Gema got defensive. Then he said, "I heard you dumped Martin and Pattie had to pick up the pieces. A few people talked about that. Come on, Gema. You've got to tell someone. Tell me. I'm nicer than the other guys you'll have to talk to."

Pete did not expect what happened next. Gema burst into tears. It was quite a while before she was able to talk to him, but when she did, it was about a love story gone bad.

"I was in love with him. He said he would marry me. I was so young and so careless. I got pregnant, and he dropped me. I keep hearing, over and over and over, how I dropped him, but it was the other way around. I left the circuit for a year, had the baby, put her up for adoption, and thought I could move on. But I didn't know where to go or what to do, so I came back to my jewelry and these blasted shows."

Gema paused to blow her nose and wipe her eyes. She took a deep breath. "I hated him. I hated him for years. But that was just a drain on my energy and my creativity. I finally gave my problems to God, and, well, I was able to go on. If you were to press me about it, I guess I still hate him. But I didn't murder him. You already know where I was."

Pete, gathering information about Martin, learned some interesting things about Pattie. Since Martin stayed at the Sunset Breeze, Pete interviewed Howard. Howard surmised Pattie might be a stalker. She made her reservation at the Sunset Breeze after Martin made his. He thought she seemed to know that Martin would be there.

The relationship chart had a darker line from Pattie to Martin, so Pattie was on his list. She cried throughout the interview. Not in the same way as Gema. Pattie cried like a woman who never got to first base.

She wailed, "I couldn't have killed him! I loved him! I still do!"

Pattie had a verified alibi. She spent an hour or so at Sassy P's with Nelson and Kristina before walking to the grand opening.

Pete questioned everyone from the rock and gem show and got little more than a confirmation that Janet's relationship chart was fairly accurate. No one liked the man, but no one had an obvious reason to want him dead.

Almost everyone knew about the three men, except, of course, Dwight, but no one knew who they were or how to locate them. Gema had first names, but nothing else.

Several told Pete to show up after everybody else left the show. The three men would pack up Dwight's gear then. That didn't happen this week. On the last day of the show, Dwight packed his own gear for perhaps the first time. He seemed to be a fish out of water as he tried to pack products into the boxes that came with him. He needed to go to storefront after storefront, begging for more empty boxes.

Pete had to question George and Candice and Felicity. Those interviews were…well…Pete was glad he could mark them off his list of suspects because they were at work.

In the course of running background investigations, he learned a few things that made him revisit three people. Gema, Adam and Dwight. And then he learned the alibi crafted by Gema, Garry and Dwight didn't hold water. They were seen together at the Inn, but others saw Garry at Sassy P's with Geraldine before he went to the grand opening. No one saw Dwight or Gema.

For some reason, Garry had lied for Dwight and Gema. Upon further questioning, neither Dwight nor Gema could give him a plausible explanation for the lie. Nor could they give him alibis that could be verified.

Cyril tried several times during the day to point Pete toward Adam and Dwight for the murder. Cyril had not been near enough to the body to get a whiff of the murder weapon. He chastised himself for that mistake. But he knew what the cats had seen. Adam and Dwight, in Cyril's mind, were the persons of interest.

At the end of the day, when Pete leaned back in his chair and talked to himself, Cyril was upset to learn Pete might be going off-track. Due to the lack of alibi and possible motive, Adam and Dwight were still persons of interest, but Pete's number one suspect was now Gema.

27

Jenny Howe was to meet two people at the Bon Vivant Grille this evening, her friend, the Lieutenant Governor, and an especially invited person from the Governor's office.

The Lieutenant Governor had a particular dislike for the Governor's Chief of Staff. She made an offer the Chief of Staff could not refuse. Come to Chelsea with me for the evening to have dinner at the now infamous, if only in its third outing, Bon Vivant Grille. Let's talk about your future in the Governor's Office.

The Chief of Staff had no legitimate reason to say no and every reason to say yes, as the Lieutenant Governor would in all likelihood be the next Governor.

On their way to Chelsea, a drive of about an hour and a half, they sat in the back seat of the limousine and talked about current news, including the last two days' coverage of several businesses in Chelsea. The Lieutenant Governor was not worried, of course, even though horrible things were being said about Tiger Lily's Café and the Bon Vivant Grille. She had a very good friend – "who will be joining us this evening" – who had nothing but the wildest praise for the establishment.

Howard had reason to rejoice. Soon, Annie's businesses would be his! He called to make reservations at Bon Vivant for himself and his wife, Geraldine and her husband, and Hank, who said he would bring a date. Howard had to wonder who would stoop to dating Hank.

Neither Geraldine nor Hank had anted up for the venture. Hank may have to be dropped from the partnership, but Geraldine assured him just this morning she would have cash in hand shortly.

Howard chuckled again to think of the footage run during the news. All day long he was able to watch as Annie ran from the cameras, out of sight and probably up those stairs. The look on her face before she got away was priceless.

Annie almost didn't want to go, but she had been told of Howard's large reservation. There was no way she would miss it. And Jenny had been in touch. She had been successful in getting her friend and her friend's enemy to come.

Annie made another large reservation for her, Chris, Nancy and Sam, Henrie, Pete and Janet, Cheryl – Ray was still on his cruise – Mem and Frank, Clara and Ramon, and Laila.

This would be priceless. She wanted her friends to have front-row seats.

Annie and the cats, minus Kali, Ko and Mo again, arrived early. She wanted to be able to see everyone enter, and she wanted a clear view of the tables. Trudie and Felicity were putting the finishing touches on her table as she arrived.

"You've got the best seat in the house. We'll all be waiting for the show to start."

Tiger Lily ran to each of the tables set up for reservations. Finding everything in good order, eventually she went to the hostess stand to join her siblings. Fiamma and Cyril would be here tonight, and she had invited Tillie to come if she could, and Fat Cat and Scaredy Cat.

She needn't have worried. Carlos, Jerry, Teresa, Holly and Jolly and Diana came in at about the same time and asked Felicity to put some tables together for them. Tillie and the cats came with them.

Chris arrived and ordered a bottle of wine to share before dinner. He sat with Annie and listened intently as she told him what her mother had said this morning. They were so intent on the conversation, they didn't notice Howard arrive.

When they heard Geraldine, they looked up. Howard and his wife were seated at their table. Geraldine stormed in, Everett trailing behind. Geraldine had something in her hand. It looked like she wanted to throw it, but she couldn't find an appropriate target.

"That man! I went to the Inn to find him and he had already checked out. He's gone, I tell you! Gone! And to think I was going to give that store to him! We were going to cut Gema out! But now he's a rat and the rat is gone!"

Annie checked her phone. Sure enough, Henrie had sent a text. She opened it to read that Geraldine had arrived looking for Garry, saying something about a piece-of-trash ring. Annie hid a smile behind her hand and passed the phone to Chris.

"Aren't you glad you didn't buy that ring for me? I know you thought about it."

"Did not."

"Did too."

By now, Geraldine had calmed down somewhat. She was in public. She had to maintain her composure. She sat next to Howard and leaned in. Annie could hear Howard's voice but not Geraldine's.

"What? What do you mean you've got no money? ... You have a stake in this ... He has to give you something valuable ... That woman had money ... Why can't we work with her?"

Juanita, a reporter for the Marsh Haven daily newspaper showed up, met Annie's eyes and nodded slightly. She took a seat close to the door and got out her cell phone. She appeared to read some posts.

The door opened and Jenny appeared, followed by her friend, the Lieutenant Governor, and her friend's enemy, the Governor's Chief of Staff. They were shown directly to their reserved table. The path took them past Howard's table.

Howard looked up in surprise; the Chief of Staff looked down in surprise; Juanita was up, clicking away with her cell phone's camera.

They kept walking. When they reached the table, Jenny and the Lieutenant Governor sat down. Jenny slid a piece of paper out of her purse and handed it to her friend, who read it carefully, pretending to be seeing it for the first time.

As the Chief of Staff started to sit, he was stopped by the Lieutenant Governor. "I think you won't be joining us after all, Gene. This is an interesting press release; it came from your email account. I think you can just go over there and sit with your friends."

Juanita continued to click away, getting as close to the table as she could for the best possible recording from the microphone.

"What?"

"I said sit with your friends. The Governor sends his regrets that he is unable to terminate your employment in person. Your office has been cleaned out by now. Stop by the office of the Capital Police to pick up your personal items. Any time after 8:00 Monday. And your email account, computer access and key cards have been terminated."

"You can't do this!"

"This conversation is over. You can probably call someone to pick you up, or maybe your friend Howard can return you to the capital. Frankly, Gene, I don't care how you get back."

Juanita continued to click and record, click and record, moving the camera to Howard's table, catching he and Geraldine together in some very unflattering poses.

One of those was the lead photo in the next morning's paper. And several other papers and television studios and online news reporting outlets.

Juanita had a surprising amount of information, including statements from the state and federal agencies that conducted investigations and an interview already given by the Lieutenant Governor on the unfortunate circumstances leading to the loss of the Chief of Staff's job. There was even a statement from the Governor disavowing any knowledge of his now former Chief of Staff's activities in this regard and a promise to file an ethics complaint for the use of state email to send false information.

Included in the coverage was another story, one that spoke of a lawsuit to be filed Monday against Geraldine, Hank and Howard, and an application for restraining orders against all parties. In the application, and in this article, were included previous grievances against Geraldine and Hank, none of which had resulted in findings of criminal fault.

Yes. Annie was done being nice. Now she was in a fight and she was in it to win.

Annie had asked Juanita for one more favor. For a free meal, she conducted an honest review of the Bon Vivant Grille. With the exception of a server not refilling her glass of water quickly enough, the review was outstanding.

Yes, Cookie was on fire! In that separate article, the stringer included a photo of Cookie standing behind the hostess stand and a very proud Tiger Lily.

Of course, crowded on the hostess stand with her were Mr. Bean, Sassy Pants, Oscar McMurphy and Simon Finnegan. Even Little Socks jumped up for the photo opportunity. The tip of her tail was cut off of the photo, but otherwise, she pronounced it excellent.

28

Sunday was a lazy day at the Inn. Even Fred Calendar was gone; he went home to open his restaurant. He planned to hire a manager so he could come to Chelsea to visit every now and then. Chris had stayed the night. He was up early to purchase a number of newspapers to pass around. Henrie set out pastries from the Confectionary and made coffee. Sam and Nancy came over to eat, read the paper and watch the news stories, for once, positive about Annie and her businesses.

"Thank goodness everyone is closed today, or we would be mobbed. By tomorrow, we'll be into the next news cycle and it won't be such a big deal."

When they walked to church, followed by all of the cats, Annie had Mo in a carrier. He was anxious to get out, but it wasn't time yet. This would be a full-church Sunday for Teresa. The day was clear, bright and headed toward a glorious seventy degrees. The sidewalks on both sides were filled with people walking to services, from all of the buildings on The Avenue, the campground and The Marina.

Following services, several people stopped on the meridian, happy to be outside on such a pretty day. That's where they were when they saw it.

The Escape. Maybe it was The Escape. It was the same shape as The Escape. And someone looking awfully like Ray was at the wheel waving his arms at the crowd on the median. But the boat itself?

It was painted in rainbow colors. Everything. The hull, everything on the deck. Everything. All of Annie's

SASHET colors were there. First, there were looks of amazement, then laughter, then cheers. What a sight.

Of course, Ray and Cheryl joined their friends for a Famous Avenue Pot Luck Dinner that evening to tell them about the make-over. Claire and Honey Bear joined them that evening, to the sadness of Mo. He watched, dejected, from a tent, as Claire made googly eyes with his uncle. And the lovely Fiamma was there, much to the delight of the big boys.

The story was simple. The crew arrived, having made a down payment, but they didn't have enough cash – or enough on their combined cards – to pay for the cruise. Ray made a deal. He would take them out, and they could play in ports along the way on Friday and Saturday night, but they had to paint the boat. All day, every day. Friday, Saturday and most of Sunday.

Jock shared the story with his friends at the same time. To hear him tell it – mostly to the lovely Fiamma – he was a hero. He kept them working by nipping heels if necessary, or carrying a thermos of water if he felt compassionate. According to Jock, that didn't happen often.

Fiamma was duly impressed. Cyril snorted. The cats and Tillie tried very hard to keep from laughing.

Honey Bear, in a tentative admission that he was not all-powerful, said, *"You all have such great adventures. I would like to get outside once in a while."*

Claire, curled up next to him, agreed. *"But I don't know where I'd like to go first. You talk about so many places."*

Honey Bear nodded thoughtfully. *"If we break out once, they'll never let it happen again. The first time will be the last. It has to be great, if we can figure out how to do it."*

Fiamma ventured an opinion. *"If you get out, you have to go to the lighthouse."*

"How do we do that?"

"Get out to the beach. Then, once you get the lighthouse in view, you can see where the path is to get out to it."

Honey Bear and Clair looked at one another, then looked at Tiger Lily.

"You can help, right?"

Tiger Lily smiled. *"I have a plan."*

29

Gema was finally able to take a break from the toddler's play area. She left the park area behind the Café and walked around to The Avenue. The street was still filled with people of all ages. Blocked for traffic, animals and children could safely walk the street. And they were certainly doing that, with adult children as well.

Bergamasco had just come off a break and was doing a cover of Wes Montgomery's "Four On Six." Gema saw Annie and Chris at a game table on the median. There was room to sit. She asked if she could join them and of course, they said yes.

Gema looked at the necklace. Yes, she had done some excellent work. They turned out just as she had envisioned, and Chris couldn't have been happier.

"It's beautiful, Gema. I can't believe how well you matched the ring. I can't wait to get that back."

"I hear the guy is going to go for a plea bargain. Maybe you'll get it soon."

"Everyone's agreed to it but the Judge. As soon as that signature is on whatever it needs to go on, I'm headed for that evidence locker! How is the shop coming along?"

"We're almost finished, believe it or not. This is coming together pretty quickly. It helps to know the owner of a B&B that can put you up for a while."

"Did you decide on the mirrors?"

"Yes. Frank was afraid it would look like a bordello, but I showed him some mirrors with gold and silver designs throughout. It will look classy, and I'll have the effect I want, making the shop look bigger."

"This is going to be as good for Frank as it is for you."

"And Frank has been so helpful. He already had some antique display cases that really set off my products. They're in his shop for repair right now. We'll be able to move them down early next week. I'm going to have to make jewelry to fill the cases. I've never had to have so much product before."

"Will you be done in time for the grand opening?"

"It may be a little light, but still, like I said, it will be more product than I've ever had."

"You'll get that morning sun to set off your corner, so it will be light and bright before the heat of the day. That will be helpful."

"Yes, it will. Oh, I see Greg. I need to ask him about my house."

Greg was working one of the food booths for the Rotary Club. He had enlisted the help of almost all of the members for this charity event. He was also in the middle of making a deal so Gema could move out of the Inn and into a small home of her own.

As Gema left, Clara joined them. "Wow. Did you buy this for her, Chris? Because I know her taste isn't that good. And by the way, how is it that we can bring our drinks outside today. I thought that wasn't legal."

"We got the wet zone permit we requested. They refused it at first, but after the alcohol folks got a close look at our operations, they revisited the application and approved it. We can't let anyone take drinks off The Avenue. They can go anywhere as long as they stay inside the police barricades."

They chatted for a while until Clara finally asked, "So what do you think about the band?"

"They are fantastic."

"And what do you think about Ramon."

"The same. Fantastic. What do you think about him?"

"I asked him to move in."

"What? How long have you known him?"

"We aren't children, Annie. We've both been around the block a time or two. We know when we've found something special."

"And this is special?"

"Yes. Special."

"So, what did he say?"

"He said I need to consider his schedule, that he is here, then he's not, and that's how he makes his money. He wants to know that I can handle it. And all the stuff that comes with being in a band, like women flirting and, well, doing more than flirting."

"The question is, does he flirt back?"

"No."

"Can you live with that?"

"I don't know. Right now, when we're together, it's good, and when we aren't, I still have my life here, and he has his life. I don't know what it's going to take for me to figure it out."

"You have time. It sounds like he wants you to take the time to make the right decision."

Chris said, "It seems like he and Fiamma would always be welcome here. She and the boys – and Tillie – are great friends now."

"Thank goodness everyone is fixed."

Chris looked up at the apartment above Mo's Tap. "George and Candice are back. Were they gone for a week?"

Annie shielded her eyes to look in that direction. "No. Just a few days, really. They left Monday morning. Thank goodness Georgia started working for us. She handled that bar like a pro."

Clara waved her arm and yelled, "Get down here!"

Candice returned her wave and in minutes, they were downstairs and on the median.

Clara leaned in close to Annie. "Look at that left hand."

Annie looked and broke into a smile. When they reached the table, Annie got up and gave George a hug, then Candice. "So, what is it? An engagement? A pre-engagement? A promise that maybe you'll think about engagement?"

George reddened. "We skipped over all that. We got married."

"What?"

Clara ran to the bandstand at the end of The Avenue. She waited until the song was over, then got up on the stage and went to the microphone.

"May I have your attention, please? Every woman who thought she was in love with Handsome George, and every man in love with Candice, get ready for some heartbreak. They're not only taken, they're legally taken!

Congratulations, George and Candice, on your marriage, and I will never forgive you for not getting an invitation!"

A group of friends entered the median from Sassy P's, where they had purchased a couple of chilled whites and a couple of reds to share. The game table was getting a little full, so they moved under the awning of Mr. Bean's where two adjoining tables were free.

"How are your cases coming, Pete?"

Pete sighed. "There is no rest for the weary, that's for sure. I did make one arrest yesterday. I was going to tell you about it, Annie. I arrested Howard for conspiracy."

"What?"

"The State Police found his nephew yesterday, and he sang like a bird. Seems he was scared to death he'd killed the cook, and all he meant to do was start a fire. Like his uncle paid him to do."

"You're kidding! What did he do that for?"

"He thought it would put you over the edge, so you would sell the business."

"Well, he almost succeeded in putting me over the edge. How about those burglaries?"

"We've building a good case against Dwight. Good enough that when the State Police interviewed him last, he gave up the names of the three men working with him. He's being held right now; we have another forty-eight hours to put an actual charge against him. They've got them for a string of burglaries all over the Midwest, wherever that show has been for the last five to seven years."

"Why did he start to talk?"

Pete looked around the group and chuckled. "I gave them a piece of evidence to show him. It's a ring that we found…well…I won't go into that right now, but we found it, and we got a print off it. The print was Dwight's. He was…well…let's just say he was shocked to learn we found it, and that we found it at his exhibit table."

"Did he say anything about it? Confess?"

"He didn't confess, but I understand he was looking at the evidence bag, and he turned to his attorney and asked, 'Is that cat hair?'"

Annie laughed.

Chris said, "Don't tell me. The cats gave you the ring?"

"No, Cyril showed me where to find it. And it was covered in cat hair. Annie's cats' hair.

"How do you know? Did you get a DNA test?

"I tried. Took it to one of those places you can go to check family relationships. They do cat DNA, but not on hair that has been shed. But I could tell just by looking. The hair we got from behind her refrigerator is the same. It won't hold up in court, but I know."

Annie turned around. Tiger Lily sat on the window ledge behind her. She looked at Annie, then at Pete, and she gave that beautiful long, slow blink. This time it meant, "Good job, Pete. You're training up nicely."

"And the murder?"

Gema and Greg walked by, talking, heads together, paying no attention to anyone around them. Pete watched as they walked by.

He turned back to the group. "We're going to make an arrest soon. We're just putting the finishing touches on the investigation."

"Who is it?"

"You know I can't say anything. This is an active investigation."

"Can you tell us a motive? Anything?"

"Why are you still my friends? You know I'm not supposed to talk."

"We aren't going to run down the street announcing it." "Come on!" "Pete, you can trust us!"

"Okay, okay." Pete looked around checking that he knew where everyone was on The Avenue. Then he leaned in.

"We were down to three suspects, then two, and now we're focusing on one."

Pete stopped and looked around again. "This doesn't feel right. We aren't there yet."

"Pete!"

"Okay! Well, it seems Martin made most of his money blackmailing folks. He was blackmailing Garry, you know, the jerk with the fake jewelry?"

"It was Garry?"

"No. Garry was one of the people he was blackmailing. About his fake jewelry."

Everyone laughed.

"And he was blackmailing Dwight about the burglaries. He knew about the three men, and he knew they were ripping off homes in every town they had a show."

"Who else?"

"Well, lots of people. I'm not going to tell you about everyone. That wouldn't be right. But the person we'll be arresting was paying him for years. Sometimes in cash, sometimes with expensive products that Martin could then sell."

"Pete, are you never going to give us a name?"

"Only if you promise to say nothing."

"We promise." "Cross our hearts." "We'll take it to the grave."

"If you mention this to the wrong person, word could get out."

Annie said, "Pete, I can't stand it! Was it someone staying at the Inn?"

Pete gave in to this group. He always did.

"Annie, for once you're clear on this murder. It was Adam. He stayed at the campground."

"Thank goodness! He was the messy one, right?"

"Yep. The messy one, the one with the best stones, the one that supposedly made more money than anyone else. But it seems he never had any money to spend on himself."

"What was the blackmail?"

"Martin had a recording of Adam confessing to killing his first wife. They were drinking one night, and it appears Martin rarely went anywhere without a recording device. This was done prior to cell phones. He must have had a mini recorder in his pocket. Seems Adam was tired of paying him. He took a chance. He probably didn't know for sure if the evidence would be found after Martin died, but that's exactly what happened. Martin had a safe deposit box in his home town."

"And how did you figure out it was him?"

"The campground manager went outside the gates for a smoke one night, and he saw Adam and Martin having a conversation. It was animated. He saw Adam hand something over, then walk away angry. The manager ducked back inside the gate, so Adam didn't see him. The week after the murder, this guy saw Martin's picture in the paper, and he came to the office to tell me what he had seen. We went from there. The state forensics lab identified some trace evidence from the body, some DNA. I'd given everyone I interviewed a bottle of water. It matched to Adam. By the way, that's how we got Dwight's fingerprint."

"Did you always think it was Adam?"

Pete laughed. "No, my friends, no. I am not the infallible investigator you all believe me to be. I almost made two big mistakes that week, and I'm not going to tell you anything more."

Nancy and Sam walked up, carrying the canvas chairs they used when listening to the band. They set up the chairs and accepted glasses of wine from Ray. Nancy asked, "When are we ever going to visit you, Annie, that we don't talk about a murder?"

"I'm not sure, Mom." Tiger Lily jumped to the table, swishing her tail and pawing Annie's shoulder. Annie opened her arms and the soft cat jumped to her lap, draping herself from shoulder to hip.

Nancy smiled. She suddenly sat up in her chair. "How did she get here?"

"Who?"

"Tiger Lily!"

Nancy looked around frantically, then turned toward the lake as everyone heard Frank's voice shouting, "Claire!"

Nancy rushed toward the sound of Frank's voice. He was trotting toward the walkway to the lighthouse, following Honey Bear and Claire, free from bondage and enjoying the sand and water.

As Nancy and Frank ran to corral their "indoor" cats, Sam chuckled to himself.

Pete said, "If I were a better man, I'd go help them. But I'm going to sit right here. And what's so funny, Sam?"

"It's that cat. I should have known she was up to something."

"Tiger Lily?"

Sam nodded. "She was sitting outside the door as we left this afternoon, and she had that little dog with her, Tillie. They practically begged us to let them in, and of course, Nancy thought they wanted to play with her precious Honey Bear. As if they ever played together. And now, everyone is out."

Annie stroked the big girl's back. Tiger Lily arched her back into the stroke. "Big girl, we're all onto you and your tricks. One of these days you'll learn how to unlock those cat doors like Tillie, then no one will be safe."

Tiger Lily curled in, tucking her head into Annie's neck and sitting in the crook of Annie's arm. She curled her paws around the back and front of Annie's neck and purred like a V8 engine.

Annie held her close and rocked. "My sweet girl. How would I ever live without you?"

Thank You For Reading!

The family of cats and the author hope you enjoyed reading this book as much as we enjoyed writing it!

About The Author

Kathleen Thompson was raised on a small family farm in Indiana. She has an undergraduate degree in Sociology from Manchester College (now Manchester University) and an MBA from Indiana University South Bend.

In a variety of towns and circumstances, she served as a probation officer, parole agent and juvenile residential counselor before moving into administrative, marketing and fund raising positions in human service organizations. Ms. Thompson took a break from human services for seven years to own and operate a bar and restaurant. Let's be honest; that's another type of human service.

While making plans to return to her rural roots, Kathi and her mother discovered an injured kitten at the family farm. The kitten, whose face was a mass of injuries, decided to make Kathi her guardian. She wrapped herself around an ankle, purred like a V8 engine, and wouldn't let go.

Against the advice of her mother, Kathi took the kitten home and to a veterinarian. The vet diagnosed road burn serious enough to take all the fur from the left side of her face, and the kitten – Tiger Lily – eventually healed and took a huge piece of Kathi's heart.

Tiger Lily was joined by the rest, rescue kitties, all: Little Socks (thank you, Aunt Mary); Kali, Ko and Mo (thank you, Connie); Sassy Pants (thank you, Ant Sherwy); and Mr. Bean (thank you, Pulaski Animal Center). Recent arrivals Speckles (thank you, Tennille) and Moriah (thank you again, Pulaski Animal Center) have joined the cast but will not live at the Inn.

Tiger Lily's Café rattled around in Kathi's brain – there isn't much else up there – for all of the years since, sometimes as an actual café and sometimes as a book. It was less expensive to write the book.

Connect with Kathi and her family of cats at their website: www.tigerlilyscafe.com, or find them on Facebook: www.facebook.com/tigerlilyscafemysteries.

Find us on the web: www.tigerlilyscafe.com

Find us on Facebook: Tiger Lily's Café, A Mystery Series by Kathleen Thompson

Text to join: Emails are sent every two weeks. You can opt out at any time. LILYSCAFE to 22828 (You may also sign up for the emails from the website.)

www.ingramcontent.com/pod-product-compliance
Lightning Source LLC
Chambersburg PA
CBHW062008170626
46813CB00001B/74
* 9 7 8 0 9 9 8 4 0 2 3 4 5 *